Only for You

Sherry Ewing

SAN FRANCISCO, CALIFORNIA

Kingsburg Press
P.O. Box 475146
San Francisco, CA 94147
www.kingsburgpress.com

Publisher's Note: ONLY FOR YOU is a work of fiction. Names, characters, places, and incidents are a product of the author's imagination. Locales and public names are sometimes used for atmospheric purposes. Any resemblance to actual people, living or dead, or to businesses, companies, events, institutions, or locales is completely coincidental.

Editor: Barbara Millman Cole

Book Cover Design by Fiona Jayde Media, www.FionaJaydeMedia.com
Book Layout ©2013 BookDesignTemplates.com

Ordering Information:
Quantity sales. Special discounts are available on quantity purchases by corporations, associations, and others. For details, contact the "Special Sales Department" at the address above.

Only For You/Sherry Ewing -- 1st ed.
ISBN 13 978-0-9905462-5-2
ISBN 10 09905462-5-X
ISBN eBook 978-0-9905462-4-5

Library of Congress Control Number: 20159000982

DEDICATION

In loving memory of my youngest daughter
Robyn Ashley Ewing

Our beautiful R.A.E. of sunshine, my pride, and my joy!
You remain forever and always in our hearts
Until we meet again...

ONE

The Year of Our Lord's Grace 1179
Bamburgh Castle, England

COUNTESS KATHERINE DE DEVERAUX SHOOK beneath the calm façade plastered on her face. Never in all her twenty-six years had she felt so much animosity in one room and, apparently, it was all directed at her. It certainly wasn't her fault if she was married to one of the most gorgeous men who had ever walked the face of the planet, was it? From the looks she was receiving, without hesitation any number of the women in the king's chamber would have given up their soul to the devil himself to be standing in her shoes.

She took her free hand and tugged at the silken wimple, wrapped so securely around her neck and chin it was choking the very life from her, and she felt as though she was suffocating. Pulling harder offered no relief, and she regretted having listened to the older woman who had informed her that all the ladies would be dressed in a similar fashion. The woman had tied and wound her hair in such tight, uncomfortable braids around her head that even her skull ached. It only added to her distraught feeling she couldn't breathe.

Gazing around the room, she noticed there were plenty of other women with their hair unbound and only a small veil covering their heads. Even their bare chests showed more skin than was allowed by the high necked gown she wore. She should have dressed as she had seen fit, rather than cave in to a servant with whom she was not familiar. Katherine felt as if she were dressed like a nun instead of the vibrant young woman that she was.

With narrowed eyes, she espied the maid who had attended her. Katherine instantly cringed inside when the old biddy walked up to a group of what she would have termed high maintenance girls. They turned as one to look in her direction and promptly burst into rambunctious laughter. If there had been a hole big enough for her to hide in, she would have willingly fled to its safety. They continued to glare at her with utter hatred until their attention was drawn to the knight walking beside her. Maybe she should have thought of them as bitches in heat, given the stares they gave her husband while they all but undressed him with their eyes.

Katherine supposed it wasn't really her fault she had screwed up by trusting the maid. She was completely out of her element here at court and already didn't care for the intrigues swarming around her. Maybe if she had grown up in this time period instead of over eight hundred years in the future, she would have stood a fighting chance with these vicious, catty women. Where in the world was that spirited lady of modern times, who didn't take crap from anyone and stood up for herself, she wondered? Surely, things were far more complicated in the future than what was found here in twelfth century England. What was wrong with her?

Katherine glanced behind her to fondly watch her dear friend Brianna, who had decided to remain with her here in the past. She laughed inwardly, since she had the feeling Brie, as she was endearingly called, had truly stayed here due to her own infatuation with her husband's younger brother Gavin. That hunk of handsome, blue-eyed man candy, his brown hair streaked with blond highlights, was currently escorting Brie about the hall and hanging on her every word. Katherine gave her a slight smile that Brie returned. From her friend's look, she too had her own reservations, clearly evident on her beautiful face, regarding the tension in the room.

Inwardly, she sighed, knowing they shared a common bond and at least had each other to lean on when things became too complicated here in the past. Was it really only several weeks ago that Katherine had watched her other dear friends Juliana and Emily, along with their own knights Danior and Tiernan, disappear through the time gate in one of Bamburgh's towers? She shuddered with its memory. If it hadn't been for her sisters of her heart, Time would have reclaimed her, as well. The thought of only being able to see the love of her life while she was sleeping caused her to shudder. It was no small wonder she wanted to leave Bamburgh as quickly as possible. They had tempted fate enough as it was.

He must have known her thoughts for his hand brushed gently over her own before he gave her a reassuring squeeze. She clutched at his arm to prove to herself that he was truly standing next to her. It was something they were both still trying to get used to...this strange connection between them that Time had blessed them with. She gazed up into his deep blue eyes and got just as twitterpated as the first time she had seen them in her dreams. She had never seen the color on another and doubted she ever would again.

Awestruck, she took in his handsome, muscled physique and hair as dark as the midnight sky. Silently, she wondered how on earth a man could appear so gorgeous, tall, and all powerful yet not be a conceited bore. There was nothing vain about the man she had married that she had seen thus far in their relationship. Katherine was still in a state of shock she could call this man her husband and that he loved her. She attempted a smile for his benefit despite the agony she was in. From his expression, she was sure it came off as a grim look of complete displeasure.

"Stop fidgeting, Kat. All is well, my love," he whispered for her ears alone.

"Easy for you to say, Riorden," she retorted in a snit, although inwardly she was pleased with his nickname for her. "You're not the one smothering with this death trap wrapped around your head."

He gave a merry chuckle. "A thin veil of silk is nothing to complain about, Katherine. Try wearing a helmet and armor made of iron, during the heat of the summer day, whilst you heft a sword just to stay alive. Then, I will listen to your grievances with a bit of cloth."

"Are you mocking me, sir?"

"I would never dare, my lady. I was just trying to prove my point that there are worse, more annoying things than a little fabric," Riorden explained. "Besides, you look beautiful."

"Ha! You just don't understand at all," Katherine complained, ignoring his compliment. "I'm not used to being covered from head to toe in an amount of material only the dead would feel comfortable wearing. I never could stand to even wear a t-shirt close around my neck without feeling claustrophobic."

His dark brows arched in confusion at her words. Leaning down, he kissed her cheek. "I still must needs get used to your language, Kat. Your speech is passing strange sometimes."

"I just don't know why you wouldn't let me wear hose, tunic, and boots. I sure as heck would have felt more at home."

"I sincerely doubt the king would have approved, my dear, but do not worry overly much. You can change soon, once we are again in our chamber."

A groan escaped her lips as perspiration began forming on her upper lip. Was it just her, or did the room quickly become stifling with unbearable waves of heat?

"Katie, are you all right?" Brianna inquired in concern.

"She does look a mite pale, brother," Gavin chimed in.

Katherine wiped at her dampening brow. "I think, I'm going to pass out," she whispered in a low, miserable tone.

Katherine felt herself being ushered to one of the windows where a faint breeze brushed lightly across her face. It barely calmed the panic overcoming her. She began to breathe faster, trying to take in great, big, gulping breaths of air, but it seemed her lungs just wouldn't fill to satisfy her need.

"Come here, Katherine," Riorden offered, placing her in a chair. "Let us see if we can get you more comfortable.

Katherine made a strange wheezing sound. "I can't breathe—"

"Put her head down between her knees," Brianna ordered. The two men looked at her as if she had lost her sense. "Truly...it helps."

With Brianna and Gavin providing a mediocre of privacy as they blocked the view from curious eyes, Katherine didn't care what Riorden did to her, as long as this insufferable cloth was removed from her head. Without delay, he swiftly removed the silk wrapped around her chin, but the dress collar close around her neck only added to her distress of not being able to inhale. If she didn't calm her breathing, she was going to hyperventilate and really give everyone something to talk about when she fainted in a heap on the floor.

Riorden seemed to understand her sense of emergency and made quick work of tearing the fabric to give her more air. The dress was ruined, but she didn't care as long as she didn't feel tied up like a Christmas goose! She at last was able to take a deep breath and looked at her hero with worshiping eyes. He in turn only stared at her with a frown upon his handsome face. "What?" she asked with a still shaking voice.

He placed his fingers on his chin, contemplating her until he at last replied. "Why did you allow that old harpy to bind your hair so, *ma cherie*? You know how I love to see it flowing freely down your back."

Before Katherine could answer, he set to work again, and, in no time at all, the braids around her head were unbound in a riot of tawny colored waves, much to her delight. Perhaps there was hope for her after all.

"Is that better?" he asked.

"You have no idea how much better this is," she replied in relief with a grateful shake of her now free hair.

Laughter rumbled in his chest. "You might be surprised how much I understand, Kat."

She felt his touch upon her shoulder, and slowly her breathing began to return to normal. Looking down, she was appalled to see the actual condition of her torn gown, now that her moment of crisis was at an end. At least the king had not as yet summoned Riorden before him; although, she wondered how much longer they were to wait for an audience. She was tired of just hanging around this castle, doing nothing, and wanted to go to her new home. Riorden had tried to assure her it wasn't anything out of the ordinary to linger for weeks on end at the whim of King Henry II. His Majesty did everything in his own time, and waiting was all part of showing one's fealty to one's sovereign.

As if Murphy's Law suddenly decided to play a spiteful prank on her, Katherine felt a sudden hush come over the room. Horrified she would be presented to the King of England with her neckline sagging around her breasts, she hastily grabbed at the ripped fabric, trying, to the best of her ability, to make it appear presentable. She was failing miserably.

The knights and ladies in the Great Hall all began to bow and curtsey, as was customary when in the presence of their monarch. Katherine could do no less as her worst nightmare came to pass. As if Karma were paying her back for some offense, she heard Riorden's name being called. The words, reverberating throughout the chamber and in her head, sounded much like a death summons. Again, the room began to swirl around her. Only God above would be able to help her if she passed out now!

TWO

RIORDEN TOOK ONE LOOK AT HIS WIFE and was concerned
for her welfare even as his name was announced a second
time. The paleness of her skin did not bode well, and he
watched as beads of sweat broke out again on her forehead. He
took her shaking hand and kissed its back.

"Wait here and rest, Katherine. The king knows nothing of
you or our marriage yet I must advise him immediately afore he
learns of it from the whisperings of others," he said, stroking
her hair to offer what comfort he could.

"We'll look after her, won't we, Gavin?" Brianna answered
with a cheerful smile.

Riorden nodded his thanks. "You will be well, my dear? Perchance, you would care for something to eat?"

He watched in dismay as Katherine brought her hand up to
her mouth. Was it his imagination or did she turn slightly
green? She was clearly not well. "Urp...no, I couldn't stomach
it. Go on...don't keep him waiting, for heaven's sake, Riorden,"
she declared. He continued to look on her with doubt. "I'll be

fine, really. Brie and Gavin are here to look after me. I'll be all right."

He leaned down, kissed her cheek, and, with much reluctance, left her side. He had not gone but a few steps when a far from quiet conversation reached his hearing.

"What does he see in her, do you suppose?" one woman asked another.

"You would think a man of his wealth and looks would be with someone more beautiful than some plain miss who brings nothing to their marriage," was the snide reply.

"She's hardly a hag, my friend, although there are certainly women far lovelier than her here at court...myself included."

"Ha! She does not even know how to dress to impress a man of his stature!" the woman at her side returned. "I would certainly know how to keep a man such as that at my side."

"I have heard tell he has married her—"

Aghast, the second woman turned to the one who had spoken. "He would not dare do so without consent from the King, would he?"

"—and 'tis a love match," the lady continued, giving her companion a scathing look for interrupting her.

"Love?" the woman scoffed. "Bah! What does love have to do with anything if she does not bring wealth to his coffers?"

Riorden did not wait to hear the reply, knowing he would pay heavily for his impudence to his liege. As he made his way forwards to the raised dais where King Henry was impatiently pacing back and forth, he espied his squire Patrick and Patrick's older brother Aiden. With a nod of his head, they fell into step behind him 'til all three knelt down afore their sovereign.

He waited there with head bowed, and yet still King Henry did not address him. Wondering at the delay, he raised his eyes to see his Majesty glaring down at him with an angry expression upon his visage. He gave Riorden a brief nod. Rising to his feet, Riorden waited for the inevitable.

"I am displeased, Riorden de Deveraux," the King began. "Perhaps you are not fit to hold the title of the Earl of Warkworth after all."

He stood tall and would not cower, not even to his liege lord, nor would he regret his decision to wed with Katherine. "I can explain, sire."

"Explain?" King Henry bellowed. "You did not ask my permission to wed, and yet I hear from others that you have done so. Why I am not hearing such a confession from you first hand is beyond my comprehension!"

"She means all to me your majesty. I—"

"Do you think I care what you feel for this woman?"

"My pardon, sire," Riorden answered in respect, "but the marriage has been consummated and cannot be undone."

The king began his pacing again. "I had plans for you and Warkworth, and it certainly did not include marrying some woman with no wealth or lands to call her own!"

"An adequate dowry was bestowed upon her, my liege," Riorden answered and turned to Patrick, who handed him a pouch of considerable wealth. He stepped forwards and handed the bag to one of the king's aids. "Surely, this will compensate for my slight to the crown."

Riorden watched as the king's man tossed the pouch to assess the worth of the contents with the confidence of someone who had done so numerous times in the past. The man nodded to the king, who sat down calling for wine. His chalice was quickly filled, and Riorden waited with bated breath for his fate to be determined by an irate king.

After several moments, the king placed his chalice down on a table and began drumming his fingers on the wood in a show of impatience. "Well?" he asked.

"Sire?"

"Bring her afore me! I assume she is here, is she not?"

"Aye, sire, she is here...but not feeling herself at the moment," Riorden replied with worry, wondering how Katherine would get through an interview with the king.

Conversation stumbled to a hushed whisper 'til silence descended inside the chamber. All eyes turned in his wife's direction, including his own. He was only slightly surprised to see her, not where he left her, but standing several paces behind Aiden and Patrick. Riorden supposed 'twould not be the last time she would be defiant to his requests by not remaining where he had told her to stay put.

King Henry flicked his fingers, and Katherine came forward then dropped down into a deep curtsey. Riorden helped her rise when she was bidden to do so and held her arm to steady her stance. They waited together in silence, not daring to speak. He did not miss when Katherine raised her head a notch in a display she had more courage than her health, but a few moments afore, would have determined. He could not have been more proud of her.

"What is your name, my lady, since your disrespectful, impudent husband has not seen fit to give one to me?"

"Katherine, Your Grace," she answered calmly.

"'Tis a lovely name," King Henry replied whilst he scrutinized her gown.

"You are most kind, Your Majesty."

"Harrumph! Mayhap your husband will see a seamstress brought to Warkworth so you may be more adequately attired when next we meet," he suggested with a stern look.

Riorden bowed. "Of course, sire. It shall be done. We welcome the opportunity to serve thee at Warkworth."

Chalice in hand, King Henry stood again and came to stand afore Katherine. "And from whence to do you hail, dear lady?" he inquired in mild curiosity.

"I am from far abroad, my liege," she returned softly, lowering her blue-green eyes.

The king took her chin and raised her head. "And will you so swear your fealty to me, Katherine of Warkworth?"

"Most assuredly, Your Grace," she replied, with no hesitation.

Riorden looked on as his wife once more went down upon her knees and the king held out his hand to her. He had a moment of uncertainty as to whether Katherine knew what was expected of her. He should not have doubted her. She gave a brief smile, took the king's hand, and placed a kiss upon his signet ring.

He helped his wife once more rise from the floor and felt her slight wobble. Placing his hand about her waist, he brought her a step closer to his side in a unified show to all who witnessed them that this was indeed his wife. It seemed to placate their king.

"Since I have said this to you afore, hopefully I shall not have to repeat myself again. Get yourself to Warkworth, Riorden, and set your estate in order. Do not let me learn you have once more gone north to Berwyck lest I have given you leave to do so," King Henry ordered meaningfully. "You understand my words, do you not?"

"Of course, sire," Riorden answered.

"'Tis good, then! You will be busy enough, settling the affairs with your father's widow Marguerite. I know you will be able to handle the situation, as delicate as 'twill be, and get her situated in her dower house," King Henry stated, still showing a look of disappointment. "Since you have disrupted my plans, I suppose 'twill be the best place for her now."

Riorden grimaced at the mention of the woman he had thought to be in love with afore he learned in truth what kind of a deceitful wench she truly was. Even years later, he was still bitter she had chosen to marry his father. 'Twas the day she did so that he cut off all ties with his sire.

King Henry interrupted his memories by clearing his throat as though he waited again for an answer. "Your Majesty?"

"Well...whatever are you waiting for? See to the packing of your belongings. I expect your departure come the morn."

Katherine and Riorden looked on as their king took his leave of the chamber. Several knights attempted to follow behind him, bowing and scraping to gain his attention, but to no avail. Apparently, the King had better things to do today than play the games that court life entailed.

Riorden took Katherine by the arm and their group left to find their chambers. He needed to ensure Katherine rested err they travel come the new day. He knew he would have his hands full once he got to Warkworth. Marguerite may be one of many obstacles to overcome in their near future, but there was one far more daunting in Riorden's eyes that could possibly even be dangerous. First, afore all else, he would have to get Katherine on his horse. He did not look forward to the argument he knew would be forthcoming when she learned of their mode of travel.

THREE

KATHERINE HELD THE BED POST and stroked the heavy wooden frame, almost reverently, as if to memorize the feel of it beneath her fingertips. Rough in places, it wouldn't always remain this way. She smiled in remembrance of the first time she had seen this room.

The chamber really hadn't altered all that much from now to when she was in Bamburgh with her friends more than eight hundred years in the future. Some of the furniture may have changed over time, but she still marveled that their placement was exactly the same centuries from now. She leaned her forehead on the dark oaken post and closed her eyes. She could still feel the utter despair of when she had first seen Riorden here in this chamber. She remembered reaching out to touch him, yet he had been nothing but a shadow of what could have been if only Time had not played such a horrible hoax on them.

The sharp sound of a trunk closing as the lid dropped into place brought her back to the present, and she watched in fascination as Riorden ran a hand through his mussed, shoulder length hair. He reached for a goblet of wine and took a sip until his attention immediately flew to her over the cup rim. There was such intense longing in his gaze that Katherine's heart flipped, as it always did whenever he looked at her in such a manner. She knew he was reliving his own disquieting memories of her in his chamber as a ghost.

They continued to watch one another, transfixed by the haunting nightmare they had once shared. The image he presented, however, was so reminiscent of their past ghostlike encounter that a small thrill went through her, knowing he was really standing right before her in the flesh. She could touch him anytime she so wished, and forevermore would she be grateful that Time had bended to their most heartfelt desire. It wasn't every day that fate brought her a gorgeous chivalrous knight to call her very own. She had waited her whole lifetime to find him, and she would take advantage of such a gift!

His eyes traversed up and down her body until a lazy grin developed on his face that generally was Katherine's undoing. Since she could stand the handsome distraction he presented no longer, she shortened the space between them. Her eyes never left his as she came to stand before him. Taking the goblet from his hand, she took a small taste where his lips had but recently met the edge and placed the cup carefully on the table. The heady wine slid down her throat, warming her stomach. It was nothing compared to what he was unintentionally doing to her emotionally. The room grew hot, and yet still they spoke no words. He looked down at her from his towering height. His eyes told her what he wanted, but she only gave him a seductive smile.

She expected to be ensnared in his embrace and taken to their bed. He surprised her when instead he held his palm face up to her, and she knew for certain he, too, had been reliving the experience of their past encounter. With her shaking hand, she placed her own palm face down to hover but inches over his. She shivered when tingling sensations rushed up her entire arm. It was still there...that connection between them that even Time would never separate.

She could almost hear his thoughts. They mirrored her own. A small jolt of excitement went racing through her body when she began running her hands up his muscled chest. They halted when she tugged at the barrier of his shirt that was in the way of the prize she sought. She licked her lips in anticipation of how she really wanted to spend their last afternoon at Bamburgh.

Her hand slowly skimmed upward to caress the nape of his neck. His skin was warm beneath her touch. "Kiss me, my dearest Riorden," she said in a husky whisper.

With the slightest pressure from her fingers to encourage him, he leaned down to place his lips on her own. This kiss was no different than any other he had given her over the past month. It was just as explosive, setting her entire being on fire, and had her begging for more than just his mouth on hers. Was it just her, or did he seem to breathe life into her very soul?

She yanked at his tunic so she could further explore his skin with an urgency born of almost sheer desperation. He groaned, making quick work of the garment by pulling it over his head and tossing it onto the floor. She began to lightly trace the lines of firm stretched skin on his stomach until he grabbed her hands as if he already couldn't stand the effect such a small act of pleasure had on him. He crushed her into his arms with his own sense of eagerness, and Katherine felt as if she had died and gone to heaven. Such a cliché of a term, but there really was no other way to phrase how this man made her feel.

Riorden's hands tore at the fabric of her gown, and she heard, more than saw, the ripping of the neckline that surely was beyond any form of repair now. She could have cared less, especially when she felt his hands reaching beneath her bodice like a bloody pirate after a coveted treasure sunk beneath the waters of the deep blue sea. He easily captured her breasts in his hands and leaned down to tease her nipples with his tongue until they were taut little buds in his mouth. His lips made a trail up her neck until he nipped at her earlobe, making goose bumps explode up and down her arms and spine. Good God Almighty! She was about to crawl out of her skin, she wanted him inside her so desperately.

His tongue darted out now and then, adding to her agony until she heard him begin to murmur in his deep baritone voice what she could only assume were words of love. She wouldn't know, since he spoke them in Norman French.

"Riorden?"

"Aye, my love?" he answered but seemingly gave no thought to halt the blinding kisses he continued placing on her neck and the white mounds of her breasts.

"I can't understand you."

She watched him as he looked up, momentarily confused until it dawned on him. He gave her a wicked smile and pressed himself against her. His manhood was rigid with his own need, and she felt it throbbing against her.

"I want you."

It was a simple statement that rushed to her heart, making her feel flushed and giddy at the same time.

"Riorden?"

"Aye, my love?"

She sweetly smiled at him while he waited for some kind of a response from her. She wouldn't make him wait long for her answer. Pulling his head down once more, Katherine blew softly in his ear and felt him shiver in anticipation.

Riorden waited with what little patience he had left and curiosity as to what Katherine wanted to say. He swore if he did not plunge into her softness soon he would shatter completely out of his senses. She began blowing in his ear 'til her tongue darted out to tease him further. He could not stand much more.

"Don't stop..."

She spoke so softly, he almost did not hear her words, but her answer hung in the air, as if Time itself seized this moment for them to always remember. 'Twas all the encouragement he needed. He knew not how the connection between them could be so entrancing, but Katherine's touch was pure magic. She always knew just what he wanted of her, at times without his ever voicing a word.

He lifted her dress and his calloused palms skimmed the smooth length of her silky thighs. Touching her soft skin only added to the friction building between them that had all began with but a single glance into her eyes. His fingers barely stroked the very essence of her when he listened in satisfaction to the whimper of small catlike sounds of pleasure only she could make.

Riorden glimpsed into Katherine's lust filled eyes and knew she was more than ready for him. Keeping their gazes locked together, he easily lifted her, and with no hesitation, she wrapped her legs around his waist. She must have thought he would take her to their bed, but he had another idea in mind. He did not go far, but her eyes beheld a brief look of surprise when she felt the stone wall brush up against her back.

Her chest heaved against his whilst her breathing accelerated. He held her stare, since they were now eye to eye, and watched her expression of startled surprise turn to one of desire.

Reaching out, she grabbed a hold of his hair as if to use it for support. Her tongue slid across her upper lip as he leaned forward to capture it with his own.

She broke their kiss abruptly and held onto his shoulders. "Hurry, Riorden! Don't make me wait any longer," she ordered as she frantically tried to reach the fabric of her gown. "Get this infernal dress off me so I can feel you against me."

Riorden chuckled but offered no further assistance. "Such a demanding woman have I married," he mumbled as he began fumbling with his hose.

"I want my clothes off, babe!"

"I am sorry, Katherine, but I cannot delay that long." His manhood sprang to life when finally free of the restraints of his own clothing and Riorden took advantage of the situation by plunging into the hot wetness that was all Katherine. She was so tight he almost unmanned himself right then and there.

She cried out as he filled her completely and again put her lips to his in a searing kiss. He was already frantic for her and feeling on the brink of climax with only a few long strokes. He attempted to slow their rhythm to ensure his wife would reach the heavens alongside him, but she would have none of it.

He grabbed a hold of her waist and turned so now his back was on the cold stones. Widening his legs for support, he helped her quicken their pace for he could barely put off any longer the urge to fill her with his seed.

"Oh God, Riorden!" she called out in a rush as she opened her eyes to stare into his.

He watched her passion filled eyes light up with wonder of what was about to occur. "Soar with me, Katherine. Let us see the miracle of the stars together, my love."

'Twas if his words to her unleashed the dam she held back, and she arched her back with her release. With the feeling of her tightening and pulsing around his shaft, he too felt his body shatter, as if the stars above exploded all around them with their energy of light coursing through his own body, until they both were spent.

She wrapped her arms around his neck when he began to take them to their bed. Taking a quick peek at what remained of her gown, Riorden reached over for a dirk, lying on a small table, and sliced through what remained of the fabric. Katherine gave him a contented sigh when the material was lifted off her body. He pulled back the coverlet on the bed, and as he laid her down to rest, she made a lunge for his hand when he made to leave her.

"No way, buster," she muttered. "You can't leave me after something that earth shattering. I want to cuddle."

He kissed her forehead, took off the remainder of his garments, and came to lie down next to her anyway. She snuggled up to his side, much like a cat would have done. "We must away come the morn, Katherine, and there is much to do."

"Don't care." He listened to her yawn. "It can wait. Let's just take a short nap."

Riorden chuckled, knowing he would rather spend the remainder of the day with his wife than see to other duties. He, too, gave a yawn and felt his eyes begin to droop. He barely grimaced at the ever so slight tug of his hair when she began to twirl a lock between her fingers. He smiled, knowing it had become a habit of hers.

"Oh...and Riorden?"

"Aye, my love," he said with a sleepy voice.

"Just remember that Karma is a bitch, and she always pays you back when you least expect it," Katherine mocked knowingly. "Recollect that, sweetie, the next time you are fully clothed, and I'm as naked as the day I came into this world!"

Riorden's eyes flew open at her words, and, suddenly, he was wide awake. He glanced hesitantly around the room, not sure what to be looking for, but did not see anything to overly concern him...at least for the moment. He pondered what his wife had said to him. Though he knew naught of this Karma Katherine spoke of, he would be most leery of it. The last thing he needed was for it to come at him unannounced and bite him sharply in his sorry arse!

FOUR

KATHERINE STOOD FIRMLY ON THE GROUND with her arms folded over her chest. She glared furiously up at her husband. "No way, Riorden! Not again!" she fumed and stomped her foot for good measure.

Aiden's laughter rang out in the courtyard. "Is it just me, or have we done this afore?"

Katherine glowered at the man, who had been traveling with them for some time. "Shut up Aiden! Don't make me go find a stick and use it on your head!" she threatened with a shake of her fist.

He only laughed harder, causing Katherine to turn her back to hide her own smirk as she thought on her association with a certain red headed Scotsman, or Englishman she supposed, since Berwyck now fell under English rule.

Aiden had rescued her dear friend Emily from ruffians, bent on doing their worst to her. Although at first it was thought Aiden held a certain attraction for her friend, it was quickly established between the two of them that they were more like irritating brother and sister, who were constantly at each other's throats more than anything else. Emily's heart, in the end, had belonged to a certain Irish rebel. Katherine continued to wonder how Emily and Tiernan fared.

Aiden started to squirm in his saddle when Katherine turned again to once more level her steady gaze upon him. She just couldn't help herself from staring, since the resemblance to his twin sister Amiria was so uncanny. Truth be told, she already missed the friendship that had formed between herself and the lady of Berwyck Castle. Hopefully, they would be able to travel north again soon, since Katherine was sure that in many ways Riorden missed his life as Captain of the guard for his friend Dristan.

She blew a lock of hair that had fallen across her eye, annoying her. Travel...ha! What she wouldn't give right about now for a good old fashioned car with enough fuel to drive anywhere she wanted to go. She mentally smacked her head, realizing that England was an island, so she really wouldn't have been able to go far. However, anything was better than the alternative that now stood in her way of getting to their destination.

"Come Katherine," Riorden urged gently. "The day awaits us."

"I know it must seem as though I'm whining, Riorden, but can't we take that lovely carriage we came in?" she pleaded.

Before he could answer, Ulrick, one of Dristan's guardsmen, who seemed to have adopted them of sorts, urged his horse forward. "I am most sorry, my lady, but we sent the carriage back to Berwyck a se'nnight ago."

Riorden leaned down from his saddle and held out his hand to her. "'Tis not far, Katherine. If we ride hard, we can be there afore nightfall."

She looked at his outstretched limb until his massive, pitch-black stallion glared at her with mocking, evil eyes. The steed was built to carry the weight of a knight in his armor and was bigger than any horse she had seen before. "He hates me," she pouted, trying to think of some excuse to not have to ride atop such dizzying heights.

Riorden laughed at her words. "Beast hates no one and is most obedient. Besides...he is just an animal."

Beast pawed at the ground and lifted his front hooves in the air, causing Katherine to wisely step back several paces instead of being trampled. The horse continued to snort his displeasure and bare his teeth, as if he understood his master's words. Riorden calmed the animal and patted him on the neck.

She took a few steps closer to the war horse and gave her husband a sheepish look while he sat high above the ground in the saddle. "It's as if he remembers, Riorden..."

"Remembers what, *ma petite?*" he interrupted her with a quizzical frown on his features.

Somewhat hesitant, she looked about her to ensure no others overheard their conversation until she continued in a quiet tone. "...that he once saw me as a ghost."

Her thoughts wandered to that day, not too long ago, when she had first seen Riorden riding up to her on the beach while she sat beneath the shadows of this very castle. From the look he gave her, he too relived the memories. Funny how Time had interlaced their lives, as if eight hundred years never separated them at all, just so they could stand before one another.

"Interesting," Riorden murmured.

Reaching behind him, he scratched Beast's rump. The horse's lips began to quiver in bliss, and, if a horse could smile, Beast was grinning from one ear to the other. Thinking it was safe to approach, Katherine stepped forward, only narrowly missing the bared set of teeth that snapped in her direction. Beast was obviously displeased that his pleasure from his master was being interrupted.

Katherine jumped back and shook her fist at the animal. "Bad horse!" she scolded, as if talking to a dog. And why not? He was behaving like one.

The blasted animal had the nerve to laugh at her, nickering merrily away.

"Beast, be nice," Riorden commanded, holding out his hand for her to take once more.

The horse threw her what she deemed as another condescending look before she took Riorden's hand in her own, knowing she really had no other choice in the matter. She was efficiently lifted and placed in front of her husband where he made her comfortable in his lap. Since she didn't know how to ride, there really was no other option. She certainly didn't relish walking all the way to Warkworth.

She held on for dear life when Riorden pulled on the reins to turn the animal beneath them. The rest of their party was already mounted. Ulrick and Nathaniel, another of Dristan of Berwyck's guards that now seemed destined to follow Riorden, appeared bored and impatient. Aiden and Patrick were having their own heated argument, for Patrick kept telling his brother about the ghosties residing in Bamburgh's passageways.

Everyone seemed to be waiting for her to get her act together so they could be on their way. Even Brianna was sitting prettily atop a beautiful brown mare, as if it were nothing to be perching on something with four legs instead of wheels made of rubber. Katherine had to admire the animal her friend was to ride, however. The horse's coat gleamed in the morning sunlight and it was clear the steed had been well cared for.

"Look what Gavin gave me, sissy!" Brianna smiled brightly, patting her horse's neck. "Isn't she just beautiful, Katie?"

Katherine choked back an answer when Beast moved suddenly from the slightest pressure of Riorden's knee. With one last backward glance at the towering height of Bamburgh's keep, she gave a silent farewell to the place and offered up a small prayer of thanks to the heavens above. She never wanted to get near a time gate again and risk the chance of losing what she had found.

Trying to maintain her precarious balance, Katherine tightened her hold around her husband's waist. Keeping her focus on the road ahead of her, she felt Riorden place a kiss on top of her head. She was one lucky woman. After all, what more would she ever stand in need of when she had her knight forever at her side?

FIVE

RIORDEN PACED WITH AN IMPATIENT STRIDE, back and forth across the forest floor. The fallen, dying leaves crunched beneath his boots as he trod upon them, disintegrating into unidentifiable specks of dust. That they no longer resembled their original forms was a testament of how long he had been kept waiting. Fall was in the air, and there would be many things to see to at Warkworth afore the snow fell. Truly, how long did it take for two women to complete their private business?

They had not traveled far afore their progress came to an abrupt standstill. Clearly, they were nowhere close to the proximity of his lands. At this slow pace, they would have to camp this night and attempt the distance again come the morrow. Still, Riorden was worried. After his wife's startled cry to stop what she called *the demon from hell beneath them*, Katherine had jumped from the saddle without any aid afore Beast even came to a halt. She ran towards the trees and away from curious eyes with her hand covering her mouth. Brianna followed ot well, especially since she had not even given a second

closely on her heels. 'Twas abundantly apparent his wife was not well, especially since she had not even given a second thought to the height she had easily dropped down from.

"Perchance, it will ease your mind, Riorden, if you go check on them," Nathaniel suggested whilst sitting on a log, tossing a dirk end over end in his hand.

"How about a go at it, Nathaniel?" Ulrick asked, taking his sword from its scabbard. "At least we can be of some use and train whilst we await the women."

"Why not? We are not used to idleness, since Dristan runs a tight garrison...no offense, Riorden."

Riorden waved the two men off, and they went but a short distance. The distinct sound of clashing swords and taunting curses between the two caused Riorden to smirk. At least the men were being productive. He watched Patrick's dark head as the lad took a stick and poked its end in the dirt at his feet. There must be something better the boy could be doing during this endless waiting.

"Take your brother, Aiden, and show him that move I but taught you recently," Riorden ordered, "but go slow. I would not want to be in need of a healer err we get to Warkworth, nor answer to Dristan for an injury done to the lad."

"Hooray!" Patrick quickly leapt up, dropping the stick, and his eyes sparkled in anticipation of hefting his weapon. "Come on, Aiden!"

Riorden chuckled as he watched his eager squire depart, practically pulling his older brother to hurry so they could be about their swordplay. His gaze went to his own younger sibling and what few memories the two of them had growing up together.

"'Tis been some time since we have talked...just the two of us, and privately, that is," Riorden began and went to sit on the now vacated fallen log. He made a slight motion, and Gavin joined him. The silence between them was slightly awkward 'til Riorden took note of the look on his brother's visage. "What bothers you, Gavin?"

He seemed unsure where to start. "'Tis just that you have not been home for many years now, and 'tis not been the same since you left. There is much going on at Warkworth, or so I have heard."

"I am sure, you, of all people, know the reason I stayed away."

"Aye, of course I do, nor do I blame you. I would most assuredly have done the same, given the circumstances."

"I am glad to hear you understood my reasoning."

"I comprehended your action, Riordan, although it did not make the situation any easier to bear, knowing you would not return to claim your birthright," Gavin said with a brush of his hand through his hair.

"Since I wanted no part of it, the title and lands could have easily been passed on to you."

"You know I could never take your place, brother, especially in the eyes of our sire. Father had often inquired after you and any news I could offer him," Gavin rushed on, "not that I had much to tell him, since I was on my own travels with Danior on the king's business."

"He made his choice," Riorden replied gruffly.

Gavin ran a hand through his hair yet again. "Aye, he made his choice, and 'twas a bad one at that. He regretted it every day 'til he drew his last breath."

Riorden stood abruptly and clasped his hands behind his back to stop himself from any attempt to throttle his brother. "Are you trying to make me feel guilty I did not rush to his death bed to hear his confession? 'Tis what a priest is for."

"Nay, brother. I would not endeavor to make you feel as such. However, Marguerite has been most unpleasant since his passing."

Riorden's brow rose with skepticism. "Really? More so than her usual rantings of not getting all she desires?"

"Harrumph! She has not changed much over the years, but 'tis more to it than that."

"She has no one else to blame but herself for her fate, since she chose wealth over marriage to me," Riorden said, pacing again. "I suppose, now that I have Katherine as my wife, I can say that she did me a favor. Though at the time, I did not think of it as such."

"Well, you may wish to know, 'tis said he still walks the passageways in search of you," Gavin uttered as he came to stand with feet apart and hands folded upon his chest.

"Who does?"

"Why father, of course," Gavin replied in confidence.

"You speak as if you have seen him yourself," Riorden declared, staring at his sibling, who only gave him a smirk of satisfaction.

"I am not the only one who has been graced with his presence. Marguerite has claimed he haunts her at all hours of the day and night. I fear she is going quite mad, and the situation may be more dire than you realize."

Riorden only gazed on his brother, as if he was not right in his head. "Such drivel you spout. Ghosts...and at Warkworth, no less? 'Tis most unbelievable."

Gavin chuckled with a hearty slap to Riorden's back. "Given where your wife and Brianna hail from, I should think that you more than anyone else, dear brother, would believe in ghosts!"

"Aye...well...how often can what happened between Katherine and I truly occur?"

Gavin took out his sword and headed towards the knights who were training. "I might as well join them. Who knows how long the ladies may be."

Riorden watched after his brother, only to realize he had never answered him, but, mayhap, time would answer it for him.

He turned his attention to the more pressing matter of continuing their journey and began making his way to find his wife. The bushes rustled as he brushed past them 'til he came to a sudden stop to listen to the unmistakable sound of someone retching. Given how she had been feeling of late, he did not have to guess who was not well. After several minutes, he snuck closer in the direction to eavesdrop on the women's conversation. What he heard was so unexpected, it caused him to break into a muffled, but merry, laugh of delight.

"Katie, you're gonna have a baby!" Brianna exclaimed in excitement.

"Shh...not so loud, Brie. You'll give me a headache."

"I would think a headache would be the least of your worries. I can't imagine you have anything left in your stomach, you've hurled so much," Brianna said, giving her a small pat on the back. "Here...try to eat this apple."

Katherine looked at the fruit as if it were poison. "I just couldn't."

"How far along do you think you are?"

Katherine raised her watery eyes and placed a hand on her abdomen. "I can't be that far along. We haven't been married much longer than a month and a half."

"Have you told him?"

It seemed as if the forest became eerily silent of a sudden. Katherine rolled her eyes. "How could I when I barely guessed myself?"

"Katie, are you nuts? Why wouldn't you tell him you think you may be pregnant, you ninny? He loves you for heaven's sake!"

Katherine ignored the name she had been called and wondered if her stomach had at last settled down. "I didn't want to say anything until I was positive. Besides, with our knowledge from the future, you know how easy it is to lose a baby in the first trimester."

Brianna looked at her with a sad look in her eyes. "I would think you'd be happy and want to share the news with him."

"Well, as astute as Riorden is, I'm sure he'll figure it out, especially if I have to stop every five minutes so I can puke my guts out."

"Ewww...that sounds so nasty when you say it like that," Brianna complained, holding her hand to her mouth.

"Sorry Brie, but don't worry. I'll be sure to tell him once we get to Warkworth and we have a private moment to ourselves."

"Be sure that you do," Brianna declared and began fumbling in a small pack she had brought with her. "Here...I don't have much left, but it will surely taste better than anything else that's still lingering in your mouth at the moment."

Katherine looked at the tube Brie was holding out to her and held out her finger. Brie squeezed out a smidgen of toothpaste, and Katherine gave a contented sigh at the sight of the luxury that would soon be gone. "You're an angel Brie. I'm so thankful that you're here with me."

They linked arms, as friends are wont to do, while Katherine put her finger in her mouth and brushed her teeth with the minty paste. She was going to miss this, among other things.

"It's too bad Juliana didn't stay," offered Brianna. "Her nursing skills sure would have come in handy come your delivery time."

"Ugh! Don't get me thinking about that as yet, Brie, or I'll never make it through the pregnancy. I keep having visions of some quack wanting to bleed me, as if that will actually make things better."

"Did they do that in this time period, or sometime later?"

Katherine shook her head. "I have no idea. Where is Emily when we need her and her love of history?"

"I'm sure she would have been useful, as well. I could call you a pansy if it will make you feel any better."

Katherine gave a lighthearted laugh. "No thanks."

Brianna giggled. "In any case, there's nothing for you to worry about, sissy. We'll make it through this together."

With misty eyes, Katherine turned to her friend. "I know I've said this a hundred times, but I really am so very thankful you're here with me Brie. I just don't want anything to happen to this baby."

Katherine felt her sister's arms enfold around her. She gave another laugh, hugging Brianna right back until the sounds of the rustling bushes drew her attention. At first she was on edge, not knowing who was approaching, but sighed in relief when she saw it was Riorden. From the look on his face and his silent stare, she knew he had overheard their conversation.

Brianna must have guessed their need for privacy, since she quickly rose. As she passed by Riorden, she gave his arm a small squeeze before she happily left them alone. Katherine observed him standing there, saying absolutely nothing, with only the sound of the birds chirping away in the treetops high above their heads.

She could stand the silence no longer. "You heard."

"Aye."

"And..."

"And what?" he asked with a strange look of puzzlement plastered on his smirking face.

Her disapproving look that for once he could not figure out her thoughts must have amused him further, since he began to laugh.

"You clod, Riorden! Have you no care for my tenderhearted feelings, especially given my delicate condition?" She tried to keep the laughter from her lips, but, when his smile only broadened, it bubbled forth like a lovely melody to show the joy she felt, knowing she carried his child.

"Come here, my lovely wife." He opened his arms to her, and she ran willingly into them.

He held her for several minutes, just the two of them standing there with him lightly caressing her back. The only sound between them was that of the peaceful tranquility of nature's song.

"Katherine?"

Her name coming from his lips held an almost reverent quality to it, and she took a step back so she could fully see the expression on his face.

"Yes, Riorden?" There was so much love shining in his brilliant blue eyes that she was humbled by the appearance of so much devotion. His hand lowered and he placed it gently on her stomach.

His voice caught when he spoke, and she could have sworn she saw tears of happiness hovering in his eyes. "I am most pleased about the babe," he said with a hushed tone, as if to not break the spell that surrounded them.

Before she could reply, her strong warrior knight and husband went down on his knees, placing his head lightly against her stomach as if to listen to his unborn child. He embraced her around her waist. She grasped his head and stroked his hair, giving a deep sigh. Her own tears fell freely down her cheeks at his gesture that was one of the most romantic moments in her entire life. They said not a word, for what was there really to say? Katherine gave a contented sigh and raised her eyes to the heavens in thanks. They were indeed so very blessed.

SIX

T HE REMAINING RIDE TO WARKWORTH was done at a
more leisurely pace due to Katherine's condition and quea-
sy stomach. Riorden was not going to take any chances with
her health. She had laughed at him on numerous occasions the
day afore, trying to ensure him she would not break and would
feel better come the afternoon. Morning sickness, she had called
it. He had not been certain 'twould be the case when they had
to stop several times so Kat's stomach could settle. It seemed
Beast's gait was not helping her plight.

They had spent the eve under the stars with Riorden making
his wife as comfortable as possible. She did not seem to mind
not having a mattress underneath her last night, especially
when she and Brianna entertained their group with their gift of
song. When their journey continued again in the morn, however, their progress was again delayed as Katherine, with all
haste, made for the bushes. 'Twas only now, as the afternoon
approached, that she was beginning to feel her normal self.

Riorden knew from the view afore him that they drew nearer to home. Home...he had not thought to ever again inhabit the walls of the keep of Warkworth Castle. Yet still his heart leapt when he caught glimpses of the fortress in the distance as the forest began to thin. Reaching the edge of the tree line, Riorden held his breath at the sight afore him. He had not thought he had missed the place so much 'til 'twas once more within his vision.

The open, grassy terrain with scatterings of small groups of trees reminded him of his youth, now long since passed. The castle nestled high on a hill, along with its walled barrier, looked achingly familiar, as if 'twere only just this morn that he had passed underneath the postern gate. The meandering Co-quet River flowed steadily to the ocean and separated the keep and village of Warkworth from the remaining countryside.

He listened, momentarily, to the inner yearnings of his heart that he thought he had buried for all time. He swore his imagi-nation was running away with him, since he could almost hear his own laughter as a young man whilst he rode with his broth-er and sire. Did his ears deceive him, or could he actually hear his father's voice, telling him again of his prospects whilst he looked upon his protégée with pride shining in his eyes. They had ridden their land often whilst his sire boasted regularly of how one day 'twould all belong to him, as his heir and the fu-ture Earl of Warkworth. He could almost see his younger self and father, standing in this exact place, as his father's arm swept the terrain afore them.

'Twas a long time ago. Had it truly been ten long years since he stood in the shadow of his birthright? Harsh memories of the last time he had seen his father suddenly invaded the more pleasant ones of his youth. Their last meeting had severed any ties between father and son, and all because of a woman filled with greed and ambition.

Most would not blame him, or so he had told himself over and over again throughout the years. If he thought on it long and hard enough, he could close his eyes and envision himself and Marguerite as they rode through the gatehouse and into the inner courtyard that warm summer day. Her sweet, tinkling laughter had rung in the air and had been so pleasing to his ears. He remembered the joy he had felt, knowing he loved her.

How could he have known that her feelings for him would be so shallow and would so quickly change? She would take but one glimpse of the vigorous and muscular appearance of his father and realize she did not wish to wait as long as 'twould take for the title to pass from sire to son. Obtaining the title of Countess had become her obsession, and Riorden soon knew that his love for her meant nothing in comparison.

The past and the present blurred angrily afore his eyes 'til he felt his wife's reassuring hand, coming to rest gently on his arm. Her head was slanted upwards as if she was studying him. And he wondered how long she had been staring into his face that surely held his mixed feelings of returning to Warkworth. Her own expression was full of concern, and he watched as she attempted a small smile on his behalf. He had the feeling she knew exactly what demons possessed his mind at this moment as he attempted to come to terms with what he would now be facing, a home without his father's presence yet with his unwelcome widow, who would surely make life a living hell. 'Twas not something he looked forward to.

He pointed out to Katherine the castle settled on the hill, almost as if she could not see for herself the place she would now call her own home.

"Let's hurry, Riorden," she exclaimed in excitement. "It seems as though I've waited a lifetime to see Warkworth up close and in all its glory."

He gazed down into her radiant face and chuckled. "You would think I am giving you a present to open. Do you always get this high-spirited to view a pile of stones?"

"A pile of stones?" she repeated with a horrified expression. He watched in amusement as she crinkled up her nose at him, as if put out that he insulted their home. "Riorden, I'm going to be living in a castle...your castle. It's not just a bunch of rocks to me."

His melancholy mood left him of a sudden, and he tried to envision the castle as if seeing it for the first time through her eyes. He leaned down and placed a kiss upon her forehead. "Very well, *ma cherie*," he whispered affectionately and watched her smile brighten. "Let us away with all haste so you may see Warkworth for all 'tis worth."

Riorden made a motion of his hand, and their party moved forward. They quickly shortened the distance to the castle. The thundering hooves of their horses whilst they galloped by in a blur alerted the serfs working in the fields of their arrival. Katherine's laughter rang out, and, for the first time, it appeared she was actually enjoying the exhilarating ride as Beast lengthened his stride, as if to appease his mistress and her desire to be home.

They had almost made it to a narrow bridge, separating the countryside and the village, when Riorden slowed his mount after coming upon a small, familiar wagon. A young boy and girl were jumping up and down in excitement and pointing in their direction. Katherine began to wave to the children, calling out their names.

He brought Beast to a halt and jumped down from the saddle. Lifting up his arms, he helped his wife down, and she all but ran to the children as if they were long lost family. Riorden came at a slower pace and watched the father take his cap from his head, holding it as if he was ready to be thrown into the gallows.

"I's just knew he would find ye, milady," Mary exclaimed with all the enthusiasm of a ten year old child.

"I's did too," her brother Peter shouted. He puffed his chest out, as if to prove he was just as smart at only six summers.

The mother tried to corral her children into some semblance of order. "Now children, do not be pestering 'er ladyship. Me apologies, milord," Mabel muttered, bobbing her head up and down. She quickly brought a wooden chair for Katherine to sit down on.

Katherine laughed, breaking the tension filling the air. "You have nothing to worry about Mabel. Isn't that right, Riorden?"

Riorden nodded his head and turned his attention to the nervous man afore him. "I had thought you to be living within the safety of the castle walls afore now, John. Did you not give my missive to the steward?" Riorden inquired, and wondered if he had erred, offering this stranger work at the Warkworth.

John began shuffling his feet. "Beggin' yer pardon milord, but that was just it. The steward done run off, and the Countess would not e'en let us past the front portal."

Riorden shook his head. Not even inside his own gates, and already she was vexing him. "I see," he murmured calmly, although that was far from how he was truly feeling. "Well, I am here now. Follow us when you are ready. I shall see that you are set up with lodging for you and your family. A mason needs to be close to his work now, does he not?"

After helping Katherine to rise, Riorden walked with her back to Beast, and, this time, his wife gave the animal an affectionate pat on his neck. Once in the saddle, they again began to make their way across the wooden bridge. 'Twas not long afore they called out to the guard and waited as the drawbridge was lowered so they could cross the moat.

"Can you believe it, Brianna," Katherine quietly whispered. "Just look at it! It's so spectacular; I'm almost at a loss for words."

Riorden waited as Brianna came abreast of them and handed her friend an apple. "Your mother would be shocked you can't find your tongue, but you had better eat something, Katie. I can almost hear her now, telling you to take care of yourself and the baby."

He urged his horse forwards and had barely made the outer baily afore Katherine asked him to stop where they were. Riorden watched her expression and was not sure if she was happy or about to shed a river of tears. He had only seen such a look once afore on her face, and 'twas when they had only been shadows to one another.

"Katherine?"

She squeezed his hand yet did not even bother to take her gaze from the view afore her. "I'm all right."

Afore he knew what she had planned, she swung her leg over the saddle and slid gracefully to the ground. Her hand rested on Beast's neck, as if she never had an aversion to his earlier demeanor towards her. She patted his neck, never taking her eyes off the surroundings in front of her, and held out the apple. His horse gave her a momentary look of doubt that did not even register on his wife's face. As if he deemed such an offering safe, Beast gently took the apple from her palm and began munching on the unexpected, but welcome, treat.

The courtyard became instantly silent as all eyes turned to Riorden and his traveling companions. He could only imagine the thoughts running through everyone's head at the sight of the prodigal son, who had finally returned. But that was of no concern to him at the moment. He was more interested in Katherine's reaction to what she saw as she carefully made her way towards the Lion Tower whilst her friend joined her. They clasped hands, staring up at the stone structure, oblivious to the now silent courtyard as everyone halted their duties.

'Twas not 'til Katherine fell to the ground and began weeping as if in complete misery that conversations quickly resumed at a ferocious pitch whilst everyone began to have speech at once. Riorden rushed to her side, wondering in fear if her reaction was because she thought she had made a horrendous mistake by staying with him in the past.

SEVEN

Katherine's hands were shaking while she covered her tear soaked face. She was so overcome with a jumbled mess of emotions that she barely heard Riorden calling out her name. That his voice was getting closer by the second still meant nothing to her, at least for the moment. All she could comprehend in her poor, feebleminded head was that the castle was whole. Warkworth Castle, a medieval wonder as far as she was concerned, was completely intact and whole.

She felt, more than saw through her blurry vision, Riorden help her rise off the hard ground where her knees had buckled beneath her. Taking the sleeve of her tunic, she ran it lightly across her eyes as she continued to adjust to the wondrous sight in front of her. The keep stood there, almost begging her to hurry and come within its welcoming walls. She could already envision her reaction once she stepped inside the entryway. This would be a place she would call her home and raise her family until the end of her days. She gave a merry laugh in her excitement to begin her new life here with Riorden at her side.

"Katherine...what is amiss? Is it the babe?" Riorden questioned, full of worry since he obviously mistook her tears for ones of sadness.

"The baby's fine, Riorden. Just give me a few minutes to myself, would you please?" she asked, turning her gaze on her husband and Brianna, who shared a similar look of astonishment on her face. She watched them both nod their consent then she turned back to take in the splendor of Warkworth.

To say that it was breathtaking would have been to do it an injustice, and yet it was magnificent in its simplicity just the same. True, it was nowhere near the size of Bamburgh, but Katherine was thankful for that. She couldn't imagine attempting to control something of that magnitude. She had had a hard enough time keeping her tiny apartment in the future clean as it was.

She closed her eyes and listened contently to the everyday sounds of a working castle slowly coming back to life after the obvious initial shock its inhabitants had just experienced with Riorden's return. Ever so slowly, she again took in the view. And, for the briefest moment in time, everything froze in place as the present and the future intermingled with each other. For a split second, the ruins of Warkworth as she had last seen them, centuries in the future, were before her, and yet, with a quick blink, they just as rapidly disappeared, replaced by this magnificent, twelfth century spectacle.

As she looked around, she noticed the people, who hastily turned back toward their duties that were briefly left unattended when they realized the lord of the manor had finally come to claim his birthright. Knights stood proudly at their posts on the various towers, ensuring all intrusions to the fortress would be recognized before they even came close to its walls. Horses nickered in the distance as young lads came to take their mounts to the nearby stables. Even the slam of hammering steel in the blacksmith building was a welcoming sound to her ears.

She took a deep breath, and the air, as it left her lips, did so shakily. Entirely overwhelmed by her emotions, she stood in the sunshine, watching the black lion standard of Warkworth flap in the afternoon breeze high above on the tallest tower of the keep. She let her hand come to rest on the Lion Tower wall. For an instant, she again watched in bewilderment when she could see its future, crumbling form. She had not expected to actually be able to feel the soft green moss, growing between the cracks of the stones that time had not been kind to. It was with a great sense of relief that she could look upward and see the perfectly shaped stone carving of the lion instead of only its glaring head...basically, the only thing that had survived the aftermath of age come the twenty-first century.

Katherine shook her head to clear her vision and gazed in amazement as the moss beneath her fingertips disappeared from view. She caressed the rough edges of stone to ensure they were really within her reach then sighed in relief and turned back to Riorden with a welcoming smile.

His brow rose in an unspoken question that she should declare her feelings to him and she went to him, linking her arm through his. "I don't know how to explain it to you, Riorden, except to tell you, there is so much joy in my heart to see Warkworth standing."

She watched as he looked on her and then raised his own eyes to the castle and grounds before him. "'Tis been standing for many years, Kat. It looks the same as it always has with one exception," he replied and turned to his brother. "What was father building err his demise that stands between the courtyards?"

Gavin came and took Brianna's hand, bringing her to his side. "I heard tell, he was building a church. Remember, I too, have not been home for many months, Riorden."

"What was wrong with the chapel? 'Tis of adequate size and always served our needs."

Gavin only shrugged. "In all honestly, I cannot tell you what I do not know, brother."

Brianna gave a little, lighthearted laugh. "Well I, for one, am pleased to see the castle grounds in their original form."

"It's a miracle, to be sure," Katherine whispered.

Riorden only grumbled underneath his breath. "I am afraid, I do not understand what you women are talking about."

Katherine squeezed his arm. "Sorry...I should explain."

Her husband gave her a look that told her to hurry up and speak her mind. Even Gavin had an impatient look for her to begin its telling. Brianna only gazed on her with sparkling eyes.

"The last time Brie and I saw this place, it was a crumbling pile of ruins. The keep was still there, but mostly a lot of the building was just opened up to view the sky. Even this Lion Tower holding your crest was a decaying mess." Katherine sighed in pleasure while she once again reached out her fingertips to caress the rough stones. "I would have never dreamed to see it like this, but then again, who would have thought time travel was possible."

"We literally had to pick Katie up off the ground," Brianna chimed in, "much like you did just a few minutes ago, Riorden. For the life of us, we couldn't figure out what she was so upset about."

Katherine took Riordan's arm while she stared up into his handsome face. "It's like I told you at Berwyck," she began. "In the deepest recesses of my mind, I was remembering what this place had actually meant to me. What it meant to us. This is the place where we built and lived our lives together, my love."

Riorden remained silent and began to lead their group through the small tunnel separating the inner and out baileys or courtyards, depending on how you perceived things. The closer they got to the keep, the more excited Katherine became to see the inside of her new home.

"You are pleased, then?" Riorden leaned down to whisper tenderly in her ear.

She shivered as she always did whenever she heard the deep baritone of his voice; its seductive tone seemingly reached into her very soul. They had climbed the wooden steps leading to the keep's door, and she held her breath in anticipation of the main wooden portal opening.

"It's beautiful, Riorden," Katherine exclaimed, urging him to let her at last see inside the keep. She was so excited, she was practically jumping up and down.

He gave a chuckle while observing her enthusiasm. At last he opened the oaken door, and, as it swung open, a foul stench reached their noses, wiping any other thoughts from their minds. Katherine practically gagged at the smell while they walked through the vestibule and into the Great Hall.

"Bloody Hell!" Riorden roared. "'Tis a cesspit!"

Katherine turned and buried her nose in her husband's chest. Unfortunately for her delicate senses, she couldn't agree more.

Riorden felt Katherine trembling in his arms and was at a loss for what to say. His fury was barely controlled as his eyes swept the interior of his hall, and his temper almost shattered in a thousand directions. He had not felt such raw, unrestrained anger since the last time he stood almost in this exact same place.

Was this Karma coming to get him that Katherine had been telling him about?

'Twas a tragedy to witness the condition of his home, and even more so that he subjected his new wife and her friend to the dwelling. The rushes were a slimy mess beneath his boots, and he was almost afraid at what he might encounter were he to pass across the floor. Platters of rotting food had been left on several of the tables. He did not wish to speculate on how long it had remained thusly.

Cobwebs hung from the dusty tapestries and unused candlesticks, as if the spiders had enjoyed weaving their silvery death traps to their hearts' content, since no one had disturbed their busy work. The torches hanging in the wall sconces were unlit and only small shafts of light shone down from the few upper windows, giving what light there was to the chamber. It lent a gloomy quality to the room that even he did not wish to linger in. Taking in the conditions around him, he would have thought the place had not been cleaned since his father's passing. Surely, this could not be true.

A sudden high pitched shriek rent the air and vibrated off the keep wall with an eerie echo. 'Twas then he heard his name being called. Once...twice...thrice. Riorden tried to steady the uneven beat of his heart, knowing just who was calling his name. For an instant, he failed, as he remembered what this woman had once meant to him.

Her feet virtually flew down the stone steps at the far end of the hall. She was a vision of loveliness with her long black hair flowing behind her in a cascade of long loose curls. She took one look at him when she reached the last stair and gave a happy cry of relief. Her pale blue dress all but floated behind her as she ran to him with tears streaming down her face.

Riorden felt Katherine flinch at the sound of another calling his name. He watched her emotions play across her face whilst she gazed upon what she most certainly must consider a rival for his affections. It could not be further from the truth. Then he felt his own feeling of disbelief when Katherine's grip was ripped away and she became dislodged from his arms. He saw her mouth open in a display of her own sense of shock as she was rudely pulled then pushed away from him when Marguerite reached his side and deftly took her place within his arms.

"Riorden, you have come back to me!" she voiced in a rush, flinging her arms around him. "I always knew you still loved me and would return so we could be together."

Everything had transpired so abruptly that Riorden found himself in an unpredictable and awkward dilemma as he held the now sobbing woman from his past. But 'twas the deep hurt in Katherine's eyes as Gavin and Brianna were about to usher her from the hall that would haunt his dreams and waking hours throughout the months to come.

EIGHT

"Hold!"

Katherine's steps faltered at the sound of Riorden's command. She took a deep steady breath to calm her nerves, despite the smell that penetrated her senses. It almost caused her to lose what little was left in her stomach from breakfast. Looking at the floor, it didn't appear that it would make much of a difference if she added to the decaying mess beneath her feet.

Raising her chin to prove, at the very least to herself, she could handle the situation, she turned. Good Lord above, who was she kidding? She couldn't handle the situation at all! Her breath left her, as if someone had punched her, while her heart leapt to her throat upon seeing another wrapped in her husband's comforting embrace. In an automatic reflex, her hand immediately went to her stomach as if to protect his child she carried within her. For whatever reason, Katherine knew her baby would be in danger once Marguerite became aware of her condition. A cold feeling of dread filled her with a premonition of what was to come. It shook her to the very core of her being.

He quickly disentangled himself from the clinging arms firmly wrapped around his neck. Marguerite was far from pleased. She almost appeared appalled that Riorden did not fall to his knees to worship the ground she stood on. Katherine almost smiled, thinking even Riorden would not subject his hose to what would be forever left within the fabric if he were to do so.

"Do not leave, Katherine," Riorden proclaimed as he came to stand next to her, taking her hand.

"What is the meaning of this, Riorden?" Marguerite screeched.

Katherine felt herself being pulled to his side as he gently raised her hand, bringing it to his lips.

"Riorden!" Marguerite whined loudly.

He ignored the offensive woman, much to Katherine's delight. "Forgive me, *ma petite*," he murmured softly in her ear.

"Please tell me that will never happen again, Riorden," Katherine answered in a hushed tone. "I don't know if my heart could stand it."

Marguerite stomped her foot. Katherine was afraid to see what disgusting objects went flying onto their clothes. "Would someone tell me just what is going on here? Riorden, you have much to explain. Who is this woman?"

Katherine gave him a small smile of understanding and watched him turn back to the woman he once proclaimed to love.

"I have been remiss in introductions it seems, although you hardly gave me the chance," Riorden began. "Marguerite, may I present my wife. This is Katherine."

" *Wife?*" she screamed.

"Aye, we wed at Berwyck over three fortnights ago."

"But the king promised me that we would wed," Marguerite pouted and began wringing her hands. "He gave me his word."

"'Tis clear His Majesty spoke his intentions afore he was informed of my wedding, but that is of no consequence now," Riorden said, and Katherine observed Marguerite's face turn red with rage.

"Of no consequence?" Marguerite gasped.

Katherine listened as Marguerite began sputtering away in Norman French. It was apparent the lady wasn't pleased, and she supposed, if she were standing in the woman's shoes, she might have felt the same. Her arguments continued, with Riorden now joining in, as the two verbal combatants began shouting at one another. Katherine's eyes narrowed, and her brow furrowed when Marguerite began shaking her fist in her direction. This aggressive act was followed by laughter, leaving Katherine wondering what she had said. Based upon Riorden's reaction, Katherine could only surmise that she had just insulted his wife.

"Enough, Marguerite!" Riorden declared, holding up his hand to silence any further speech. He turned to his brother. "Gavin, please do me the favor of escorting our ladies from the stench of this place and see if the Garrison Hall is in any better shape. I will not allow Katherine to become ill from the filth residing within these walls. 'Til this hall meets my approval that it has been sufficiently cleaned, it remains off limits to Katherine and Brianna."

Katherine felt slightly miffed that he would be ordering her on what she could or could not do, but if it got her out of this room before she threw up, she was all for it. She tugged on his sleeve to get his attention, and he leaned down so she could whisper in his ear. "I don't trust her, Riorden."

She felt his lips as he kissed her forehead. "She is naught but a woman, my dear, and no longer has any hold on my heart. Rest assured."

"I will not rest assured anything, darling, until you send her on her merry way," Katherine huffed. "Be careful."

"There is nothing for you to worry your pretty head about, my sweet."

"Ha! You obviously haven't heard about the fury of a woman scorned," she replied sourly. She took one last glance at Riorden before she reluctantly left the hall without him. A feeling of unease overcame her. She had the notion the green eyed monster of jealousy would be rearing its ugly head to taunt her far sooner than she would have expected!

Riorden took one last look at his wife whilst she left the Great Hall afore turning back to a woman who was already trying his patience. She was still just as lovely as he remembered her, albeit ten years older. For the most part, the years had been kind to her, and, based on the way she was attired, she still ensured she was dressed in her finest to impress. He wished he could say the same thing about the state of his hall. There was nothing impressive about the filth surrounding him.

As she stood there in the gloomy interior, her eyes began to dart to and fro with worry, and he wondered what was going on inside her head. He didn't have to wait long but should not have been surprised when she gazed at him yet again as she all but silently implored him to save her from the horror of her life. Her eyes held a look of fright, and he thought mayhap his brother was right when he stated she was going mad.

She reached out her hands to him. "Please...I beg of you Riorden! Take me away from this place where we can be together."

He ignored her. "Why does my hall smell as if the contents of the garderobe have been dumped here?" Riorden demanded.

Marguerite began yanking at her hair. "'Tis him. He has warned me not to touch a thing."

"Who would dare such?"

Her tear filled eyes beseeched him to understand. "'Tis your father, Riorden. He never gives me a moment's peace if I leave my chamber. He said I would pay if I touched the hall. He wants it the way 'twas at his passing."

Riorden cared not to hear any more of her babbling whilst he looked about at the remnants of the feast that had been laid out many months afore. He took her elbow and began ushering her towards the stairs. "Are the upper chambers in any better condition?" he inquired with hope.

"Just mine," she whispered. "He only allows one serf to come and see to my needs. The rest are afraid to go against his wishes."

"What of the kitchen and cellars below? Are we prepared for the coming winter?"

"How am I to know this, Riorden?" she hissed with frustration. "Are you not listening that he has basically made me a prisoner in my own keep?"

"Show me where you rest." He followed her lead whilst she clung to his arm as if 'twas the only thing that protected her from whatever evil tortured her mind. He opened the door to one of the smaller chambers and ushered her inside. She seemingly grew in confidence and became the old Marguerite he remembered once in the safety of her chamber.

Her eyes were cold as a winter storm when she turned to him. "Get rid of her," she commanded then turned her back to him and crossed the room.

She went to a nearby table, picked up a brush, and began running it through her hair. 'Twas as if she specifically reminded him of how he had once told her he loved to watch as the brush made its way through the length of her tresses.

"Nay. She is my wife and goes nowhere."

"Bah! She is a plain little hen who dresses as a man. Any true lady of worth should not display herself so. As you can see, I am far more attractive and know how to dress to keep your attention."

"She is beautiful to me, and how she dresses herself or anything else concerning her is none of your damn business, Marguerite," Riorden voiced, trying to calm his anger that rose whilst she insulted his wife.

"You deserve someone with beauty to rival your own rugged handsomeness...you deserve me."

"Harrumph! I believe I made that mistake once afore, Marguerite. I do not plan to travel down the same road again," Riorden announced. Did she actually think him so shallow that seeing her lovely face would make him forget their past history and her betrayal?

She put her brush down and came back to him with a hungry look in her eyes. "Put her away somewhere then, Riorden," she purred, running her fingers up his tunic, "and we can be together, like we should have been years afore."

As he did earlier, Riorden removed her hands from his chest with a scowl. "'Tis you who will be leaving, Marguerite," he declared, making his way towards the door. "Prepare yourself to move to your Dower House as soon as it can be arranged."

"But, Riorden, you do not understand," she cried out. "He vowed to make my life as miserable as I made his if I dare leave Warkworth or this room."

He turned and looked her straight in the eye without compassion. "That, Marguerite, is your problem, not mine."

Riorden left her standing in the middle of her chamber, sputtering words about his demise and damning him to hell. *Merde!* He did not have to worry about how his afterlife would be spent. With Marguerite around, he already was living in perdition!

Marguerite's eyes narrowed as she watched Riorden leave without a backwards glance. She plopped herself down on her bed in a huff. By the Blessed Virgin Mary, the man was even more handsome than she remembered. Afore he was still young at heart with the foolish notion that love would make all aright. But now...now he had gained the maturity of a man full grown and in command of all around him. She would do all in her path to have him once more.

She felt a cold chill pass through her, as if her late husband were displeased with her thoughts. If she had known what her life would now entail, she would not have played such a role in her husband's early demise.

A low moan filled her chamber that was not her own, and she rushed to the bed, throwing the covers over her head in protection. She knew not how, but she had to leave Warkworth, and soon. If she stayed much longer, she was not sure if her sanity would remain intact, or if she would have much left of her mind.

NINE

KATHERINE AND BRIANNA MADE THEIR WAY through the
postern gate with their guards walking several paces both
in front and behind them. Wildflowers in their hands, they
shared a whispered secret between themselves about the handsome men who had accompanied them today. Their laughter
rang out, and they quickly covered their mouths to hide their
merriment when two of the knights looked to see what amused
them so.

The morning had started out lovely, and, with the rising sun,
Katherine had felt the need to put their bed chamber in order.
Used to modern day nick knacks, the room seemed barren, and
she had wanted to find something to brighten up the place. Still
trying to adjust to the time period she would now be living in,
she had found Riorden and asked if it would be all right for her
and Brianna to walk the grounds outside the castle walls. She
should not have been surprised when he assigned her a half doz-
en knights to ensure their safety. This need for constant protection still took some getting used to.

Espying young Mary, she motioned to the girl and asked her to find two vases for their flowers. The young girl quickly scampered off to do her bidding. Taking their blanket they had brought with them, Katherine spread it out on the grass in the inner bailey. Sitting down, she crossed her legs and gazed around her, enjoying the view. It wasn't until a soft clearing of one of the guard's throat broke into her musing that she realized he awaited her notice.

"I'm sorry," Katherine spoke in embarrassment, having forgotten all about her guard and now trying desperately to remember his name. "Did I forget something?"

He gave her a short bow. "Will there be anything else I may do for you, Countess de Deveraux, afore I return to my regular duties?"

"Please, call me Katherine," she urged.

Aghast, it took him a moment to compose himself before he could answer her. "I would never dare such a liberty, my lady," he at last mumbled. "Will there be anything else?"

She tried not to laugh while she listened to him speaking so politely to her. "Oh, I think Brianna and I will be secure enough, now that you've returned us to the safety of the castle."

"Then I will take my leave of you," he replied.

"What's your name?" Katherine inquired, halting his progress to leave their side. He seemed taken aback that she would worry about knowing the name of one of her guardsmen.

"'Tis Caldwell, my lady, and I am ever at your service."

"Thank you so much, Sir Caldwell, for everything you do for us here at Warkworth. I know what a great sacrifice it is to serve another at the cost of your own life. I am in your debt for guarding us today and every day," Katherine murmured sincerely.

Katherine saw he was again surprised at her words, since she could clearly see the shocked expression written all over his face. It was evident he had never been thanked for doing his duty.

"The honor is mine, my lady." With another quick bow, Caldwell left them to enjoy the remainder of their day.

Brianna's muffled laugh caused Katherine to turn her questioning gaze on her friend.

"What's so funny?" Katherine asked.

"Did you see his face?" Brianna giggled again. "He really was out of his element, but you did your mother proud by thanking him for his service. You could really tell he wasn't used to receiving a compliment for just doing his job."

"No matter the time, he's still our military and a soldier of war. I think these knights deserve our thanks when you think about the hand to hand combat they have to train for just to keep us safe." Katherine gave a shudder. "I suppose war is war, and there's always a price to pay for the cost of someone's freedom."

"Let's not think about war. It's too depressing. Did you ever ask Riorden about the painting you found of him at Bamburgh," Brie asked, conveniently changing the subject."

"I asked him about it and if it was somewhere here at Warkworth. He seemed confused given the description I gave him and told me he knew of no such portrait," Katherine answered.

"Oh what a shame. It was such an awesome picture of him," Brie replied with a heavenly sigh.

"Yes it was, wasn't it? Maybe his father had it done after their falling out, and it's in hiding somewhere," Katherine guessed. "We'll just have to look for it once we're allowed back into the keep. I love that picture, and we just have to find it."

"Considering its size, it can't be that hard to locate," Brie surmised.

They both became lost in thought again and enjoyed the warmth of the late autumn sun. It was the sound of the keep door creaking open that drew their attention, causing Katherine to inwardly curse. Was it just her, or did Brianna flinch, as well.

"Ugh! Her Majesty is about to grace us with her almighty presence," Brianna declared, giving voice to Katherine's own troubled thoughts as far as Marguerite was concerned.

Katherine's eyes squinted in the bright sunlight as she watched the woman who once held Riorden's heart. With her head held high, she practically floated across the grounds with a confident air of one who was used to drawing the attention of every single man in sight from her looks alone. Marguerite was no different than those other high maintenance women from Bamburgh who had looked down their aristocratic noses, making Katherine feel inferior. She began to doubt she would ever fit in here.

Katherine gave a weary sigh. She had only just recently met the woman, and already she hated her, knowing from their first glance that the feeling was mutual. Katherine knew Marguerite's type. She'd seen it a hundred times before. Marguerite would stop at nothing until she claimed Riorden again as her own. It made no difference that the man was already married.

As if to confirm her worst fears, Marguerite made her way to Riorden, who was in a conversation with John the mason. Before she interrupted them, their heads had been bent over a table while discussing the plans that Katherine knew were for renovations on stabilizing the castle walls. Although she couldn't hear whatever it was she was demanding, Riorden was obviously not buying into Marguerite's request. She stomped her foot, but Riorden only went back to work, ignoring any further protests.

Katherine had a brief moment of relief that Marguerite's pleas fell on deaf ears until the woman's eyes leveled on her from across the yard. Another cold chill went through her, and she watched in dismay as Marguerite began to make her way to the inner bailey.

"Good Lord, here she comes," Katherine stated while a feeling of doom hung over her like a terrible thunderstorm about to ravage the ground around them.

"Well...it *was* a pleasant day," Brianna murmured.

"I just know it's going to take everything in me not to want to pull her hair out by the roots!"

"She'll be gone soon, sis," Brianna replied. "Buck up now. Don't let her get under your skin."

Katherine leaned back on her elbow and portrayed a completely relaxed demeanor when Marguerite came to stand in front of them. She watched the woman's eyes narrow to mere slits while she maintained her lounging position. Katherine supposed it was the ultimate insult that she didn't stand to meet her rival on even ground.

"Did you need something, Marguerite?" Katherine asked with a slight smile on her face. She took one of the flowers and brought it up to her nose, inhaling the delicate fragrance, as if she didn't have a care in the world. Outwardly, she hoped she appeared calm, but inside, her heart was rapidly beating in her chest, like a loud, big brass band. Raising her chin a notch, she would not give Marguerite the satisfaction of knowing how much she feared her past relationship with her husband.

"Do you have no sense about you woman that you would not rise when one of your betters stands afore you," Marguerite sneered.

A strange garbled sound escaped Brianna, making it evident she was insulted by the remark. "Oh, you did *not* just speak to her like that!"

Brianna made to rise, but Katherine put a steady hand on her friend's arm to restrain any further outbreak. "Brie, I've got this."

They exchanged a silent look until Brianna resumed her relaxed position. Katherine returned her attention to the older woman, standing there with her fists clenched at her sides. She looked her up and down but stayed where she was. Marguerite's face began to turn purple with rage.

"You will stand in my presence!" Marguerite shouted, pointing her finger in Katherine's direction. "I am the Countess of Warkworth, and I demand your respect."

"As am I...or have you forgotten something of such significance," Katherine replied sarcastically, before she continued. "Have you never heard the saying that respect is earned, Marguerite? So far in our very short association, you haven't bothered to show me much, so I really don't feel the need or desire to extend the courtesy."

"How dare you talk to me as if you are above me? Just you wait. You shall be leaving these grounds and going back to wherever you came from. You might as well begin your packing. You are not wanted here."

"I beg to differ with you, Marguerite," Katherine said and finally rose to stand toe to toe with the woman. "You had better get used to the idea that *I* am now the mistress of Warkworth, and I can assure you, I'm not going anywhere."

"How dare you speak to me that way, you insignificant piece of fodder?"

"If you think to get a rise out of me by calling me names, you're wasting your time. I have better things to do than listen to someone with no class," Katherine said and sat back down, turning her attention back to Brianna. "Now, what were we talking about, Brie, before we were so rudely interrupted?"

"Just wait 'til I tell Riorden how you are treating me!" Marguerite huffed.

Katherine couldn't hide the smirk that suddenly plastered itself onto her face. "Well, turn around, dearie, because here's your chance."

Riorden's stride could only be described as determined as he quickly made his way across the baily to reach Katherine's side. He could not believe the audacity that Marguerite would dare confront his wife at her own castle. *Merde!* He could not get rid of his father's widow soon enough. She was trouble in the making, and the sooner she left the keep, the better everyone would be.

Whatever words Katherine had just said to Marguerite caused the woman to scream out in outrage. As he came up behind Marguerite, he reached out, grabbing the arm she had raised to slap his wife. He yanked hard until she spun around and all but threw herself into his arms then began sobbing...again. Was there no end to this woman's ploys?

"Enough, Marguerite," he snarled, pulling the suddenly distraught woman away from him.

"Oh, Riorden, thank goodness you are here!" she cried out. "You have no idea how insulting your wife is, and how she has treated me. Me! Your father's widow. How much more agony am I supposed to endure?"

Taking Katherine's hand, he pulled her up from the ground and brought it lovingly up to his lips. Smiling into her eyes, he wrapped his arm around her waist and held her close. He nodded briefly towards Brianna then he turned his steady gaze back to Marguerite.

"In case I did not make myself clear, or you misunderstood my words, this is my wife, Marguerite, and her lady friend," he said through clenched teeth. "If you so much as ever raise a hand to either of them, I will dispatch you to Dunhaven Manor whether 'tis ready for your arrival or not. Do you have any doubt of my words?"

"But Riorden, she—"

"I have had enough of your tantrums this day and care not to suffer your presence any longer than necessary. I am sure you can find something to occupy your time inside the keep."

He dared her to voice her objections with a raised brow, but, for once, the woman clamped her lips shut tight. Her skirts swirled in her haste to leave them, and Riorden finally felt as though he could draw a breath of fresh air.

"Goodness, how does anyone stand that obnoxious woman?" Brianna complained with a toss of her head. "I mean really, has she always acted in such a vile manner and been so callus?"

Riorden took a lock of Katherine's hair that had fallen across her brow and pushed it behind her ear. Kissing her cheek, he looked behind him to ensure Marguerite did indeed return to the keep. "I personally cannot account for her behavior, ladies. I am most distressed to subject you both to her outbursts. I can only pray that your interaction with her will be at a minimum 'til she departs."

"We'll be fine, Riorden. Don't worry about us," Katherine replied softly.

He observed her for a few moments, and he could tell she was forcing a smile for his benefit. She was troubled. Of that he had no doubt, and he could hardly blame her. 'Twas not the best situation in which he would have wanted to introduce his wife to her new home, but they would need to make the best of it.

He took both her checks in the palms of his hand. Leaning down, he kissed her gently, not caring if anyone saw their display of affection. "I love you, Katherine," he whispered, "just in case you forgot."

This time her smile lit her eyes. "Sweetheart, how could I ever forget something as wonderful as that?" she said laughingly. "I love you, too."

Giving them a bow, he left them to return to his duties although his gaze returned to her numerous times as he watched her from afar. She was a beautiful distraction, and he was thankful she belonged to him.

TEN

HER LUNGS BURNED IN HER CHEST as she continued her frantic race from her worst fears. How was she to outrun the turmoil going on inside her own head? Her mind screamed at her to hurry with her quest. She must find him before all she had gained was lost to her forever. Time would not be so cruel as to take him from her now that they were to at last start their life together, or would it?

She fled head first into a dense white and obscuring fog. Coming to a sudden halt, she became disoriented and confused with her surroundings. She knew not which direction to turn, nor where to further her search. Which path would lead her to him, and how on earth was she to find it if she couldn't see what was right before her eyes. Had she, in truth, already lost him when he espied the woman from his past?

"Riorden!" she screeched out his name, but the sound only resonated all around her, as if she were standing captured in the middle of a tunnel with the walls closing in all about her. Her voice sounded sharp and harsh, even to her own ears. It *certainly did not have the lilting quality of the one he used to love. She knew within one heartbeat that she hated the woman for what she had meant to her husband.*

The vision of his ex-lover skimmed the recesses in her mind, but it was enough to blind her to everything they had been through just so they could be together. Jealousy began to course through her, taking physical shape in the form of a towering, green scaled, hideous monster. A scream of startling proportions was ripped from her very soul, even as the demon's claws came to take hold of her. Once within its deathly grip, she knew for certain all hope was lost. For jealousy, the root of all evil when it came to the game of love, began to greedily consume her. Her trust in him gone, she surrendered the battle to fight for him, along with her will to allow love to conquer all...

Katherine awoke after she did a head bob. Trying to get her bearings, her fuzzy brain scanned the room, attempting to determine where she was only to realize she had dozed off in a chair. She couldn't have rested long, but it was more than enough to give her a kink in her neck, which she began to rub. Given the troubled dream threatening to disrupt her resolve to remain strong, she was relieved her nap had been a short one.

Going to the window, she opened the shutter and took a deep breath of air, hoping to calm her frayed nerves. *It was only a dream*, she reminded herself. Just because her past visions were almost a premonition of what was to come, didn't mean this one, in particular, would be true.

Her memories of her conversation with Amiria of Berwyck flashed quickly across her mind. She had understood the situation would be dire, at best, but how could she have known how much it would hurt to see Marguerite thrown into his arms.

Seeing it for a second time was almost her undoing. Although it certainly wasn't as if Riorden had welcomed her attention.

However, it didn't lessen her sense of foreboding that currently plagued her. Trouble was on the horizon. She could feel it, and there was nothing she could do about it other than have faith that everything would work out as it should. She would *not* let that menacing woman get the best of her. She had only just arrived on the castle grounds for heaven's sake!

With a new sense of purpose, she leaned out the window to observe the goings on of castle living and practically drank her fill of every miniscule detail swimming before her vision. She gave a happy laugh with the thought that she had actually done it! She was living in twelfth century England with the man of her dreams. Life was going to be so very good for them.

As if she conjured him from her very thoughts, Riordan came from the smithy. He pointed to several areas of the castle defenses until the knight by his side ran off to follow whatever orders he'd just been given. Although she wanted to call out her husband's name, she didn't want to embarrass him in front of his men just so she could gain his notice. She shouldn't have been surprised when he spotted her.

A small thrill went through her as his gaze fell upon her, even at such a distance. From his grin, she had the distinct impression he was undressing her with his eyes. A devilish twinkle lit her own with the thought of how she would welcome Riordan to their chamber. She crooked her finger toward him to join her in their room. He held up one of his own with an indication he'd be there shortly. She smiled, blowing him a kiss. He in turn pretended to catch it and laid his hand over his heart.

It was a loving gesture that sent Katherine's heart to skip a beat or two in excitement of how they would spend the remainder of the afternoon together. She began taking her clothes off, leaving a trail of them behind her like bread crumbs for him to follow as she scampered to the bed. Grabbing one of the long stemmed wild flowers, she placed it on his pillow before crawling over to her own side.

She closed the bed hangings, plunging herself into darkness until he found her. The thought of his reaction of seeing her lying naked on his bed made her giggle. With thoughts of how she would tempt her husband, she smiled, wondering how he would react to what she had planned. It wasn't as if this would be something a normal twelfth century woman would ask of her partner, but Katherine figured what did she have to lose anyway? It was time to give Karma a helping hand.

Riorden climbed the stairs of the Garrison Hall after ensuring John and his family were settled in their new living quarters. Since there was nothing he could do to change the fact that he and Katherine would not be sleeping this night in the keep, he had made it perfectly clear that come the morrow the Great Hall would be scrubbed 'til it shined. He had been informed their temporary chambers in the Garrison Hall would be adequate for their needs 'til the keep had been cleaned. He supposed occupying his father's chambers was the least of his worries.

Opening the door, he closed it behind him with a soft click and slid the bolt into place, ensuring their privacy. His eyes widened, seeing his wife's garments on the floor, and a roguish grin plastered itself on his face. His only thought throughout the day as he went about conducting his duties was when he would be able to at last hold his wife in his arms. *Merde*, but that woman knew him better than he knew himself sometimes.

The lit candles cast soft shadows about the room as dusk began to overtake the land. But there was enough light for him to clearly see his way to the bed. Pulling back the drapery, he thought to espy his lovely wife fast asleep and under the covers, since he had taken longer than anticipated to join her. He was pleasantly surprised to see her seductively lounging there and wide awake.

"Hi ya, handsome," she whispered with a sly catlike grin.

"Good eve to you, my lady."

"Business all taken care of for the day?" she inquired sweetly whilst twirling a lock of her glorious tawny colored hair between her fingers.

He watched her intently, even as he felt a part of him rise to the temptation afore him. "Aye," he replied, unbuckling his belt and propping his sword up against the wall near the head of the bed.

"Then you're all mine for the rest of the night?"

"'Til the morn, if you so wish it, my lovely wife."

She gave him a smile that radiated clear to those beautiful aquamarine eyes he so loved. Reaching over to the small table next to the bed, she pulled at a length of dark silk then grabbed the flower from his pillow. His gaze traveled the length of her body as she crawled her way across the coverlet, much like a lioness on the prowl. He swallowed hard, intently watching her luscious and firm round bottom come closer to his side. He stretched forward to touch her perfectly shaped backside only to have her playfully slap his hand away. She laughed at the expression he must have given her and proceeded to wag her finger at him, as if he were naught but a child caught stealing a sweet afore supper.

"No touching, dear heart." Her words lingered in the air. Reaching out, her fingertips grazed along his tunic, causing desire to rush through him like a river overflowing its banks, as she all but devoured him with her eyes. "Would you like to play a game, babe?"

His laughter rumbled in his chest. "Most assuredly, Kat."

She rose up on her knees to face him. "And do you trust me?"

"But of course, my love."

She gave him a quick kiss. "Then sit down, and close your eyes." His brow rose in question at her ploy, but she only laughed again. "Go on, now. I won't bite...at least...not much."

Curious as to what this modern woman had in store for him, he sat at the edge of the bed. His breath left him when she all but molded herself against his back, and he peeked at her from the corner of his eye to see what she was about. She must have anticipated him cheating, since she attempted a look of stern disapproval at his glance over his shoulder. The laughter shining in her eyes gave her away.

"Tsk, tsk, Riorden. We haven't even begun yet, and already you're not playing fair," she said in a feigned show of being put out. "Now, be good, and let me have my wicked way with you."

"Is this that Karma you spoke of, my sweet?"

Her tinkling laughter rang out in the room, sending chills of pleasure skimming down his spine. "Most assuredly, my lord," she declared brightly, echoing his words but moments afore. "Close your eyes."

He obeyed her and felt her wrap the silken cloth around his eyes. She quietly asked him to raise his arms. He lifted them obediently and his tunic was removed from his torso. Her hands lightly skimmed across the breadth of his shoulders, sending goose bumps racing along his flesh. The bed dipped, and he knew she left his side to come stand between his legs. Her hair tickled as she leaned up against him to whisper in his ear.

"I've heard it said that your senses are heightened when you can't see what's going on."

He wondered what she would do next, but did not have long to wait afore he felt her brush the petals of the flower up and down his chest. She soon replaced it with her hair, and the tresses were like the touch of the softest butterfly's wings as they kissed their way lower on his body.

"Is it true?" she asked in a hushed tone.

"You do not know?"

"No." 'Twas a simple statement.

"Then you have never done this to another?" he asked quietly, hoping she had never had such an intimate experience with someone else, like they were about to share.

Her lips brushed against his, and he felt as if his soul took flight. "Only for you..."

Far into the night she made love to him until she at last allowed him to regain his sense of sight. He returned the favor by punishing her just as sweetly 'til they were both exhausted. Never in his wildest imagination would he have thought a woman, let alone his wife, would instigate such a dramatic and sensitive game in the bed chamber. He looked forward to whatever she would come up with next, since she continued to be full of wonderful surprises. His last conscious thought afore he fell fast asleep was to thank the stars above for sending him such a miracle as his Katherine. He could not have asked for a better wife to share his life.

ELEVEN

KATHERINE FELT THE SLIGHTEST TUG on her hair while Brianna wove a pretty yellow ribbon through her blondish-brown locks. Her sister of her heart was a marvel at such things as making ones hair look nice without even trying. She wished Riorden had let her keep her pocket mirror, but he had thought it might fall into the wrong hands. She took the metal one he had given her, but her image was distorted and only made her grimace when she tried to make out her reflection. She gave a big sigh. She knew her hair must look wonderful from the kiss Brianna gave her on her cheek.

"All done, Katie," she said joyfully. "I know he'll just love it."

Katherine gave her hair a final pat. Reaching up, she could feel how Brie had braided some of her hair to form a crown of sorts, leaving the rest of her mane to fall loosely down her back in a lovely cascade of waves. She moved her head back and forth and felt its length sway right alongside her.

"Do you truly think so," Katherine asked breathlessly. She had dressed carefully for the evening meal, hoping to keep her husband's notice focused more on his wife than his father's widow, who constantly begged to be the center of attention. Even Aiden, Nathaniel, and Ulrick were aware of that woman's ploys, as they tried to stay clear of Marguerite whenever humanly possible. Her hands subconsciously smoothed the soft silk fabric of the yellow and earth toned gown, hoping against hope Riorden would approve of her choice this evening. She had chosen this gown in particular, since she had dressed to please him.

"Well, of course he will, silly! Besides, the color becomes you Katie and looks marvelous on you."

Katherine blushed at the flattery and linked her arm through Brianna's. "Have I mentioned lately just how good you are for my ego?"

Brianna laughed. "Just about every day, sissy!"

Katherine gave one last look about the chamber and noticed everything was in order and put away. Riorden, she had learned, liked everything to be in place, so she tried her best to pick up after herself. They left, closing the heavy wooden door behind them. Their soft shoes silently marked their way down the passageway until they made the short trek down a flight of stairs and entered the Great Hall. A miraculous change had overcome the hall in the past month, and she stood with pleasure, taking in the sight of it.

She never thought they would get it clean enough to suite Riorden's determination to put his hall in order. She now understood how he had performed as Captain of the Guard under Dristan's domain. Nothing went unnoticed by his eagle eyes as he went about inspecting every crevice that might hold any leftover refuse he did not care to step in. Everyone scurried to do his bidding, just to please him.

She had defied him only once during the cleaning process when she thought he was preoccupied elsewhere on the estate. At the time she had just wanted to be of some use instead of lounging around while everyone else was scrubbing away the grime of the keep. She had been standing on a chair, busily dusting the cobwebs from one of the wall sconces, when she had been suddenly scooped up into Riorden's strong arms. He hadn't been pleased to find her thusly and had set her near the hearth with needle and thread to do a bit of mending. With an order to stay put, he had kissed her soundly then promptly had ordered a serf to take up where his wife had left off.

Katherine smiled with the memory of how she had looked at the foreign object in her hand, wondering where to start. Sewing was something that had always escaped her, and she would have rather cleaned a toilet then sew a button that had fallen off one of her blouses. She couldn't say she hadn't given it a try, though she had failed miserably. Starting over several times had not improved her efforts and when she caught Riorden staring at her with a smirk of satisfaction plastered on his handsome face, she knew he had given her this task purposely. She had given a merry laugh then had blown him a kiss.

Bringing herself back to the present, she took a seat next to the hearth. It had almost become a place she could call her own. Trying to find a moment's privacy anywhere besides their bedchamber was a chore with so many serfs milling about, either performing their duties, or asking how they could serve her. She welcomed the silence that descended in the hall, uncommon to be sure, but welcome all the same.

She heard Brianna saying she was going to check on her horse in the stable. Katherine waved her off and began staring off into the flames of the fire at her feet. The fireplace was a work of wonder with engraved figures of a lion's head placed in both corners and looping vines of ivy making their way to the center piece. Another masterful work of art portrayed the face of a man who wore the head of a lion, almost like a cape of sorts. It was truly magnificent, and if she were to guess, she imagined the figure was of a relative of Riorden's. Someone had been very talented to have carved something so detailed out of solid stone.

A shriek rent the air, and Katherine gave another heavy sigh, knowing Marguerite must have attempted to leave her chamber. At least she had the peace of mind that whatever, or whoever, continued to haunt the woman's mind was doing a fine job making sure she rarely left her room. To be honest, she was glad her time was limited in Marguerite's company. That woman gave her the creeps, truth be told, with her crazed eyes. There was no way on God's green earth she would ever desire to be in Marguerite's place with whatever demon's plagued her. She must have done something very dreadful indeed to have a ghost haunt her from the afterworld.

She almost laughed aloud with the thought of ghosts. If someone had asked her, even a year ago, if she believed in them, she would have thought they were making a joke. But seeing as she had already lived the experience herself and had been thrown threw a time gate to find the love of her life, what was there not to believe?

Almost as if she wished it, she blinked her eyes several times to ensure she was really seeing what she was seeing. Was it a vapor, or just her overly active imagination, since it appeared as if smoke was beginning to take shape before her eyes? Maybe she was asleep and dreaming the whole thing. But no, she was awake, and she felt goose bumps race up her spine as the unmistakable form of a middle aged man came to at last stand in front of her. She rubbed at her eyes on the off chance she was really dreaming she was awake, or if maybe someone had snuck up on her. Yet she just had the strangest feeling that another ghost had come to pay her a visit. Sunlight from one of the upper windows almost made him sparkle as its glowing rays went through his transparent form that became more and more solid by the second.

Katherine continued to keep her seat and waited while this ghostly apparition looked her up and down. His brows drew together when they lingered on her stomach, and she blushed, thinking he could see inside her to determine if she would birth Warkworth's next heir. It did not take long for his perplexed expression to change to one of pure pleasure. At last he looked her right in the eye before performing a most courtly bow.

"Lady Katherine," he voiced inside her head, "'tis a pleasure to make your acquaintance." She made to rise, but he lifted his hand to cease her motion. "Nay, there is no need."

Katherine relaxed back into her chair and watched in amazement as he conjured up one of his own with a clap of his hands. There was no mistaking who now sat across from her, and she now knew where Riorden had received his striking good looks.

"My Lord Everard, the honor is mine. May I be so bold as to ask why you have appeared afore me?" she declared honestly, trying to remember to speak as though she belonged here and not eight hundred years in the future. He chuckled, more to himself, she thought, than for her benefit as he continued to stare at her. She began to wonder if he knew what was going on inside her head.

Everard sat back in his imaginary chair before he at last answered her question. "Thought it time I met my daughter-in-law. You have come a long way to be with my son."

Her smile surely must have reached her eyes. "You do not know the half of it."

He returned her grin with one of his own, leaning forward, as if sharing a deep dark secret with her. "Well, dear lady, as a matter of fact, I do. I suppose that comes with my current state of being. But please, you do not need to try and have your speech be anything other than from where you come from. 'Tis not as though I would give such information away. You are, after all, family."

"You are too kind, my lord. I'm sorry we weren't able to meet under different circumstances," Katherine said sadly, reverting back to her modern day pattern of speech.

"Yes, under different situations would have indeed been more preferable and accommodating, but I fear Riorden would not have brought you afore me if I yet lived."

"I'm sorry for the disagreement between the two of you," Katherine answered. "However, I can't in all honestly say I'm not pleased it was you who married Marguerite, and not Riorden, despite his feelings for her at one time. If not for you, I would never have had the chance to find him, since he would have already been married."

"He was better off without her," he muttered with frustration, "not that he ever gave me the chance to explain."

"Sometimes, when your heart has been betrayed, it's hard to see anything other than the hurt and anger that overtakes all else. It's been my experience that even the voice of reason tends to take a back seat when your feelings have been crushed."

"You have no reason to be jealous of her, my dear. Anyone can see how much my son cares for you," he said, as if reading her thoughts. He stood, and his chair disappeared with his standing. "She poisoned me, by the way."

"*What?*" Katherine exclaimed, rising shakily from her own chair that wobbled in place until she reached out a hand to steady it.

"'Tis nasty business, poison. 'Tis easily hidden in food and wine. One day you are fine in the prime of your life, and the next thing you know, you are slumped over dead at your evening meal," he murmured in disgust. He must have noticed her frightened expression, since he began shaking his head. "My apologies. 'Twas not my intent to frighten you but only to warn you to beware of her. She is not to be trusted."

"I'll be careful."

"See that you do."

Katherine heard the keep door shut and from her peripheral vision, she saw Riorden had entered, along with several others who followed behind him. She took another look at his father who began to disappear again.

Lord Everard gave her another cocky smile of encouragement, so reminiscent of his son, she returned it with ease while he bowed to her again. "I should be on my way. I must needs go make my wife's life as miserable as possible whenever I get the chance. 'Tis one of the few pleasures I allow myself."

Katherine dropped down into a deep curtsey. "It's been a pleasure to make your acquaintance, Lord de Deveraux. I hope we shall see you again soon," she murmured politely.

She watched him turn to stare at his eldest son, and her breath left her when she saw so much regret visible in his eyes. He turned once more to face her. "As do I, Lady Katherine," he said in sorrow, and, in the instant of a heartbeat, he disappeared from her view in a wispy, vague bit of smoke intermingled with the haze of the hall. He disappeared so quickly, she almost wondered if she had really seen him at all.

TWELVE

RIORDEN STOPPED DEAD STILL in his tracks whilst he
watched Katherine sink into a curtsey to an empty room.
What is she doing, he thought to himself? He stood dumbfounded when she continued a conversation with no one but herself...or so it appeared.

"Who is she talking to?" Riorden questioned Gavin hesitantly.

"'Tis father, of course. Do you not see him?" he replied with knitted brows.

Riorden looked about his hall but saw no one other than Katherine. "Nay. I do not."

Patrick began jumping up and down. "Aiden," he called. "'Tis a ghostie! Do you see him?"

Aiden exchanged glances with his brother. "I am afraid not, Patrick."

"But how can you miss him? He's right there, or he was," Patrick said with his eyes eagerly darting around the room. "Aw, he is gone now."

Brianna rumpled Patrick's hair and waited until the young-ster offered his arm. "Come on, Patrick. Let's go see what Cook has in the kitchen."

Typical! Even a ten and three boy could see his sire, and yet he was too cowardly to appear afore the one man he should be making amends with. Riorden barely recognized that everyone had left him standing there, staring at his wife 'til she finally turned to him with a small smile. He could hardly move, know-ing the ghost of his father had been having a conversation with his wife, if his brother's words were to be believed. What was there to doubt, given he too had seen an apparition afore.

He finally came out of his daze and, with an angry stride, came to his wife, grabbing her arm roughly. 'Twas not what he had intended, and her eyes narrowed on his hold of her 'til he loosened his grip. He had not meant to hurt her, but his emo-tions were raging inside him. Though that really had nothing to do with her, but more with a situation he could not control.

"Why are you so angry with me?" she cried out, almost knowing where his thoughts had wandered. He supposed his face was not that hard to read.

"I do not want you talking to him," Riorden demanded as he began pulling her from the hall towards the vestibule.

"Are you telling me who I can or can't talk to? And where are we going?"

"Anywhere! I need to breathe!" he all but shouted at her as he led her outside towards the stable. He slowed his pace when he became aware she was all but running to keep up with him.

"But what about dinner?" Katherine asked.

He slammed his fist into the stable door afore yanking it open and entering the dimly lit room. With an angry stride, he began grabbing Beast's gear so he could get the hell out of the boundaries of Warkworth. He needed to clear his head of these troubled thoughts that were getting the best of him.

"About what?" he asked with a furrowed brow. He became irritated with himself for not understanding her future words.

"You know...dinner...the evening meal," she said carefully, afore placing a comforting hand on his tense arm. It had the desired effect when he stopped his movements and finally turned to look at her. "I had something special planned," she continued quietly.

"You did?" he replied and noticed for the first time the extra care she had given with her appearance this day. She was always beautiful in his eyes, but the yellow tones of the dress seemed to truly compliment her. It reminded him of autumn and the brilliant colors of the fall foliage. 'Twas no wonder he had chosen a golden fabric for her wedding gown, for the color favored her.

"Yes, for just the two of us."

Riorden watched her gaze upon him with such hopeful eyes and could only imagine how she had felt of late, knowing that Marguerite still resided at Warkworth. He had learned that her Dower House was nowhere near prepared for the coming winter, but neither was Warkworth. How could he send the woman there, despite his feelings for her, knowing the castle was not ready for her to dwell therein? Still, 'twas not a good excuse for ignoring his wife. He had been so busy trying to manage the estate that he had not spent much time alone with her in the past two fortnights. And now his father was appearing afore his Katherine, making him furious with uncontrolled anger.

He took her hand and pulled her into his arms. He felt her own tighten around his waist as if she never planned on letting him go. He kissed the top of her head and lifted her chin to look at her.

"I have been a most neglectful husband of late," he whispered.

Katherine shrugged and attempted to hide the hurt that flashed momentarily in her beautiful blue-green eyes. "You've been busy."

"Aye! Apparently too busy to ensure you are comfortable as can be expected under the circumstance in your new home," he muttered, almost embarrassed that he put her in such a position. "I am sorry my father has bothered you. I hope he will not burden you so again."

"He didn't bother me, and he certainly wasn't a burden."

He ignored her comment, entered the stall, and began saddling Beast. He was yanking so hard on the bridle, it caused Beast to snort his displeasure at the rough handling from his master. He watched as Katherine went to the horse and began caressing his neck. Not only could her gentle touch cause his own anger to lessen, but it appeared she now had a way with Beast, as well. Apparently, she had come to some unspoken understanding with the animal.

"Where are you riding to?" she asked quietly. 'Twas obvious she could no longer disguise her disappointment he would not stay.

Riorden led Beast from the stall and out into the courtyard whilst she followed meekly behind. "Come with me. Let us away to the shore," he suggested, "and perchance 'twill do us both some good to put our moods at ease."

Her gaze swept her gown 'til her fingers touched at the material in indecision. "I'm hardly dressed for a ride right now, Riorden."

He pulled his cloak from off his shoulders and swept the garment around his wife. She pulled the edges of the collar together. He smiled seeing her contented look as she smelled the cloak and felt the warmth from his own body surround her.

"Will you ride with me, Katherine?"

"You know I will. To the ends of the earth if need be," she breathed.

He settled himself in the saddle 'til he reached for Katherine and made her comfortable in front of him. "Ready?" he asked and watched in delight as her whole face lit up with excitement.

"Absolutely!" she exclaimed. "Let's see if we can try to catch the wind today, Riorden."

He laughed and kicked Beast into motion. 'Twas as if even his horse was in need of a brief respite from the rigors of staying stagnant in one place. He tossed his luxurious black mane and gave a snort, as if to hasten their departure.

Riorden flicked the reins, and once they left the barbican gate far behind, along with the village, he let Beast have the lead. They galloped at full speed with their troubles getting farther and farther behind them 'til they reached the ocean shoreline. He would not think of what still caused his anger to rise to the forefront of his mind for the rest of the day. Instead, he would enjoy this time with his wife and worry about the rest on the morrow. 'Twould have to be enough for now.

Katherine sauntered over to a small table and poured wine into a chalice. She took a tiny sip before turning back to stare in fascination at her husband, leisurely lounging in their bed. The blanket barely covered his naked hips, and she stopped herself from licking her lips, since he looked so damn inviting. He read her mind, of course, the naughty rogue, for the look he gave her caused her to blush from the top of her head down to the tips of her bare feet, not to mention everywhere in between. She impulsively gathered the edges of her robe close together to hide her embarrassment of having him watch her so openly. She would have thought she'd be used to it by now. He chuckled in amusement.

They had shared a lovely afternoon, just the two of them, sitting silently on the beach and listening to the waves crashing into the shore. The ocean had always been one of her favorite places to just sit and find the inner peace that everyone stood in need of from time to time. It seemed to have had the same calming effect on Riorden, since they both had seemed lost in their own troubled thoughts. She had seen him angry once before, but somehow today had felt different.

Thoughts of his father had rushed through her mind, and she could only wonder what their last conversation held between father and son that they'd never spoken again. She knew the cause of said argument and that it had merit, but still...it had to be more than just Marguerite for Lord Everard to continue to haunt this world. It was apparent he still had unfinished business, preventing him from finding his own peace in heaven.

She had actually been surprised they had left the grounds with no other guards following. Katherine had made mention of it, but the stormy look Riorden had thrown her silenced any further comments. He had grumbled to her that he was more than capable of keeping her safe. That she thought he was incapable of doing so had seemed to put a wedge between them. It had been the first instance since Time had brought them together where Katherine felt awkwardness settle around her heart.

She hadn't known what to say to make things better, so she had kept her thoughts to herself instead of giving them voice. It should have been a perfect opportunity to air their feelings and concerns, but Katherine had been too hesitant to speak them aloud. She hadn't wanted to watch the anger that simmered right below the surface of his calm façade explode into something she had not been prepared to deal with. She had let the matter rest. Although she knew they would need to talk things out eventually, and it would need to be done soon.

They had sat there silently upon a blanket, just holding hands, lost in their own thoughts. Since Katherine no longer owned a watch, she really had no idea of the time. The setting sun brought with it a cool afternoon breeze, indicating they had been there longer than she had thought. The chill of the wind must have brought Riorden out of his daze, for he had unexpectedly gathered her in his arms and had kissed her soundly. Nothing had seemed to matter after that except his mouth being on hers again. They both had felt they couldn't make it back to the keep fast enough.

"Katherine, come back to bed, *ma cherie*. You shall catch a chill." His voice brought her back from her reminiscing.

She shivered, as if proving his point, but it had nothing to do with the coolness of their chamber but everything to do with hearing him speak to her thusly. The baritone in his deep, husky voice always did this to her, not that she was complaining.

She went to the hearth and put a log on the fire then waited for the dry wood to ignite with a crackle and pop.

"Katherine, that can wait."

"I'm coming," she said, smiling at his impatient tone while she looked over what was left from their repast. "Can I bring you something?"

"Aye."

She turned to look at him and waited for him to respond. He all but devoured her with his hungry eyes. Surely, he would be able to hear her erratic heartbeat clear across the room though she tried to remain immune to his charm. "What can I bring you? Some fruit perhaps?"

"Nay."

"What, then?" She hid back a satisfying grin, knowing his answer, the scoundrel. He always knew he could throw her senses completely off balance with just one look.

"Just you," he commanded, holding out his hand for her.

She let the robe float to the floor and watched in satisfaction as his eyes ignited while she strode to his side with a seductive sway to her hips. Her hand had barely made contact with his strong, warm fingers before she found herself beneath him. His hands slowly stroked wherever he could touch her skin, and she began running her toes up and down the calf of his leg.

"Do you think it will always be like this between us, Riorden?" she asked, reaching up to play with his hair. "I mean, it's just so perfect, don't you think?"

He kissed her lips and began nuzzling her breasts. "Aye, everything about you is perfect."

She gave a little laugh, thinking about how big she would soon be. "Well, you may not think so when I am fat with child, and you can get nowhere near me with my enormous stomach between us."

"Since 'twill be my child growing within you, we shall indeed be blessed." He placed his hand on the hardness of her belly. "The babe grows strong within you."

Katherine couldn't help the smile that lit her face. "I wish you could feel the little flutters going on inside right now, and just wait until the baby starts to kick. I can't wait to see your face."

He returned her smile. "'Tis most unusual for a woman to openly discuss such things, Kat, even though 'tis with your husband. It takes some getting used to."

"Well, I'm not your everyday, twelfth century woman here, so you don't really have a lot of options other than to go along with the flow."

"You and your passing strange ways, Kat. I just never know what you shall say next," he laughed. "You are positive we will not harm the babe by making love?"

She gave a tug on his arm until he moved between her legs. Her heart skipped a beat in anticipation. "The baby's fine, Riorden. There's no need to worry about him, or her. We'll have to think of other ways to make love once I get bigger, you know," she hinted with another smile.

"I am sure we will think of something," he murmured as he began kissing her sensitive skin.

"You won't tease me about my stomach leading the way, will you?" She was suddenly self-conscious about how much weight she would put on with her pregnancy.

"Nay."

"I mean, some men find pregnant women fat and ugly."

"You are beautiful to me, and I am not one of those men." He continued on with his assault on her senses.

"I can only hope you still think so when I'm near the end of this pregnancy," she muttered glumly.

He leaned up from where he had been nibbling at her neck and tucked her hair behind her ear. "Kat?"

It took several stolen breaths from staring at the intensity of his blue eyes before she could answer him. "Yes?"

"Has no one ever said you talk too much, my sweet?"

Embarrassment caused her to blush again. "I suppose, once or twice."

He began kissing her, and any further thoughts were completely gone from her mind. Heat flooded her entire body as she

experienced the dreamlike enchantment Riorden always managed to weave around them. She gasped as he entered her.

"Riorden?" Her throaty murmur as she tried to catch her
breath when he began to move sounded foreign in her ears.

"Aye, my love?" he said just as hoarsely.

"Speak to me in French," she urged, raking her nails playfully down the muscles of his back. "It always drives me wild."

He looked up at her with a completely wicked grin. "As my
lady commands."

It was several hours later, after Katherine was completely
drained, that she curled up next to her husband and listened to
the soft snores passing from his lips. She closed her eyes, content. She would worry about their troubles and her concerns
another day.

THIRTEEN

*S*HE CLAWED HER WAY UP *to the edge of the riverbed, gasp-*
ing for air. She wasn't sure how she had made it, only that
she had. Looking back at the river, its current seemed so inno-
cent. She swore, for how could she have known that its true
force lay underneath the surface as it attempted to suck her
down into its watery grave.

But truly, had she had any choice, other than leaping into
the frigid water? The answer was a simple one. No! Not if she
wanted to save herself and her unborn child. Jumping into the
river had seemed like the most logical choice at the time, and
yet, given her aversion to water, what had she been thinking?

Her feet slipped as she tried to plant them on something solid
to pull herself from the cold stream. The slime squished between
her toes. She groaned at the feeling while trying not to think of
what her feet were encountering, having lost her slippers some-
time during her frantic flight. Her only thought now was to get
herself safe and away from the river's edge, including any pry-
ing eyes that would be searching for her. Escaping the water

that had almost been the death of her had only been part of her problem. The other was far more troubling to her tenderhearted feelings than her early demise.

As she tugged at her water logged skirts, she crawled on shaking knees to the tree line and collapsed against the rough bark of a towering oak. A sob escaped her lips as tears slipped uninhibited from her eyes. That evil woman wanted him back. It was more than obvious to everyone, except the man who refused to see that she would stop at nothing to have him again, even if that meant killing his wife.

She gazed up at Warkworth in the distance with its glowing lights shimmering from the upper windows while evening quickly descended upon the earth. She had drifted farther in the river's current than she thought while her arms flayed to keep herself above the water line. She quickly came to the realization she was on the wrong side of the river, and she looked again toward the keep. What should have been a welcoming sight, brought her nothing but sorrow, knowing even now she was with him.

She gave a long drawn out sigh and stood, wrapping her arms around her to keep from shivering as the cold air went straight through her. Soon it would be completely dark, and she would need to find shelter. Luckily for her, and her knowledge of the future, she knew which direction she would be heading as she made her way into the trees.

The safe haven she sought was not easily found, this place made inside the face of a rock wall that would one day be known as Warkworth's Hermitage. With the light quickly fading, she carefully made her way up a stone path until she found the entrance to what was, at this time in history, little more than a cave. Someone, at some point, had been here, however. But the dried flowers left on what would one day be called an altar was a clear indication that the person wouldn't be returning anytime soon.

She slumped to the ground, curling her body into a tight ball of despair. Cold, scared, and feeling utterly rejected, she began to pray, even as darkness swallowed up her body, and she became one with the shadows of the night. Katherine began to weep for what she had lost. Without Riorden in her life, there was no reason for her to stay here in the twelfth century.

As if Time heard her hopeless thoughts, the ground beneath her began to quake, even while she cried out she had not meant to go where her mind had wandered. But it was too late, as those annoying little iridescent lights began to sparkle and dance before her eyes. She watched in horror as first her hands and then the rest of her body quickly became a vague ghostly silhouette. A feeling overcame her, as if she had only been tested to ensure she was worthy to be given such a gift as to travel through time in order to keep her chivalrous knight. Obviously, she had failed.

Against her will, she felt a force hit her with the energy of what it might feel like to get hit by a truck as she was instantly ripped back to where she truly belonged. Time had come to claim her, and, throughout all history, people would only remember the legend of a twelfth century woman who wept throughout time in a cave for her lost love. Brought back to the present, Katherine screamed out Riorden's name and knew only one thing for certain before she collapsed in a dead faint. Marguerite had won...

"Katherine! Awake, my love, you are but dreaming."

The sound of his comforting voice woke her, but she was still hesitant to open her eyes, afraid that she had only dreamed of him. She began to smile, knowing he was real when she felt the softness of his lips as he kissed her cheek.

"Hurry, Katherine. You may rest the day away later," Riorden urged. "I thought you wished to see me off this morn." She felt him move away from their bed.

Her eyes flew open when his words penetrated her fuzzy brain. He was mostly already dressed for travel, and her eyes lovingly scanned his broad shoulders. She heard the chink of his chainmail when he donned his tabard as it fell into place over his chest. He turned once more to face her, and her mouth became dry. Her hands suddenly began to shake uncontrollably with a feeling of unease at what his trip would cost her.

Was it just her imagination, or did his eyes seem more blue than usual? Perhaps it was the color of his cloak that had made them seem more intense. Her heart skipped a beat, as if it knew exactly what this man before her did to her senses. Her gaze moved to the lion head emblem in the center of his chest that now appeared to gaze at her with jeering eyes.

"Kat?"

"What?" she muttered, knowing she hadn't heard a word he had said, for she was remembering every minute of her nightmare and feeling every bit as scared now.

He finished buckling his sword at his side and came back to the bed. The sapphire stone in its hilt sparkled in the firelight from the hearth and reminded her of Riorden's eyes. "Mayhap, you should stay abed. I kept you up most of the night, and you still need your rest, it appears," he chuckled, kissing her cheek again, but he continued reading her face in puzzlement. "Is something amiss?"

She shook her head as if to clear the remnants of her dreams. "No...yes...I don't know, Riorden. I had a bad dream, and I'm afraid that all, or some of it, may come true, as my dreams have before." She threw back the covers and began dressing in her comfortable hose and tunic. Riorden only continued to watch her from hooded eyes.

"*Ma cherie*, there is no need to worry. Nothing will happen between us."

"Ha! It's not *us* I'm worried about Riorden but *her!*" she said angrily as she yanked on her boots. All she could think of was Lord Everard's words to be wary. *Poison!* How was she to go about detecting something so easily concealed in food or wine as poison?

"Are you perchance jealous of her? You need not be."

"Of course I'm jealous, Riorden! Why wouldn't I be, as beautiful as she is?" Her voice had risen in pitch, and she pinched her eyes shut so he wouldn't see her cry. This pregnancy was making her an emotional mess! Why did she doubt his feelings for her? She knew it was because, in a way, Marguerite was right. When it came to physical beauty, Katherine came nowhere close, nor would she ever be in the same league, as the other woman who once held Riorden's heart. She covered her eyes with her hands, trying to gather what little she had left of her composure.

"There is more to beauty than just physical appearance, my love," Riorden proclaimed, as if he had read where her thoughts had led her. "Come, Katherine. Do not upset yourself so, or you may harm the babe."

"It's not the baby I'm worried about, Riordan," she snapped harshly.

"Why then are you angry with me when I have done nothing wrong? 'Twas just a dream." He gathered her in his arms and held her tight until she felt the voice of reason bring the calming effect she stood in need of.

"Sorry."

He tilted her chin up and gave her a grin that was hard to resist. "Now smile for me, my lovely wife, and give me a kiss. I shall be back afore you even have time to miss me."

She obliged him. "I miss you already, Riorden," she whispered fervently and held tightly onto his hand as they made their way below.

The Great Hall was busy as knights finished breaking their fast. Riorden held her chair out for her, and she sat while food was laid before them. He filled a trencher for them to share, but she only took a small piece of dry bread to nibble on, not knowing how her stomach would react to food. It didn't take long for it to disagree with her, and she pushed her chair back, listening while the legs scraped loudly along the stone floor. Riorden was inhaling the heavenly aroma of his repast, but, for Katherine, the smell only made her want to gag.

He offered her a sip of watered down wine, but even that she declined with a shake of her head. His brow rose in concern she wasn't eating, but she waved him off, promising in a slight whisper she would eat her fill later. It seemed to satisfy him as he finished his meal with gusto. For her, it was done all too quickly, for that only meant she could no longer delay his parting.

Katherine stood and took Riorden's arm. Unexpectedly, Marguerite came careening down the stairs, making for the front door to the keep. Her heavy cloak flowed behind her as she rushed across the floor.

"Leave me be, Everard!" she yelled with tears streaking down her face. She ran the distance to the door as if the devil's demons from the underworld were cracking their chains about her head, ready to consume her. In the blink of an eye, she was gone with the vestibule door slamming loudly behind her.

A hush seemed to descend upon the Great Hall with her departure. Patrick crossed himself furiously, along with several other serfs who had witnessed her flight. Gavin and Brianna only looked at one another, as though there was nothing out of the ordinary going on, and resumed their meal. Aiden, Nathaniel, and Ulrick left their meals unfinished and left to see to their horses. Riorden, alone, scowled with brows drawn together in a fierce frown. Katherine could only guess at what was going on inside his head.

They left the hall with her hand placed lovingly in the crook of his arm. He was talking to her again, but, as they crossed the inner courtyard, none of his words registered in her head while she looked ahead to the outer baily. Coming out of the small tunnel, Katherine came to a blinding halt while her gaze flew to the unbelievable sight meeting her eyes.

Ever so prettily sitting atop a striking dapple grey mare with reins in hand, Marguerite looked down at Katherine from her lofty perch and gave her a smile that only another woman could interpret with precision.

Katherine felt as if her heart dropped out of her chest, and she turned to Riorden, trying to form some kind of response. The silence between them crackled with tension. Still trying to think of something to say to express her feelings, nothing came to mind, and her lips just moved soundlessly until she clamped them tightly shut in a grim line of fierce disapproval. She must have looked like an idiot!

She quickly turned her back on the woman, whose irritating laughter suddenly reached her ears. "Really?" she gasped, taking his arm and ushering him a short distance away so they could speak privately. "She's to ride with you?"

"'Tis her dower house, Katherine. You knew I would need to ensure 'twas ready so she could leave," Riorden answered.

"But why does she need to go with you?" Katherine tried to keep the hurt from her voice, but, from his look, she hadn't done a very good job of it. He put his arm around her shoulder to give her a reassuring pat.

"There are some things that Marguerite must needs see to herself. The sooner the estate is settled, the sooner she can leave Warkworth for good."

"But, Riorden—"

"But what, Katherine?" he exploded. "Have you so little faith in me that your jealousy of that woman would blind you to how I feel for you? Blind you to everything we have gone through just so we could be together? *Merde*! You carry my child. Does that not prove my love for you?"

Katherine flinched to hear how he spoke to her. "You don't understand. Your father—"

He growled at her like a wounded animal and made no effort to hide his pent up frustration that he had obviously been holding back. "For the love of God, woman, do not speak to me thusly of my sire. He is dead! Let him stay that way," he shouted furiously.

"I won't mention him again," she whispered in fright, not knowing how to handle this side of her husband. The way he was looking at her, he wouldn't hear her words about Marguerite wanting her dead in a dream anyway, let alone that she poisoned his father. She choked back her tears as she gazed at him.

"*God's Wounds!*" Riorden swore and enveloped her in his embrace. "She is nothing to me, Kat. Please try to remember that whilst I am gone."

"I will," she said slowly.

"I should be gone no longer than two fortnights, mayhap, less," he declared, wiping the tears from her cheeks.

"A whole month?" she squeaked out.

"Aye," he answered. "I will leave Aiden here for your protection and to watch over you, if that suits."

Katherine only managed a shrug of indifference. "That's fine," she said simply.

He leaned down and kissed her lips. "Stay inside the castle walls unless you have your guards and Caldwell with you and take care of our child."

He turned from her with his cape fluttering behind him in the morning breeze. He gave one backward glance in her direction until, with a wave of his hand, their horses were set in motion, leaving through the barbican gate. Her breath caught in her throat as she watched him disappear from view, but the expression Marguerite gave her was sure to remain in her memory for days to come. It wasn't a look that boded well for her good health.

FOURTEEN

RIORDEN SLOWED BEAST TO A HALT at the rise of a hill and looked down upon the land surrounding Dunhaven Manor. His father used to tell him how his mother had always loved this country estate, not far from the hustle and bustle of London. He had said she thought 'twas just far enough from the city limits to give her the feeling she was still north at Warkworth. He had been told she did not care for life in the city, nor that of court.

He shared her sentiments, not that he remembered much of his dame. Dying young, giving birth to his brother Gavin, his only reminder of her was a small portrait he had carried with him for years whilst in service to Dristan. He would see if the larger painting that once graced the Great Hall could be found. It should be hung in a place of honor. Although he would not be surprised to learn Marguerite had burned it to ashes.

She moved her horse forwards 'til she was abreast of him, almost as if she knew his thoughts had momentarily settled upon her. Sighing with pleasure at the sight below, she turned her sparkling eyes in his direction. "'Tis lovely, is it not, Riorden?"

"I have heard tell my mother always thought so," he answered, still thinking of a woman he had never truly known. Of all the estates Marguerite could have chosen as her dower house, he was unpleasantly taken aback that his sire had allowed her to choose the one place his mother had called her own. He should have not given it a second thought. 'Twas of no consequence to him where she lived, as long as he could soon be rid of this troublesome woman. He just wished she had chosen another estate.

"Aye, well...'tis mine now, and I shall endeavor to make the place my own." Marguerite reached out, placing her hand upon his arm. "You will stay, will you not, to ensure all is in order?"

"Only as long as necessary, Marguerite. I have a wife waiting for me at home and Warkworth is still in need of provisions to be readied for the winter."

She smothered a laugh with a gaze upon him that at one time he would have seen as a come hither look. Years ago, he would have taken her up on what she was silently offering. He was thankful those days were long since gone, and he now had an understanding of what true love really was all about.

He nudged Beast with his knee, and they began a slow trot down the hill. Afore long, they were dismounting, and he was assisting Marguerite from her mare. He did not care that her hands lingered longer upon his shoulders than they should have. He ignored the looks cast at him from Ulrick and Nathaniel and made for the manor's front door. Reaching for the knob, Riorden barely touched the cool metal afore the door was hastily wrenched inwards.

A gasp greeted him, along with the shocked expression on the servant's face. "Bless me soul, 'tis the young master!"

"Good day, Timmons," Riorden said with a fond smile. "'Tis good to see you still watching over the old place."

"Where else would I go, Sir Riorden, since this 'as been me 'ome for as long as I can remember?"

Marguerite pushed her way into the entryway, much like a full blown thunder cloud. "'Tis Lord de Deveraux to you!" she ordered. "He now holds his father's title of Earl."

"Apologies, milord," Timmons replied carefully and inclined his head to Marguerite. "Countess...'tis good to 'ave yer return."

"Harrumph! I should think so," she muttered snidely.

Riorden patted the old man on his back. "Can you see to having chambers aired out for the Countess, along with me and my men, Timmons? We plan to stay here to see to what stores you may need for the coming winter months afore the Countess returns to move in permanently."

"Of course, milord. I shall see to it at once."

Timmons left the entryway with shuffling feet, and Riorden's gaze swept the manor with a practiced eye. The place was chilled to the bone, and he pondered how much work would really need to be done afore Marguerite would be comfortable enough to see to her own needs. Knowing her as he did, he would not be surprised if she encouraged him to stay till spring.

Marguerite pulled her hood closer about her hair as she quickly made her way to the stables. Darkness had descended, but the cold night, for her, usually brought with it her dead husband. For once, she was glad he had not been able to follow her to Dunhaven Manor. Perchance, his soul was destined to remain at Warkworth, since that is where he died. 'Twas just an assumption on her part, but she thought it sounded logical if things of this nature ever really did make any kind of sense in an otherwise normal world.

Normal? Bah! There was nothing normal about her life of late. Haunted by a dead husband she never should have married, and her ex-lover returned with a wife! *Wife!* Who would have thought Riorden would disobey the king and get himself married without permission up near the wilds of that barbarian land of Scotland? She swore she would have him once more, no matter the cost. Drastic times called for drastic measures. 'Twould not be the first time she would use whatever she needed to ensure she receive all that was due her! He was supposed to be mine. *Damn Katherine's soul to hell!*

Watching her steps and surroundings to ensure her secrecy, she carefully opened the wooden door to the stables and cringed when it squeaked loudly to her ears. No one seemed to be there with the exception of the animals, more's the pity. He was late, and she would tell him how displeased she was with his tardiness. She could not afford to be caught this night, not if she wanted to fulfill her plan to have Riorden back in her bed. Once there, she knew her beauty alone would have him mesmerized. Then and only then, would she know that he had not forgotten her all those years ago, and that they could spend their days making up for lost time. 'Twould be of little consequence to her, knowing his wife would also conveniently disappear.

A soft whistle met her ears. She searched the darkened interior of the room afore espying a man stepping from the shadows and coming to nonchalantly lean on one of the pillars towards the center of the stable. She glared at him when she recognized his familiar face as he stared at her, as if he had all the time in the world.

"I see you got my missive I sent from Warkworth, but you are late," she hissed, "and 'tis not the first time."

He looked her up and down, admiring her form afore he broke out into a wicked grin. "Seems to me you are the one who is late, madam, since I have been waiting for you all of a score of minutes."

Marguerite looked up at his handsome profile and remembered the last time they had met. She came to stand afore him, and he reached out to caress her cheek with his finger. She shivered, despite the fact that she had no intention of tumbling with him in the hay...not that they had not done such afore. 'Twas not that it had been an unpleasant coupling, but she had other things on her mind this night that certainly did not include him.

"Not tonight, Warin," she told him with disinterest. She watched him shrug, as if it mattered little to him if he took her or not. Although she felt put out that he did not press the issue, Marguerite got back to the subject at hand. "Do you have what I seek?"

"For shame, Marguerite. Do you have no time for play? The night is still young after all."

"Nay. I will be missed at the manor."

He gave a knowing smirk that struck a chord of disdain, causing her eyes to narrow. "I doubt it, my pet."

She watched as Warin opened up a satchel and pulled out a small vial of liquid. She held out her hands, greedily, but he only lifted the container high above her head, out of reach. "And what do you have as payment for me, my dear Countess? Something worthy enough, I hope, for all the trouble I have gone through on your behalf."

"The other is set in place, then?" she inquired with a gleeful smile.

"Was there any doubt? You paid me well. Why would you think I would not keep my end of the bargain?"

"When?"

"A se'nnight, mayhap more. These things take time to set in motion. I do not wish to be caught dirtying my hands for you, no matter how fond I am of your delectable body."

"I am most grateful for your assistance, Warin," she voiced softly, and yet still wary of what price she would pay this night for his help.

"Just how grateful are you, my dear? Although you are the best tumble I have had in some time, I do not relish having my neck stretched on a rope for you," Warin pushed off the beam and walked around her, making her uneasy. "Why do you care what happens to her anyway? Was not getting rid of your husband enough for you?"

She went to slap his face, but he easily grabbed her wrist, giving it a small twist. She cried out. "How dare you?" Marguerite gasped.

He laughed in her face as he leaned down but inches from her own. "My, my, my...you have become quite the little martyr, have you not? You kill your husband and plan to get rid of his son's wife then act as if you have been the one wronged."

"Who do you think you are to judge me so?" she declared with ferocity through clenched teeth.

"I am the man who still holds something you want," he gave her a mischievous grin, holding out the flask, "or did you forget about this?"

"Will it work?"

"Again, you doubt me. I should be hurt by your refusal to take me at my word."

"Why should I trust you that it will not kill him, too?"

"If you had followed my instructions, your dear departed husband would still be alive and most biddable so you could find where he hid his gold," he said roughly. "I told you, but a drop or two would do the trick, and he would have told you anything you asked of him, but you never did listen to me."

"I have looked everywhere I could think as to where Everard may have hid his coinage, but to no avail. If I find his monies, I will pay you handsomely, as I promised you I would for helping me." Marguerite reached for the vial again. "Give it to me!" she ordered. Her eyes widened when he rubbed his manhood up against her.

"'Tis exactly what I had in mind," he said as he pulled her into the shadows of the stable and chuckled. "Mayhap, you would be worth it after all."

'Twas some time later that Marguerite carefully made her way back into the manor with a satisfied grin on her visage. Warin may be a bit of a brute, but he truly did know how to make her moan in pleasure. As she made her way to her chamber, she passed Riorden's door and fondly remembered their brief time together. With a shake of her head and the vial hidden in the folds of her cloak, she was appeased with the knowledge that he, too, would be in her bed afore long. As for his wife...well...she would not be around much longer to be a problem at all. As far as Marguerite was concerned, Katherine's demise could not happen soon enough.

FIFTEEN

KATHERINE'S LEGS WERE BEGINNING TO CRAMP. How long she had been kneeling on the cold, hard stones of the chapel floor, praying for Riorden's safety, she couldn't say. Her knees had become numb at least an hour ago, and yet still she kept her vigil before the marble statue of St. Christopher. It was the least she could do for her peace of mind, since there was little else to occupy her thoughts other than her own musings warring inside her head.

She couldn't remember ever having prayed so much in her life. Each morning since Riorden had left, she attended mass with the other inhabitants of the castle. The small chapel, located next to the barbican gate, filled up quickly, but her place as the keep's new mistress was always reserved in the front. Personally, she wouldn't have minded if she blended in with the rest of the people who crammed the benches behind her. She couldn't understand the Latin the priest spoke anyway, but she knew it was important she set a good example. At least Gavin, Brianna, and Aiden kept her company so she didn't sit alone.

She heard someone enter the chapel but continued on with her prayers...prayers she was unsure were going to be answered any time in the near future. Was she even praying in earnest? She didn't think so, since her mind continued to wander in so many directions, her heart was just plain aching.

She was ruining it all, and with little help from Marguerite! How many times had she been warned that her time here at Warkworth would be put to the test until that vicious woman would be dispatched to her dower house? Well, she was at her dower house, all right...along with *her* husband! She knew they would both be returning soon to Warkworth, as one trip wouldn't be sufficient, but it grated on her nerves that they were basically alone together. Her faith in her marriage wavered in uncertainty, knowing there was nothing to stop Marguerite from taking what she wanted most. Why she even doubted Riorden and the love they bore one another only confused her more.

Jealousy! Was there really any other emotion that could tear a relationship apart faster than jealousy? It had always been the worst emotion for her to try and control, most likely because she had been cheated on more than once in her past. It was hard for her to trust people, and, because she had been hurt in her past relationships, she was left feeling vulnerable and alone.

With her emotions raw and her current state of being pregnant, everything and anything was escalated tenfold. She was angry with the world. She was angry that Riorden, at the very least, hadn't taken her with him. More importantly, she was angry with herself for letting Marguerite get the best of her. Yet, she had no idea how to stop all these horrible feelings from rearing up in the forefront of her mind. The knife in her back twisted sharply to the point where she could almost feel someone pouring salt into the open wound. She supposed the thought of being poisoned tended to do that to a person. If only Riorden would have listened to her concerns before he rode away still irritated at her behavior.

"How long has she been at it today?"

Katherine winced hearing Aiden's voice behind her, and his loudness seemed out of place within the quiet chapel.

"Long enough," Caldwell's low deep voice answered from his constant vigil against the chapel wall. Even his tone spoke that he felt she had done her duty toward her husband from the length of her prayers.

"I can't get her to leave, Aiden," Brianna answered, clearly exasperated with her efforts that had failed. "Even Gavin had no luck."

Katherine sighed, knowing Aiden would be determined to take care of her, since she had been put under his protection. For someone younger than her by two years, he tended to be pretty bossy. In the last week, she barely had the energy to fight with him anymore.

She began to move at his gentle urging as he lightly steadied her arm at her elbow. Her legs wobbled, and if not for Aiden's arm snaking around her waist, she would have fallen.

"Easy now, Katherine. I have you," he said quietly. "Do you even have the slightest inkling in that pretty little head of yours that he shall have mine served on a platter if any harm befalls you?"

"Who?" she asked softly, still trying to get her footing as the blood rushed down her tingling legs. She gritted her teeth, not wanting to disturb the sanctuary of the chapel by stomping her sleeping feet as the pin pricks pierced each one with every step she took.

"Your husband, that is who, my lady. When he put you in my care, I am sure 'twas not for you to spend all of your days praying for his soul. I must admit, however, that I respect your dedication on his behalf. If only I could be so lucky as to have someone who loved me just as deeply."

She looked up into his violet eyes with tears shimmering in her own. "I only mean to do all I can to keep him safe, Aiden," she barely managed to say.

"I know we do not know each other well, Katherine, but I must needs ask. Where is the woman who stood up to Riorden at Berwyck not that long ago? She was a feisty wench, and I admired her spirit. I am just as sure your husband did, as well."

She shook her head sadly and sat down next to Brianna on the bench. Aiden came and sat on the other side of her. "I don't know who she is anymore. I'm so afraid..." Her voice trailed off, since she wasn't sure she should worry anyone, especially Brianna, with what Lord Everard had told her.

She watched as Aiden and Brie exchanged silent glances with one another before Aiden made a gesture that Brianna seemingly interpreted as asking her to leave. She rose, gave Katherine a brief kiss on the cheek and left the chapel.

"I will watch her now, Caldwell," Aiden insisted. "You have my word no harm shall befall your mistress."

"If you insist," Caldwell replied, clearly not sure he should be leaving her side. He seemed to be everywhere she went, and to be honest, Katherine wouldn't mind a little privacy for a change.

"I do," Aiden answered as he watched Caldwell take his leave.

Katherine took a deep breath. "Thank you for that."

"Now...we are alone, so tell me what has you so frightened that you act like a meek little mouse instead of the lioness I know you can be?" He reached for her hand, giving it a small pat until she gave him the briefest of smiles.

"Me? A lioness? I hardly think so Aiden, but thanks for the vote of confidence."

He gave a brief laugh. "Oh, I think she is still there. We must needs bring her back is all," he said. "So tell me your fears and hold nothing back, for I cannot in good conscious protect you fully unless I know what I may come up against."

Katherine gave a heavy sigh before she began telling him everything that had occurred. Once she started, she found it hard to stop as she unburdened her soul, not only from her distress of seeing Marguerite ride off with Riorden, but also for all the past hurt she had endured in her younger years. He listened compassionately until she began spilling the beans about what Lord Everard had said, and then Aiden's temper erupted.

He began to pace frantically in front of her. Katherine could only assume he forgot he was in a church, since she could have sworn she heard a curse word or two thrown in with all the Gaelic that came spewing forth from his mouth. He must have suddenly realized what he was doing, for he gave a brief bow to the altar, made the sign of the cross, and took her elbow again, steering her away from the chapel. Not until they were in the open afternoon air did he at last speak to her.

"Let us away, lassie. There is much to do afore Riorden returns, and I must needs have speech with him," Aiden declared, still ushering her across the baily.

"But he refuses to hear anything about his father. I don't think you should test his temper," she warned. "It wasn't a pretty sight, I assure you."

"I should think he had better start listening, especially if it means the wellbeing of his wife!"

He continued dragging her along until she tugged on his arm to slow his frantic pace. "Where are we going?" she asked, trying to catch her breath.

"'Tis obvious, is it not?" He waited for Katherine to answer, but she only stared at him dumbfounded. "If you are going to stay here, then 'tis time you learn to ride. At least I will know that if the need arises, you will be able to get yourself to a horse to flee the grounds."

"But, Aiden, I—"

He held up his hand to stop her and then got the strangest look upon his face. "Katherine...how do I say this without being...well...we just do not speak of such things to ladies we are not wed to."

She gave a bubbly laugh for the first time in a long while then hid her smile behind her hand. "Are you talking about my pregnancy, Aiden?" She laughed again as she saw him blush as red as the roots of his hair.

"'Tis unseemly to discuss the subject, I know, but I feel the matter must needs be addressed," he muttered in embarrassment.

"Then it's a good thing I'm a modern kind of gal, since it's no big deal to speak of such things where I come from," she said. "Would you like to feel the bump I've got growing here?"

"Eee gads, no! Riorden would have my head for sure if I dared such a liberty!" Aiden bellowed.

Katherine's laughter rang out again. "No? Well, I won't pressure you, but I assure you it's perfectly fine in the twenty-first century."

"'Tis a good thing I have no intention of going anywhere near your future world if the women are as bold as you. I do not think my chivalry would last very long with all the temptation."

"You don't know the half of it, Aiden, but what was your point of this whole conversation?"

"Just that you be careful. I would not wish to be the cause of you losing Riorden's heir."

"I will be," Katherine promised.

Heading into the stables, Aiden made to grab a side saddle, and Katherine reached out her hand to halt his progress.

"No way, Aiden. If you're going to teach me to ride, I want a normal saddle, if you please."

"But, Katherine, 'tis not seemly that you should ride thusly." Aiden stared at her as if she had lost all sense in her head. She folded her arms in front of her and gave him a look her mother would have been proud of.

"If you want me to be careful, then get a regular saddle. No woman should swing her leg over such a device and perch herself only half way on with the constant fear of falling off."

She listened as Aiden began cursing again, voicing his objections, but she ignored his grumblings. Surely, it had to have been a man who invented such a stupid convention that women must adhere to. But she would ride as she saw fit and be damned of how anyone thought of her. The only opinion that mattered anyway was her husband's.

Katherine felt somewhat lighthearted for the first time in over a week since Riorden left. With Aiden's help, they began her lessons on how to ride. She soon realized she wasn't about to become an expert horsewoman overnight, but at least she put everything into what Aiden was attempting to teach her. Her only thoughts were to prove to Riorden that he could be proud of her. She could already imagine the look on his face when he saw she had attempted to learn to ride in his absence. With that thought in mind, she smiled, knowing he would soon be coming back home...to her.

SIXTEEN

BEADS OF SWEAT ROLLED DOWN Riorden's face. Wiping his brow with the back of his arm, he again took ax in hand and swung it over his head in a downward plunge. There was an instant satisfaction, feeling the tool slice through the brittle wood with a loud smack. He performed the task again with the same results. Picking up the split pieces, he tossed them into the growing pile of logs that would heat the hearths come the winter. Just as quickly as he added to the mound, an ever diligent serf would take them away to neatly stack the logs by the rear door to the manor.

'Twas a busy, mindless job, but work that must needs be done, and who better than he to hack away at what once was a tree of some considerable size. Besides...it took his mind off more troubling matters that he did not wish to think on. Smack went the ax again, only this time wood splinters went flying, narrowly missing his head.

"Mayhap you should take a break, if you wish to keep your eyesight, *mon ami.*"

Riorden looked up and noticed Nathaniel, lounging against a nearby tree. He had been so focused on cleaving the wood, he could only wonder how long Nathaniel had stood there. He propped his boot on the solid trunk he had been using as a chopping block and gazed at his friend. "There is another ax, if you would care to dirty your hands with some exercise and join me."

Nathaniel only chuckled. "I am not sure I would want to disturb you, since you appear to be taking out your aggravation on what still needs be cut. Am I intruding? Do you wish to be alone?"

"Nay, I would not mind a brief respite from this tedious chore."

Riorden put the ax down and retrieved his tunic where he had left it on the near-dead grass. He pulled it over his head afore Nathaniel at last spoke.

"You should not give the lady the satisfaction of being able to ogle you," Nathaniel counseled. "She watches your every move, but you knew that, did you not?"

"Aye, I knew...not that I can do much to stop her gawking."

The silence stretched between them, almost awkwardly, despite the years they had traveled and warred together. One did not ride as part of the Devil's Dragon of Blackmore's personal guard and not feel a certain kinship with someone who closely guarded one's back.

"Why did you not bring her with you?" prodded Nathaniel for an answer.

"You mean Katherine?"

"Who else would I mean?"

Riorden looked up to the manor and saw the drapery flutter in one of the upper windows. 'Twas obvious Marguerite was once again spying on him. It seemed as if every time he turned around that woman was close at hand. "I did not want to subject my wife to the bitterness that consumes Marguerite's life of late."

"And you think leaving your wife behind to mull over what the wench does with you in her absence will bring her peace of mind?"

"Katherine knows how I feel about her. She has nothing to be jealous of," Riorden muttered, taking a swig of water from a flask his friend handed him.

"Ha! You know nothing of women, Riorden, if you think Lady Katherine is not feeling the full effects of your absence." Nathaniel replied. "I cannot say as I would blame her. There is something about your father's widow that is not quite right. She seems tetched in the head, if you take my meaning." Nathaniel's gesture of pointing a crooked finger at his own temple and contorting one side of his face illustrated his meaning.

Riorden ran his fingers through his hair. "She claims my father's ghost haunts her."

"Truly?" At Riorden's nod, Nathaniel continued. "That is interesting. I wonder what she did to deserve that, do you suppose."

"I do not try to guess anything where my sire is concerned, be he dead or when he was of this earth," grumbled Riorden.

"Mayhap, you should."

"Why?"

"Oh, I do not know... Mayhap, because your ex-lover is going mad from his haunting could be a good enough reason. I would think that if your wife, and even your brother, has had speech with your father, 'twould be my guess he has something of import to tell you that was left unsaid whilst he was alive. That alone should be of concern to you," Nathaniel surmised. "Take your pick of which you feel is the most critical aspect to explore."

"'Tis a moot point, since I have not seen his ghostly apparition come afore me," Riorden snarled.

"You should make the effort, Riorden. I have the notion that to continue to ignore your past, will cost you what you hold most dear in your future."

Riorden pondered his words with a heavy sigh. "I cannot lose Katherine. She is all to me."

Nathaniel gave him a hardy pat on the back. "Then make sure she is aware of this, Riorden. You have been extremely blessed to have a woman such as your Katherine brought into your life to bring you comfort. I know of no other to be as fortunate as you, *mon ami*, especially considering exactly how far she has come to find you.

"You know from whence she hails?" Riorden asked in surprise. He had not realized that they had not guarded their secret better.

"Do you not mean to say *when*?" Nathaniel chuckled.

"'Tis not a matter that should be jested about, for it could cost Katherine and Lady Brianna their lives if the wrong person learned of such knowledge." Riorden gave a brief glance upward again to see that Marguerite was still gone and not eavesdropping on their conversation. He returned his attention to Nathaniel and studied his friend for several minutes. "How did you know?"

"I learned of it whilst still at Berwyck, but have no fear. The mystery of your lovely lady's origin is safe with me. Nonetheless, I would keep Lady Katherine close, if I were you."

Riorden stared at his friend, as if Nathaniel had imparted such words of wisdom that would never have crossed his mind.

"You think Katherine is in danger? Marguerite is mean spirited, but I hardly consider her to have such evil intent."

"Then open your eyes, Riorden, afore 'tis too late! Do not be so blinded by your anger with your father and your past that you refuse to listen to those who warn you of what they themselves can see behind your back. You should watch yours, by the way, especially where Marguerite in concerned. 'Tis plane to see she wants you, but only she knows for sure how far she's willing to go afore she stakes her claim."

Riorden watched Nathaniel leave him, wondering if his comrade had voiced what even he himself had been holding back for the past se'nnight. His heart skipped a beat with thoughts of Katherine being in some kind of unknown danger, and he quickly felt the need to return to Warkworth...and his wife.

Marguerite carefully balanced the bottle and cup she held on a tray and wrapped lightly on the door afore her. With the call to enter, she turned the handle and came to a sudden halt at what her eyes beheld.

"You are leaving?" she asked in disbelief. She had thought she would have more time with him.

"Aye." Riorden gave her a simple answer and went back to his task of throwing his garments into a bag. From the looks of things, he appeared to be in a hurry and would leave afore the morn's end.

"But, I thought we were to stay here at least another se'nnight. There is still much to do, unless I misunderstood you."

He looked at her with a sideways glance, as if noticing her for the first time. He turned away from her, continuing on with his task without a care that she was upset with his parting. "You mistook nothing, Marguerite."

"I brought you something to drink," she offered in the hopes she could get him to sample the heady red wine.

"Set it there," he said with a noncommittal nod of his head in the direction of his desk.

She crossed the room, lingering slightly as she passed him. It had been so very long since she had the opportunity to be alone with him. He was so close. All she wanted to do was reach out her hand to touch and feel the strength of his broad shoulders. And yet, she would be a fool to do so and needed to exercise some patience. She poured the wine into a chalice and offered it to him. If only he would but take one sip. 'Twould be the start of her plans coming to fruition.

"I am not in need of sustenance, Marguerite. As you can see, I am in a hurry," Riorden said briskly.

"But, what about me? Dunhaven Manor is far from ready to move in completely, and most of my things are still at Warkworth and in need of arranging for transport," she complained.

Riorden stopped his busy packing long enough to look at her again.

If only she would see some small measure of love in those glorious eyes as he had given her all those years ago. But there was nothing showing within them except contempt and loathing, making her all the more determined to keep him as close to her as possible.

"Come if you wish, but if you do so, then you must needs hurry. I leave within the hour, with or without you." Riorden picked up his satchel and strode to the door, leaving her to forlornly observe his retreating backside 'til the door slammed shut behind him.

Coming back to her senses after flinching from the loud sound that ricocheted in her head, she hurriedly made her way to her own chamber to throw a few things into a satchel for the ride back to Warkworth. Inwardly, she cursed, knowing upon her return Everard would torment her now more than ever for leaving the grounds. With the small glass vial tucked in the folds of her gown, she made her way below, more determined than ever to have Riorden in her bed. She already envisioned their return to Warkworth and a start of their new life together.

SEVENTEEN

"WOULD YOU JUST LOOK AT IT, Brie? I mean really look at it!" Katherine exclaimed with sheer excitement, her eyes practically glowed as her gaze rested on the castle off in the distance.

Brianna reached over and patted her hand. "Yes, dear, I see it, just as I saw it the last twelve times you've commented on it," she said with a laugh.

Katherine gave her a sly smirk. "Well, I just can't help myself from wanting to jump up and down, knowing I'm living in a castle. It's rather spectacular, don't you think?"

"Of course, I do, silly. Who wouldn't?"

Aiden tossed an apple up in the air and caught it as they continued their picnic under the shade of a tree. "I just do not see what all the fuss is about," he murmured, taking a bite of the juicy fruit. "'Tis hardly anything to get overly enthusiastic about, at any rate, nor is it out of the ordinary. Do they not have castles where you come from?"

Katherine leaned over and gave him a playful push. "You're just spoiled because you've lived your entire life at Berwyck, and no...we may have large houses or mansions, but nothing that could compare to what I now call my home and the history behind all these castles you take for granted. Can you just imagine the number of the souls who will walk through those passageways over the centuries?"

Gavin reached his hand out to Brianna and tucked a piece of her hair behind her ear. "I suppose, in the greater scheme of things, we shall one day be counted as among those souls you now speak of Katherine."

She quirked her brow at him while the reality of his words began to sink in. "Well...that's a sobering thought." Lost in pondering life's mysteries, she began to think of the life she left behind in the future. "I wonder sometimes, even as we sit here, if maybe Juliana and Emily are walking the same ground we are, only back in the twenty-first century."

Brianna gave a sad sigh. "Don't you mean ahead, Katie?"

Katherine gave a shake of her head. "I guess, I do. It gets a little confusing sometimes, doesn't it?"

"I wonder how they're managing without our sparkling conversations brightening up their Saturday mornings at the coffee shop," Brianna mused.

"What is this coffee shop you speak of, Brie?" Gavin inquired, using Katherine's nickname for her friend. "Is there much danger in such a place?"

Brianna's laughter rang out, and she gave Gavin's cheek a quick kiss. "The only danger is having to wait in line just to get your caffeine fix," she replied briefly. He gave her another curious look before she answered his unspoken question. "I'll tell you about it later, my love."

"What I wouldn't give for a white chocolate mocha right about now," Katherine said with a heavenly look.

Aiden rose with an impatient look. "You women are making me daft with your future talk. Enough so, that I think 'tis time to get back to work."

"Oh, come on, Aiden. Let's just enjoy the beautiful day a little longer," Katherine cajoled as she lounged back on the blanket she was sitting on. She wouldn't admit it to anyone, but her backside was already pretty sore from sitting so long in the saddle all morning.

"Do not think you can get me to change my mind with such a look. It may work with Riordan, but 'twill certainly not work with me," Aiden answered, wagging his finger at her.

"But, Aiden, I—"

"Enough, and stop your whining. Your break is over, Katherine. Get yourself back on your horse, and let us continue with your training," Aiden ordered.

Katherine rose, knowing she had lost the battle. "Slave driver," she tossed over her head. Taking the reins of her horse, she put her foot in the stirrup, grabbed the pommel, and swung her leg over the saddle. She tried not to think about falling off as she once again began taking the horse through the routine they had been at before their lunch. It was a slow trot and, although she was being bounced around all over the place, she had become comfortable with the steady pace.

"Grip her with your knees a little tighter, Katie," Brianna called out, "and sit up straighter!"

Katherine took her horse around the field in a circle another time, trying to perform Brie's instructions. She smiled in delight when she felt she was doing better. She slowed the mare and brought her to a halt, giving the animal a pat on her neck in appreciation of her patience with such a novice rider. She looked down at her friend, who now sat prettily on a small stool Gavin had brought for her comfort. Gavin was just as content, lying back on a blanket at her feet.

"Again Katherine!" Aiden demanded from the tree he was propped up against. "You may not rest as yet, my lady! We have only just started again. Now, get going."

"Give me a break, will ya, Aiden?" Katherine smirked as she watched him attempt to make out her meaning. His perplexed expression seemed almost painful.

"Stop with your future words, or you will give me a headache, lassie!"

Brianna's laughter rang out, as even Gavin looked at the women quizzically. "Trust me Aiden, it could be so much worse. We're trying to be good and watch our language," she said.

Aiden only shook his head, and Katherine again tried to muffle her laughter.

"Lady Brianna, I am afraid to ask. How worse could it be?" Aiden suggested for her to continue.

"I think, I'll just keep quiet for the good of the cause," Brianna murmured and received a quick kiss from Gavin, who then rose to stand next to Aiden.

"Well, I think you are doing just splendidly, Katherine, especially for someone who has an aversion to horses," Gavin praised. "My brother will be most pleased."

Katherine gave a nod of her head. With a complete air of confidence, she turned the mare to resume her lessons. She had only gone in a circle the parameter of the field three times before she heard Aiden shout out to her again.

"Now, flick at the reins and give her another kick and bring her up into a canter!"

"Go for it Katie! You're ready," Brianna encouraged with a wave.

Nervous, but thinking it couldn't be that hard to take that next step, she did as instructed, or so she thought. She wasn't ready for the horse to bolt forward and felt herself lose her balance in the saddle. The little mare took the bit between her teeth and before Katherine knew what was happening, she lost her grip on the reins and they now hung, uselessly, out of reach. The mare began galloping away, as if she had only been waiting for the taste of freedom. Katherine screamed for help as she heard her friends' voices fade in the distance and the terrain blur before her eyes.

Katherine held onto the saddle as if her life, and that of her unborn child, depended on it, which of course it did. Tears stung her eyes and she cursed at her own foolishness that she would do something so idiotic as to risk the life of her baby.

The sound of thundering hooves at last began to penetrate the frightful experience she was having, and she was thankful that Aiden or Gavin had at last come to her rescue. She continued to cry out for help, as if they couldn't see her need. Squeezing her eyes closed, she suddenly felt an arm snake around her waist as she was pulled from her saddle and settled against a warm comforting form.

Her eyes flew open as she inhaled the familiar scent that was all Riorden. Her words of expressing her thanks and to welcome him home were frozen upon her lips as she took in his frigid, blue eyes. They held pure fury. He pulled Beast to a halt. She barely saw Aiden fly past in pursuit of her wayward mare.

"Have you lost your wits, Katherine? Explain yourself and tell me what the bloody hell you think you are doing on a horse, madam!" Riorden roared. "Is this how you take care of our babe?"

"I wanted to surprise you on your return," Katherine replied, trying to calm the fear that seemed to be stuck in her throat.

She had never witnessed him looking at her in such a manner and it scared the daylights out of her to see such an angry expression leveled, by him, on her.

"How? By getting yourself injured or losing the babe?" he bellowed.

"I would never do anything to harm our baby," she cried out, interrupting his tirade.

"Then what are you doing racing wild throughout the countryside," he shouted. "I told you I would teach you myself how to ride."

Katherine put her arms around his waist and felt his own tighten around her. "I'm so sorry, Riorden. I just wanted you to be proud of me," she whispered as tears again rushed to her eyes. She really was such a pansy.

"I *am* proud of you, Katherine," Riorden said with a big sigh. "You gave me a terrible fright is all."

Aiden came abreast of them, leading Katherine's docile mare. Katherine knew Riorden would have a few choice words for him, as well. "You and I will have speech, once we return to the keep, and I see that Katherine has rested." Riorden's tone was brusque.

Katherine gave Aiden a look she hoped came across as saying she was sorry for the tongue lashing he was sure to receive. He returned it in kind. It seemed they had an understanding of sorts between them. As they made their way through the village, Katherine had the distinct feeling, now that Riorden had returned, that her problems had only just begun. So much for what was once a very lovely afternoon.

Riorden quietly closed his chamber door so as not to disturb Katherine's sleeping form. He had stayed with her 'til she had fallen into a restless sleep. He had watched her for some time and could only ponder what nightmare was currently making her sleep so troubling. He could guess at a hundred different scenarios, any of which could be accurate. What worried him the most was generally the dreams they shared tended to come true in one form or another.

He made his way up the tallest tower of the keep to try to clear his head. 'Twas a steady climb up the steep steps, but, once outside, the view was well worth it. He inhaled deeply of the brisk fall air and scanned the horizon of what was once again his home. Though he was still not sure how he felt about being back in a place so filled with ill memories.

He knew he was being unreasonable and downright ornery towards his wife. His anger with his father was getting the best of him, making him lash out to the one person he had no wish to hurt. This place and his angry emotions that assailed him from every direction were going to be his downfall if he did not get a hold of them. He was uncertain where to even start.

Feeling as if he was putting off the inevitable, he made his way back down into the Great Hall in search of Gavin. He saw Mabel and her daughter tidying up after the noon meal.

"Have you perchance seen my brother, Mabel?" Riorden asked.

"I believe he was heading to the Garrison Hall, milord. Is the mistress well after her mishap?" Mabel asked gently.

Afore he could answer, young Mary tugged at his tunic. "Ye will not stay mad at the Lady Katherine, will ye, milord?"

"Mary!" Mabel said aghast. "Me apologies, milord!"

He gave the girl a small pat on her head. "Nay, Mary. I will not stay mad at your mistress for long."

It seemed to placate the child as she turned back to the duties her mother had assigned her. Riorden made his way outside to find his brother. He espied him just leaving the Lion Tower and met him in the outer courtyard.

"I was just coming to find you, Riorden," Gavin proclaimed with a smile. "Good news! I just received a missive from the king, granting permission for Brianna and myself to be wed. She has been busy sewing her gown, hoping for our request to be granted. I cannot wait to tell her the news!"

Riorden slapped his brother on the back. "These are glad tidings, are they not? Have you spoken with the priest?"

"Aye. I was just going to check with Brianna to see if she could be ready within two days hence," Gavin explained. "No offense, brother, but I am ready to get us wed so we may take ourselves to our own keep and be settled."

Riorden chuckled, watching his brother's enthusiasm. "I can imagine so. You have been waiting for some time now to claim your bride. I do not know how you have restrained yourself for so long."

Gavin gave him a grin. "'Tis been hard, but I know she will be worth the wait."

Riorden saw his brother's impatience to be on his way to find his lady and laughed. "Well, go on with you. Why are you standing here talking to me when you have a wedding to see to?"

Perchance, a wedding was just what he needed to take his mind off his troubles. His mind wandered momentarily to his own wedding with Katherine, and how she had been a vision of loveliness that day. He thought he could not be any happier than the day they had wed 'til he learned she carried his child. *Aye!* A wedding was just what was needed to put the past where it belonged...in the past.

With that thought in the forefront of his mind, he made his way to the lists for some much needed practice. There was more than one way to take care of the bygone days that tortured his memory, and what better way than to spend the afternoon hacking away with a sword. 'Twas just what he stood in need of.

Eighteen

THE NEW DAY DAWNED BRIGHT with only a few clouds in the distant horizon, but it was of no concern to those waiting in Warkworth's chapel. Today was a day of celebration, for Gavin and Brianna would at last become man and wife.

Standing in the shadows at the back of the chamber, Katherine gazed on her friend as Brie fidgeted with the golden belt so it was just right underneath her bosom. The gown really was a lovely blue that complimented her friend's olive skin and black hair. Her tresses had grown in the past three or so months since they had traveled to the twelfth century, and Brianna had somehow managed to upsweep even the shorter strands into a coiffeur that was pleasing to the eye. Brie truly did have a talent for anything requiring finesse; from hair styling, to sewing finery, to fending for herself, and Katherine would miss her once she left this evening to go to her new home. By day's end, Katherine would now have only herself to depend on, with the exception of her husband. The thought left her feeling somewhat bereft, considering she should be happy for her friend.

"Will I do?" Brianna asked with a shaky voice. She was obviously nervous, although Katherine was not sure why. Brie would be marrying her own glorious knight this day, her reason for remaining in the past.

"You look stunning, Brie," Katherine replied with a smile. "No bride has ever looked lovelier."

"I don't know about that, Katie," Brie giggled. "If I recall, you looked pretty surreal on your own wedding day."

Katherine took her friend's hand and held it for several moments while silence surrounded them. She tried to keep the tears from her eyes, but somehow they managed to spill over all the same. Brie wiped them away.

"Don't cry, sissy. It's not like we're never going to see one another again. I'm a day's ride inland, maybe less, and Gavin has promised, if nothing else, we can return for the birth of your baby."

Katherine gave a weak grin. "I'm just over emotional of late and can't seem to keep anything hidden anymore."

"I can't blame you, Katie, but please don't let her get the best of you, my dear. Remember, he chose you to make his wife, not her, and he loves you."

Katherine shook off her melancholy feeling and smiled brightly for her friend. "I just want you to be happy, Brie. I'm going to miss having you close." They wrapped their arms around one another before Katherine gave a merry laugh. "Come on, sis. You've waited long enough. Let's get you married!"

Katherine made her way to her husband's side, giving him a welcoming smile.

"All is well, Kat?" he whispered in her ear.

"Yes. We were just taking a couple of minutes to ourselves, since it will be some time before the opportunity presents itself again."

Before Riorden could continue their conversation, the priest began to say mass. Katherine's eyes became sleepy as she tried to stay awake, listening to the man's monotone voice. At least an hour or more later, Brianna and Gavin were pronounced man and wife, and they were signing their marriage contract. Her sister of her heart gazed up after she had proudly written her name with the quill that had been provided. Katherine had never seen Brianna look more radiant. This poignant moment they shared made her miss Juliana and Emily even more, especially knowing she and Brie had missed out on their weddings, as well.

They made their way to the Great Hall where a wedding feast was already being laid out. Riorden had found a few minstrels in the village, who even now were tuning their instruments to provide the afternoon's entertainment.

Katherine had just made a few last minutes suggestions to Mabel when she noticed Marguerite heading down a set of stairs off the kitchen area. Although she knew the cellars were below, Katherine had never wandered down into the storehouse of Warkworth's keep. Her curiosity getting the better of her, she wondered what her nemesis was up to, and she slowly made to follow her down the set of narrow stairs.

Darker than she thought it would be, the chamber was musky, reminding her of the smell of an old basement that had flooded once or twice and had remained wet with mold. She crinkled her nose and continued onward. Then she came to a tunnel of sorts, with only a couple of torches to light the way. If she hadn't felt on edge with her decision to follow Marguerite before, she certainly did now.

She remembered when she had watched a scary movie in her youth and for months afterwards, she had been terrified of the dark. She shivered, hearing the movie theme music play inside her head now. Even after all this time, that terrifying tune still gave her the willies and bothered her enough to make her swallow hard. What the hell she was doing? What was she leading herself into? She felt as though something was going to jump out at her, but even though she just knew it was going to happen, she couldn't seem to stop herself from taking another step forward when she should be turning around and going back the way she came to safety. Emily would say the feeling was like waiting for the zombie apocalypse to begin, overwhelming fear, but intense curiosity at the same time. This stupid situation seemed no different, so she continued into the darkness, wondering what Marguerite was up to.

She passed several rooms filled with food stuff, barrels of ale and wine, and all other manner of household goods. When she heard footsteps heading toward her, she quickly hid behind one of the barrels and peeked around the edge carefully to see what was going on. Her heart was hammering in her chest, and she felt like anyone and everyone could hear it, loud enough to alert Marguerite if she was near.

Katherine saw Marguerite clutching a bottle of something. She supposed there was nothing strange about that. The woman might merely want something to quench her thirst in her room. But what was strange, is that she would go and fetch it herself. If she had learned anything about Marguerite, it was that the woman liked to be waited on, hand and foot. Even the servants whispered how demanding she had become, now that Riorden had returned to dwell at the estate. Marguerite had more servants at her beck and call than she had had before, and the woman thrived on the attention and power she wielded whenever the opportunity presented itself.

Marguerite left, her footsteps quickly fading until Katherine felt it was safe to follow. Not until she was back within the Great Hall did she feel she could let out a deep breath of relief. Unfortunately, it didn't last long. Her apprehension quickly returned when she saw Marguerite linger at the table on the raised dais before she made her way up the stairs, Katherine assumed, to her room.

Riorden came to her side, and she shakily took his arm as he led her to the feast that was now ready. She saw her wine had already been poured into a chalice set at her place. Without thinking of what she had just witnessed, she reached for the cup in order to quench her thirst and calm her shattered nerves.

"Nay, Katherine!" She heard Lord Everard's voice come into her head.

Before her hand even touched the stem, she saw the goblet being tipped over and watched in fascination as the contents spilled onto the white linen, like a slow moving river of blood. Only God above knew for sure what a ghost had just saved her from.

Riorden's gaze had drifted to her, but she only mumbled an apology over her clumsiness. But the damage was done to her peace of mind. It was hard to try to enjoy the remainder of the celebration, although it was not for lack of trying on Katherine's part. Riorden took her onto the floor so they could dance to some of the slower tunes that would not overly exert her. He had been most attentive the entire night, even when the men began drinking something heavier than wine and ale.

Before too long, Gavin and Brianna began saying their farewells, much to Katherine's dismay. A feeling of sudden panic began to consume her, knowing that her only lifeline to her past life was leaving her. Not until Brianna was about to depart to start her own happily-ever-after story did Katherine realize how much she had been relying on her friend for moral support.

Standing in the outer baily with her sister of her heart held close in her arms, Katherine gave the younger girl one last hug before she stepped back and held her at arm's length. Reaching up, she cupped Brianna's face and gave her a weak smile. "Be happy, Brie," she whispered softly, trying to hold up the happy façade she had plastered on her face, and trying her best not to crumble.

"I'll see you again soon." Brie assured her.

Katherine could only give her a brief nod before Gavin came and assisted Brianna onto her horse. She had an uncanny premonition that it would be a long time before she saw her friend again. Despair settled around her heart like the darkest demon consuming the human soul. Watching their party leave Warkworth, she kept her gaze focused on the barbican gate, even after the portcullis began to lower, watching her dearest friend ride away with her new husband.

She waved off Riorden's concern and felt his hand giving her a squeeze. It was almost as if he silently told her everything would be all right. Katherine knew better. Needing to be alone, she excused herself and went up onto one of the battlement walls. It didn't take long before she saw the dust settle back into place, leaving no trace that Brianna had ever been there.

Not wanting to fight the feeling as exhaustion at last took its toll on her, she decided to lie down and rest. At least within her own chamber walls, she could feel safe and secure. She needed the comfort of finding some sort of solace that had evaded her during the daylight hours. Yet, she would only find her worst nightmare that would return to haunt her this eve. For in her sleep, Katherine shivered with dread as the mists of Time came and took back one of its own...

NINETEEN

MARGUERITE SMIRKED AS SHE OBSERVED Katherine's absence from the celebration. She was glad for it 'til she overheard one of the ladies who attended Katherine mention the current Countess of Warkworth was with child. *With child!* Was it just dumb, blind luck that continued to mar her miserable life? Wasn't it enough that her dead husband tormented her whenever she tried to live some kind of normal existence here at Warkworth? When would something go her way for a change?

Mayhap that time was now, she mused with a smile, noticing how the revelers continued to take cup in hand and be merry. That they did so was not out of the ordinary, since a wedding celebration could go on 'til the early hours of the morn. What made Marguerite extremely pleased was that Riorden had not retired to join his wife.

Seizing the opportunity that presented itself so nicely, Marguerite went to a nearby table, arranged several cups on a tray and poured draughts of whiskey into each of them. Ensuring that she was unobserved, she reached for the vial, pulled out the stopper, and watched as one small drop dripped into one of the cups.

She bit her lip in indecision if this would be enough, for it seemed like such a paltry amount to have the effect she desired. She was about to pour another into the cup she would offer to Riorden when Warin's words came back to her. Better too little than for Riorden to end up like his father. She would not make the same mistake twice.

Taking the tray in hand, she balanced it carefully with a feeling she had tried this once afore and failed. But she was determined more than ever that the time was right, so she pressed forward towards the large hearth where Riorden stood with several of his guardsmen.

"Something to drink, good sirs?" she murmured with a welcoming smile.

She rotated the tray when eager hands reached for the cups 'til only one remained. She attempted to not appear anxious as Riorden took the intended cup in hand.

"Playing servant, Marguerite?" he jeered with a smothered laugh. "I would think this was beneath you."

She gave a careless shrug, as if his words did not hurt her feelings. "I was just trying to help."

Marguerite left the men standing there 'til one of the guards, Ulrick she thought his name was, raised his goblet in a toast to the bride and groom. From the dim corner, she stood in the shadows watching as, along with the rest of his men, Riorden downed the contents of his cup. She almost clapped her hands in glee but subdued the impulse. Now, all she had to do was wait...

Riorden passed his hand through his hair, even as he tried to focus on the words Nathaniel and Aiden were discussing. He had not thought he had drunk so much that 'twould cause him to become this inebriated, but he must have been wrong. He needed to make his way to his chamber afore he passed out. If he were to do so in front of his men, he would never hear the end of it.

"I will retire," he said to his men. He thought they made a joke about him not being able to handle his whiskey, but any thought of returning their pun was ignored as he made his way to the stairs.

His vision began to blur and he stumbled whilst he made his way to his chamber. He felt a hand of support come to wrap around his waist to assist him. Looking down, he saw Marguerite looking at him with soft, doe-like eyes.

"Are you unwell, Riorden?" she whispered gently. "Here, let me help you to your chamber."

He mumbled some kind of response although his tongue and mouth were dry. His skin felt as if 'twas on fire, and the desire to lie down underneath the cool coverings of his bed was the only thought he had on his mind. His head began to spin as he felt the edge of the bed against the back of his legs.

"Let me help you with your boots, Riorden," came the silky tone of the woman, who gave him a subtle nudge so he all but fell on the bed. He rubbed his eyes when he gazed down at her hair and saw the black tresses transform into the tawny colored locks of his wife.

"Katherine, my love, come to bed with me," Riorden slurred, barely noticing her shoulders flinch as she took off one boot and then the other.

"'Tis exactly what I had in mind, my dear husband."

Her laughter rang sweetly in his ears, even though something seemed out of place that he could not grasp. Pulling his tunic over his head, he felt her helping him with his hose as he at last lay down on the softness of the feather mattress. Moments later, he felt the silky flesh of his naked wife come to lie atop him as he wrapped his arms around the woman, bringing her full length against his warm body.

"Love me, Riorden."

"I do, Katherine, for all time will I love only you," he murmured against her neck.

He heard her laughter again and was unsure what there was to jest about at a time when he was about to make love to her. Any other thoughts he may have had left him abruptly as he felt his eyes begin to roll back into his head. The last thing he remembered with any clarity was hearing a snarl of outrage from the woman at his side.

Marguerite just could not believe what she was seeing. *Asleep!* How the bloody hell could he pass out on her just as she was finally about to get everything she wanted? A soft snore passed his lips as he rolled onto his side, followed by him murmuring his wife's name. *Damn Katherine's soul to hell!* How she hated that atrocious woman!

Angrily, she rose from the bed only to stand there with her hands on her hips, staring at the man who had all but consumed her every waking thought. Perchance, she still might salvage something of the situation that she had so carefully arranged.

She began picking up their clothes and neatly folded them. Taking a small sip of wine, she gazed around the room, as if seeing it for the first time. Aye, it appeared as if everything was normal for a couple living together as man and wife. Smiling in satisfaction, she climbed back into bed and snuggled against Riorden's back. She would ensure that matters between them were set aright come the morn. No doubt, with the rising sun, Riorden would thank her for her cleaver scheming just so they could at last be together.

TWENTY

SHE IMMEDIATELY KNEW THAT SOMETHING *was terribly wrong* when she woke up alone in their bed. Her bare feet practically flew down the passageway until she came to a door that appeared before her. Her heart hammering in her chest, she stared sightlessly at the wooden door blocking her way from the one she sought. She didn't want to find him here of all places, nor did she want to enter this particular chamber. But she had no choice in the matter and knew she must for her own peace of mind.

She reached for the handle, noticing how her hands were visibly trembling, and yet still she grasped the cool metal with a feeling of dread. With the opening of the door, she began hoping against hope that her premonition would not come to pass.

The chamber was dimly lit with only a few glowing red embers from the hearth giving any kind of light within the room. Shivering, not only from the cold air, but from complete fear, she made her way to the bed and pulled back one of the bed hangings.

She gasped at what her eyes beheld. Her worst nightmare had just become a cold, hard reality. With her arms wrapped around her stomach as if they had the ability of offering her unborn child some form of protection, she tried to calm her raging emotions. She tried to breathe, but found it near impossible, for surely someone had stolen her breath with no plans on giving it back to her anytime soon. She had known she would find them together, but to actually see their limbs entwined in this lovers' embrace was more than she could bear.

The woman began to move, brushing back her glossy black hair from her face until she realized she and her lover were not alone. As if to prove her position had radically changed, she caressed the chest of the man beneath her, and Katherine watched in dismay as her husband took Marguerite's hand and placed a loving kiss upon the inside of her wrist. If it was an automatic response, since he performed the same gesture to her on numerous occasions, she could not say, but to be honest, it mattered not. The only thing that was of import was this clear, undeniable fact that he had betrayed her. She had been fooled yet again! She should have known what she had briefly found was too good to be true.

Marguerite leaned up on her elbow to stare at her rival with the complete confidence of someone who had gotten what she had desired. "He has always been mine, and as you can plainly see, he is mine yet again!" She hissed and gave an evil grin as she lay back down, putting her head to rest on Riorden's chest.

That his arm brought the woman closer to her side was the last straw of what remained of Katherine's self-control. Her tortured soul could stand no more and, with tears coursing down her cheeks, she fled.

Yes, she fled! She was a complete coward, for she would not wait to see the look in his eyes when he found out that she knew. Nor would she give him or Marguerite the satisfaction of knowing how much they had hurt her. She had come so far just to be with him. To have him betray what God and Time had given them was more than she could comprehend.

So, she fled the keep into the bright sunlight and ran to the stables, saddling her mare with more efficiency than she thought possible with her heart broken as it was. Her call to open the gate went unanswered until she threatened the guard, and they reluctantly obliged her. She fled the grounds with her horse's hooves thundering beneath her until she heard someone yelling from behind.

She turned back only once to see three men dressed all in black with sinister grins set upon their faces. Their horses drew closer and were almost within reach when her mare unexpectedly reared, its front hooves frantically pawing the air, as Katherine pulled on the reins in an attempt to keep control. She felt herself falling and instinctively curled herself into a ball as her body impacted the hard ground. Tumbling and rolling down the river embankment, she at last came to halt, bruised but otherwise unharmed. Watching in horror, she tried to gather her wits about her and to quickly figure out what she should do next. It was clear she didn't have much time to consider her options as the miscreants leapt from their mounts. One began running toward her, so she quickly managed to clumsily get to her feet.

"There she be, men!" he called out, quickening his stride to reach her. "'Twas easier than we thought as she practically has fallen into our laps!"

Remembering the street sense she lived with in the future, she knew it was better to die trying to get away than to die at the hands of an assailant. With no other avenue of safety in sight and no one to come to her rescue, Katherine took one last look at Warkworth Castle before jumping into the churning, freezing river.

Her arms flayed wildly about while she tried to ride the swift flowing channel. The undercurrent was stronger than she thought it would be, and she was not much of a swimmer. She tried to catch her breath and keep her head above the waterline but only managed to swallow great gulps of water. Choking and gasping for air, she felt her gown becoming heavier by the second until its weight pulled her down into her watery grave...

Katherine clawed at the wet sludge of the riverbank as she attempted to pull herself up out of the churning current. Turning her head, she vomited huge amounts of water that she had swallowed during her escape from those she knew would have easily killed her.

Having awakened from her dream, she had had no other recourse than to prove to herself that it was only a nightmare. How she wished it had been.

Espying a tree root sticking out from the mud, she used the last of her energy to loop her arm around it so she wouldn't float away or sink back into a watery grave. With all hope lost, exhaustion overtook her, and she remembered no more.

Riorden began to rouse himself from his troubled sleep and rub his eyes, as if that would clear his head. His thoughts were fuzzy at best whilst he tried to remember why his body felt as if he had been through the rigorous, daily training that Dristan demanded. He swore his form felt like it had been pummeled and bruised to the point of sheer exhaustion. The nightmare he had been having did not help matters.

Scenes inside his head began to replay, but he could make no sense of the jumbled mess of images that were tormenting him. One terrifying picture was of Marguerite playing the part of a dutiful wife whilst she lay down in the bed beside him, as if they were indeed husband and wife. But 'twas the vision of his beautiful Katherine finding himself and Marguerite in bed together, fleeing the castle, and drowning in the river that had Riorden feeling thankful that everything he had envisioned had only been a bad dream. After all, he could feel every inch of Katherine's body whilst he held her close to his side.

But something was amiss...although he knew not what seemed out of place. He began to open his eyes, but the sharp, piercing morning light caused him to close them once more. 'Twas a clear reminder why he generally did not overindulge in spirits more potent than ale or wine. The next day's after effects were just not worth it.

At least Katherine was here with him as he felt her snuggle into his chest. He would need to offer her an apology for falling asleep on her last night. He had never done such afore and could not comprehend how he had become so inebriated from such a small amount of spirits.

She began to stir, and he felt her movements as she leaned up to skim his neck with her lips. He felt another part of him rising with her efforts, and he could not think of a better way to begin their day together. She rose slightly, and he wondered where she was going when he had other things in mind.

Opening his eyes, he turned to admire her beauty, but blinked with disbelief instead. Surely, he must still be living a waking nightmare, for what he beheld was unfathomable. He flickered his eyelids yet again with the hope that he would awake from the hellish scene afore him. But, no! 'Twas not to be, for the vision did not change. Bloody Hell! What had he done?

"Glad tidings, my lover," Marguerite purred, leaning over to kiss his lips.

Riorden moved faster than he thought even possible with his head pounding as 'twas. "What the bloody hell!" he roared, finally taking in his surroundings. *Damnation!* He was not even in his own chamber.

She ignored his swearing and smiled prettily at him, much to his disgust. "Normally, I would say 'tis a glorious morn, but I am afraid 'tis well into the afternoon. You were magnificent as always, Riorden. I am surprised you let us sleep at all this past night. What a performance."

"What the hell have you done?" he bellowed, rising from the bed in search of his clothes. Had she possibly drugged him, he thought furiously? How else would he be in her chamber, for he knew within him he would not have done so if he had his wits about him? Still wandering around the room in search of his clothing, he finally saw them neatly stacked by her own garments, as if they had all the time in the world to tend to such matters last eve.

She left the bed and went to a trunk, pulling out a robe. Donning it, she went to stand afore him. "What have *I* done? Surely you are mistaken, my lord. I have done nothing that you yourself did not ask for. I but was heading to my chamber, whence you came upon me and escorted me the rest of the way. I certainly was not going to deny myself the pleasure of your company, since you offered yourself to me."

"'Tis hardly likely, Marguerite," Riorden proclaimed, never believing he had erred in such a foul manner where she was concerned. He remembered absolutely nothing of the tale she told him. If Katherine were to find out, she would never forgive him. He halted his movements and thought on the nightmare he had been having. But was it truly a dream, or had it actually occurred? Riorden had the God awful feeling his wife knew all. How the hell was he going to explain this to her?

"Katherine..." his voice faded with the sorrow of knowing he had hurt her.

"She was not pleased to see us together, I am afraid."

"You planned this," Riorden accused, grabbing Marguerite by the arm and giving her a violent shake.

"How was I to know she would enter my chamber unannounced? We were sleeping after all! 'Twas obviously clear you climbed into my bed, Riorden, and not the other way around, so you must needs take responsibility for your own actions!"

"I have to find her," he muttered, more to himself than to inform the evil bitch afore him of his intentions. He pulled on his boots then rose to leave.

"Riorden! Where are you going?"

"To find my wife!"

He left her sputtering all manner of vulgar profanities, and he stammered a few of his own beneath his breath, knowing he would have some difficult explaining to do once he found Katherine. He only prayed she would listen.

TWENTY-ONE

KATHERINE'S EYELIDS BEGAN TO FLUTTER open as she attempted to figure out her whereabouts in the dark room she found herself in. A figure sat on a stool near the hearth that emitted a warm glow as he or she stirred something in a pot hanging over the flames. She tried to rise up but began coughing with the effort. Her actions brought attention to herself as the person quickly rose from the chair.

"Oh, good, you are awake." The woman's voice sounded soothing to her ears as she came closer. "But take care, dearie. You have had quite a time of it, I am afraid."

Katherine noticed she was an older woman, perhaps in her fifties, if she were to guess. The woman had a kind face that Katherine was grateful for. Suddenly, Katherine remembered all she had been through and cried out in alarm, reaching for her stomach. Relief filled her as she felt the hardness still there, followed by the tiny, butterfly flutter deep inside her.

"He is still safe, my lady," the woman answered Katherine's unspoken question. "You are one lucky woman."

"Where am I?" Katherine managed to rasp. Her throat was raw, and she could only begin to imagine the amount of water she had swallowed from her flight. Her head reeled from the torment filling her mind.

"You are on a small island, not far from Warkworth, my lady. But, have no fear," she began, "not many know of this place, nor that those few come as a pilgrimage of sorts to pay their respects to those gone afore us."

Katherine's panic subsided as she lay back on the bedroll she had been resting on. Getting her bearings as her eyes adjusted to the low light, she saw she was in the Hermitage, just as in her dream. Her dream! Why, it wasn't a dream at all...but a ghastly nightmare come true. The vivid scene of her husband's betrayal filled her mind with agony.

"Oh, God, how could he do this to us?" she cried out as the woman rushed to her side, trying to offer her comfort, not that it did any good.

"Now, now, my dear. All will be well, especially when I get you home to have your loved ones see to you," she said, gently patting her back.

"I can't go back. Someone is trying to kill me," Katherine confided to this total stranger, and her story came pouring forth. There was no doubt of her anguish as she revealed her fears to this woman, for she had nothing left to lose. Marguerite had won. Katherine had nothing left and certainly no love to give anyone with the exception of her unborn child.

"Tsk, tsk..." the woman muttered sympathetically as she went back to the hearth and spooned whatever had been cooking into a small wooden bowl. She brought it to Katherine and then returned with one of her own. The soup was soothing on her sore throat. They continued to eat in silence until they had finished.

With her meal gone, Katherine handed over the bowl when the woman held out her hands for it. She began tidying up what little there was to clean after their small meal, and Katherine felt she should be doing something to help the lady. The only problem was, she felt as if she had no energy in her whatsoever. Her mind and body behaved as if she had gone to hell and back. Perhaps that wasn't too far off as an assessment.

The woman returned to her side to feel her forehead and began nodding to herself as if she answered her own unspoken question. "At least you do not have a fever. 'Tis a good sign."

As the woman made to rise, Katherine stopped her by gently putting her hand on the woman's arm. "What is your name, my lady?"

She looked up, as though surprised Katherine assumed she was of noble birth. It was not hard to tell, given the women's mannerisms. Katherine continued to wait for an answer until the lady gazed up into Katherine's eyes with a caring smile.

"You may call me, Ella."

"My thanks, Lady Ella, for your kindness to me."

"Just Ella, my dear. 'Tis enough for now."

"As long as you call me Katherine," she suggested.

Ella patted her hand, pulled up another blanket to keep her warm, and sat down, staring at Katherine before she at last spoke. "You must needs your rest, Katherine, to regain your strength. I will keep watch, but as I said, not many know of this place, nor the solitude it offers. 'Tis why I am here. If what you say is true, then we must be careful, my dear, to keep you safe from those who would do you harm. I shall keep the hearth cold during the day so no smoke will give our location, but we should be safe with a fire at night to keep us warm until we are ready to travel."

"But, how will we leave if you said we are on an island, and more importantly, where will I go, Ella?" Katherine choked back her tears as her sadness overwhelmed her.

"As to how we will leave, I have a small boat hidden in the shrubbery, but as I said, you must rest for several days, at least 'til you are fit to travel. I am afraid I have no horse to hasten our journey, but I will do all I can to help you. Have you some-one close to you nearby? Family perchance?"

"I would not be safe there, either and would not put my friend in danger," Katherine began and put out her hand to her newfound friend, "nor would I wish anything to happen to you."

"Bah! I am an old woman who has seen much of life. Who would bother me?"

Katherine shrugged. "You never know."

"Well, be that as it may, we must get you somewhere. You must know someone who will protect you."

Suddenly, a vision of a castle sitting high on a hill with the strand beneath its rocky foundation came to mind. "Berwyck Castle! I can go there to hide, for I have friends who reside within its hall, if you could help me get there!"

Ella crossed herself repeatedly as her eyes widened in fear. "You are in league with the Devil's Dragon?"

"There is nothing to worry about with Dristan of Berwyck, I promise you Ella. He can keep us both safe, and his lady is most gracious."

"If you say so," Ella replied, but she was clearly skeptical.

Katherine lay back down while Ella went back to sit near the fire and stare off into the flames. She became drowsy again, but at least when she finally fell asleep it was a dreamless one. For what was there now to look forward to when her knight had deserted her for another?

Twenty-Two

RIORDEN WAS IN A STATE OF PANIC and knew not where next to turn. For nigh unto a se'nnight he had scouts searching for his wife, and yet still there was no word of her whereabouts. That Katherine had disappeared was all his fault, along with that evil wench Marguerite. He knew not what she did that he had ended up in her bed, but there was no doubt in his heart, he had not consciously done so of his own accord. Katherine meant all to him. He would not risk what they had found on a dalliance with his father's widow.

He had refused to believe that anything untoward would have become of his beloved Katherine, and yet his faith had faltered momentarily when her riderless horse had been found far upstream from the grounds of Warkworth and its village. Still, he ordered the search to continue. He refused to believe what everyone was beginning to whisper...that his wife had drowned in the fast moving current and lay at the bottom of the river, or, worse yet, her body had washed out to sea, never to be found. If such was the case, he would never forgive himself.

He shivered at the thought crossing his mind and continued his vigil in the chapel. He had done this once afore when God had granted him his deepest heart's desire by bringing Katherine back into the past so they could be together. How could he be so foolish as to allow any form of doubt enter her thoughts that he did not love her completely.

Arms outstretched, his body aching from the hours he had lain on the cold chapel floor, he continued his vigilant pose. For only in the form of complete submission did he feel that a higher being would hear his prayers offered on his wife's behalf. He begged for the forgiveness of his sins and continued his penitence with a humble heart. He would not beg God with false lies to save himself from eternal hell, but he would do all in his power to do so for the souls of his wife and unborn child.

As his lips moved in a continual, silent prayer, he took slight notice of someone quietly entering the chapel. 'Twas not 'til he heard his brother's voice that he raised his forehead from the floor.

"Come, Riorden. You have done enough this day, brother," Gavin urged gently.

"Nay," he gasped as he felt the horrendous pain in every inch of his body. "'Tis not enough, for she has not returned to me."

Riorden felt the soothing, cool touch of Gavin's lady as she laid her hand upon his cheek. His gaze faltered momentarily when he saw her red rimmed eyes. Her woeful expression caused his own eyes to mist up with grief-stricken emotion. "Yes, my lord, you have done enough praying for Katherine today," Brianna whispered, even as her voice caught with her own misery.

"Let's get you into your solar and have some food sent up for you to eat."

"I cannot eat, nor drink."

Gavin pulled on his arm 'til he was at last sitting on the floor. He saw anger fill his brother's eyes. "You can do nothing more for her, Riorden, and we will not lose you both! Now, get off the floor and come with us!"

They helped him rise with unstable legs, and if not for their support, he would have stumbled back onto the stones beneath his feet as the blood rushed to his legs. From the shadows cast upon the chapel walls, he had been here longer than he had thought. They began to make their way through the outer courtyard. He barely noticed John and his workers as they continued the duties of building the church his father had started. He walked as if he were in truth dead himself, and, in reality, he felt as if he had died inside. There was nothing to look forward to without Katherine at his side.

As if in a daze, he made his way through the tunnel and up the stairs to the keep. His only thought was of somehow managing to put one foot in front of the other so he could at last go to his chamber to be left in solitude, 'til he saw Caldwell passing through the portal in front of him. That the knight looked grief stricken did not faze Riorden, as his anger he had been holding in check at last erupted in a terrifying display of agony.

"I left her in your care!" he bellowed. "You were supposed to guard her and keep her safe in my absence!"

"My lord, I—" Caldwell began but got no further.

Riorden lunged for his knight's throat.

Gavin held him back, but 'twas Brianna stepping in front of him, placing her hands on his chest, that halted his tirade. "It's hardly Caldwell's fault, Riorden, so don't take this out on him.

You won't do Katie any good by falling to pieces, so get your head together and get inside so we can take care of you!"

He shook his head as if to clear his thoughts. Brianna was right. If there was anyone to blame for Katherine's disappearance, 'twas him and certainly not one of his guards. He nodded to Caldwell, as if to excuse his outburst, and entered the vestibule, feeling lost. The Great Hall was mostly empty, and he waved off Mabel as she attempted to bring him something to eat. Nothing mattered to him any longer, for without Katherine in his life, he was just a meaningless shell of a man.

A high pitched wail filled the hall, and Marguerite came running down the stairs. Her frightened features only caused him further irritation. She hurled herself into his arms. Despite his efforts to disengage her, she held on tight. How dare she even begin to think he would want anything to do with her, knowing the part she played in Katherine's disappearance?

"Please, Riorden, I must beg of you again! Take me away from here. I cannot stand him troubling my thoughts, day and night with his constant badgering." Her tears began soaking his tunic, but he had nothing to offer her as he roughly pulled himself away from her clinging ways.

"Get thee from my sight and do not come near me again, Marguerite, or so help me God, I will end your miserable life for what you have cost me!" Riorden yelled.

"But, Riorden—" she pleaded.

He came to her with all the pent up frustration that had been building in him. His hands encircled her neck and he began to squeeze. "What part of I do not want you within my sight do you not comprehend, Marguerite? If you value your life, you will stay in your chamber 'til arrangements can be made to get you to Dunhaven Manor. I will not be responsible for my actions if you defy my orders," he whispered harshly in her ear.

Pushing her away, he listened whilst she gasped and coughed for air. His gaze swept her in a silent show of contempt, and she quickly fled the hall to return from whence she came. Her shrieks continued to echo within the keep, grating on his already tense nerves, and he was not sure how much more he could take.

Apparently, he could take more than he thought as he pushed opened his chamber door. He had refused to enter their room 'til her return, but now felt a desperate need to be near something of hers. Closing the wooden door, he put the bolt in place, ensuring his privacy. He wanted no interruptions.

As he closed his eyes, he could almost feel her presence surround him as if she were taking him into her comforting embrace. It calmed him for an instant 'til his eyes flew open to ascertain she was not once more in her ghostly form. But there was no one in the room save himself, and he was thankful for the solitude. Walking to a nearby table, he lingered over her hairbrush and noticed the long strands of her tawny colored hair still captured in the bristles. Her boots still remained where he had last espied them, and he assumed she had fled in a gown instead of hose and tunic. Had she even thought to bring a cloak afore she fled from him in her despair?

He went to a trunk they shared and lifted the lid. His answer was afore his misting eyes, as he saw her tan cloak with its furred hood neatly folded on top of her remaining garments. He could smell the floral scent she wore waft up to his nostrils and fill him with a sudden nostalgia he would not soon forget. He pondered how long such a smell, which would always remind him of the one woman he had truly loved with all his heart, would remain. Digging frantically down to the bottom of the trunk, he reached for the silken night rail he had kept when they shared their first night together at Berwyck.

Memories assaulted his senses whilst he remembered how he had torn the garment from her lush body, and how they had made love all eve long. How would he ever forget the look in her blue-green eyes as she came to him on their wedding day with all the love she felt for him shining in her eyes? Or how she gazed at him so sweetly when she presented him the poem she had scripted, just for him? Their brief memories together swept through his mind like a tempest upon the sea 'til he cried out in agony.

He clutched the torn fabric to his chest, as if willing Katherine back to his side, 'til he slumped to the floor in complete wretchedness for what Marguerite's wickedness had cost him. Tears spilled from his grieving eyes, and, in the privacy of his own chamber, he shed them with no shame. The one person, who he held most dear, he had lost. She had fled from him when she had found him in the arms of another. How could he blame her when he himself would have done the same? She was gone, and he feared, never to return.

He lovingly folded the remains of the garment and put it back in place in the trunk, slamming the lid tightly shut. Going towards the wall, he inspected it with a practiced eye 'til he pulled out one of the larger stones. Reaching inside, he removed his father's metal box and set it aside. He would not inspect the contents this day. He knew he would find gold, among other objects of worth, to see him through rough times if the estate was ever in need of extra monies. Only he and Gavin knew of the whereabouts of his father's wealth, as he had shown both his sons the secret hiding places in their youth. The box inside this chamber was only one of many scattered within the stones of Warkworth. Reaching inside the hole in the wall once more, he took out a pouch of his own, strode to the bed, and let everything fall onto the coverings for him to see.

'Twas not much, but it had been hers, and he had taken special care of her items, since Katherine had asked him to put them somewhere safe. He opened something she had called a notebook and scanned the pages of her writing of a story of some kind. He could almost hear her laughter, as when she had told him 'twas a proper historical romance with a happily-ever-after ending. Pens, a wrapper from that sweet she called candy and did not have the heart to throw away, and something she said was a plastic container waited his inspection. He twisted the thing she called a cap and smiled in bliss as her flowery fragrance rose pleasantly to his nose. He closed it quickly, not wishing for the creamy lotion to spill from the strange bottle.

He thought on her machine, called a phone, she had given to Juliana, and how they had made their moving image appear on such a marvelous device. Katherine had shown him such incredible modern devices she had stashed inside that object named a purse, although, for her sake, they had destroyed the majority of its contents. Riorden hoped that at least the return of the phone had given her mother some sense of peace, knowing her daughter had been happy...at least for a while. He surmised, as far as those in the future were concerned, he along with everyone else he knew were already long since dead.

He supposed that in the greater structure of life, Time had once again played a cruel joke on them all. He wiped at his desolate eyes, put everything back in place, and went to stretch himself out on her side of their bed. He could still smell her scent on her pillow and, again, could not help but wonder how long 'twould remain. He felt something above his head and clutched at the fabric, wondering what she had been hiding. 'Twas a tiny garment for the babe she carried, and obviously she had been attempting to knit the item herself. 'Twas not perfect, but she had done a fine job, considering she was not one to take needle and thread in hand.

He closed his eyes, and in his grief he could see her, as if 'twere but yester eve that they were happy lying here in this room, side by side. Heads together, they had whispered their deepest secrets and prayers for their child. They had laughed, thinking on all the years they would spend together. If he only knew then what he knew now, including how brief their time truly would be, he could have changed events so this torment he now felt would not come to pass.

He at last began to drift off to sleep, thinking of his sweet Katherine. But 'twas the voice of his father, whispering to him to take his ease, that was his last conscious thought. With the rise of the new day, his agony and torment would begin all over again.

TWENTY-THREE

I'M SO SORRY, ELLA, but do you suppose we could stop again, please?" Katherine asked while she plopped herself down on a log. Her borrowed shoes came off, and she began rubbing her sore, tired feet. Blisters were raw on the back of her heels, and she had the ungodly feeling she wouldn't be able to walk much farther tonight. Not that they were making much progress, traveling under the evening sky. How long had they been gone?

Ella came to her, took one look at her oozing sores, and promptly set to work pulling this and that out of the bag she carried. She began mixing dried herbs together and then began looking around on the ground until she picked something up.

Katherine was appalled at what the woman was handling, as if it wasn't anything unusual to pick up off the ground. "Is that animal poop?"

Ella looked at her as if she had lost her senses. "The scat is a known cure for healing wounds and holding a poultice together.

'Twill not harm you," Ella answered and began smearing the concoction on Katherine's feet.

"I don't know about its healing effects, but that's just so disgusting, Ella," Katherine replied, but she had to admit, it did take the sting out. She was sure it had more to do with the herbs than the dung she was trying not to think about. Looking down at her feet, Katherine didn't have a clue how she would ever get those shoes of torture back on again.

Ella wiped her hands and then came to sit next to Katherine. "'Tis clear we will not travel farther this night. I am sorry the shoes did not fit better, and they are causing you pain."

"It's not your fault, Ella, and it was better than going barefoot all the way to Berwyck. I wonder how far we still need to travel." Katherine pondered with a yawn.

Ella scooted down so the log was to her back and she appeared as comfortable as one could get, given the situation. Katherine came to join her. "Several days at the least, mayhap more," Ella answered while she stared into the darkened forest.

Katherine let out a heavy sigh. She was so tired, but she refused to close her eyes, knowing what she would see if she did so.

"You cannot go without sleep forever, Katherine," Ella said, as if reading her thoughts. "You do neither yourself, nor the babe any good without a proper rest."

"I'll manage."

"I told you we should have stayed in the cave longer than two days' time," Ella muttered.

Katherine gazed at her new friend. She could still envision herself standing on the bank of the river, looking with such longing at the castle off in the distance. All she had wanted was for one last glimpse of what would never be before she turned her back on it forever. "I just couldn't stay that close in the shadow of Warkworth, knowing they were together," Katherine finally managed to say. "It was best for my peace of mind that we left when we did."

"I did not agree with you then, nor do I agree with your decision now. It certainly was not for the best, at least for your health," grumbled Ella. "You are most stubborn! Someone surely must have told you that a time or two in your young life, I suspect."

Katherine gave a small smile. "Yes...once or twice."

Ella peered at her, or so it seemed in the moonlight, since they wouldn't light a fire this night. "There is much more to your story, I think, than you are telling me, Katherine," Ella surmised.

Katherine lowered her eyes. "Oh? Why do you think so?"

"Well, your speech for one. I have never heard anyone have speech as you do," Ella said, tilting her head as if she was determining the truth to the pretense that she lived abroad. "Why do I have the feeling that when I gaze upon you, that I am looking at an old soul?"

"A what?"

"An old soul...one who is older than one gives the impression of being from one's outward appearance."

"That's ridiculous, Ella. I'm only twenty-six, for goodness sake."

Ella shrugged when she spoke of her age. "If you say so, dear."

Katherine became lost in her own thoughts, knowing she was so easily read by some. She turned to Ella and looked her in the eye but could only see someone who had been completely honest with her. Coming to the conclusion she could trust this woman with her life, she decided her story would be safe with Ella.

"What if I were to tell you that I come from a very long distance from here?"

"That would still not account for how I see you. Many travel abroad and make their home far from where they were raised. Alliances are made through marriage, girls marry young and travel great distances to live as chattel to their husbands. 'Tis nothing out of the ordinary."

"Yes, but I'm not talking about the distance of how one travels by foot, horse, or ship. I'm from a place farther than that, and I came here for a purpose."

"You confuse me. How can you be from a place not accessible by horse or ship?" Ella asked with her brows furrowed together as though she was trying to figure it out.

Katherine took a deep breath. "I'm from the future, the twenty-first century to be exact."

Ella only stared at her as though she had lost her mind, and Katherine couldn't blame her in the least. She supposed it was a lot for anyone, including a twelfth century woman, to comprehend.

Ella suddenly began to laugh. "You but jest with me, Katherine." Her laughter quickly faded when Katherine did not join in on the fun. Ella began to peer at her strangely with tight-knit brows. "Could it be possible?" she whispered, so softly Katherine strained to hear her words.

Katherine reached out and took Ella by the hand, hoping she wouldn't scare the hell out of this medieval woman who had been so kind to her. "Let me tell you a story of unbelievable proportions. It's a tale that stretches the imagination, and makes you wonder if all things are possible."

"Mayhap, 'tis good I am sitting," Ella replied carefully as she continued her strange assessment of Katherine.

Katherine wondered if Ella was about to start making the sign of the cross or if the woman was trying to figure out if her new friend was insane. Instead, Ella just sat there, patiently waiting for Katherine to tell her and Riorden's story.

"It all begins with a young woman who dreams every night of a knight in shining armor coming to her on the battlements of Bamburgh Castle. He is tall and handsome, his dark blue cape billows in the breeze with a lion head imprinted on his tabard. And his eyes," Katherine sighed in remembrance of how much she loved the man, "are the eyes of the bluest blue. Everything about him is the stuff that dreams are made of to fulfill a woman's deepest romantic desire."

Into the night, Katherine weaved her tale that, to some, would be so farfetched, she would either be burned at the stake, or welcomed into a hall as its newest bard. But with its telling, Katherine relived every glorious moment with her husband; how their dreams were interwoven while the centuries kept them apart; seeing him in the portrait and learning his name and the emotions that had come over her when she did; running down the tower stairs with Juliana, Emily, and Brianna, and being hurtled back through time; his touch...that magical first time when he took hold of her, despite the fact she had sliced her fingers on his sword; their anger at one another that only brought them closer; and the first time they had made love.

Their romance and how they fell in love spilled out, even to the last dream that had broken them apart, leaving her more bereft than she had thought was humanly possible.

"So you see, his betrayal was far worse than just taking a mistress as some men do. It's as if he killed the part of our love that had withstood the test of time itself...what had brought us together in the first place, and he threw it all away. And for what?" Katherine voiced, and for the first time her anger was the driving force behind her heartache as fresh tears fell from her eyes. "Meaningless sex with a woman he said he didn't even care for. Men! They are all such liars."

"You are most bitter." Ella noticed, shaking her head, almost as if in understanding. "I suppose, if this phenomenon were to happen to me, I would be the same."

"Do you blame me for feeling this way?"

"Nay, Katherine, I do not. And yet, I have this feeling all is not as it may appear."

Katherine folded her arms on her knees and rested her cheek upon them. "It really doesn't matter at this point how it appears, Ella. He betrayed the love we had between us by taking a lover. No matter the circumstances, or how such a travesty came about, that fact will never change. How would I ever even begin to forgive something like that, no matter how much I still love him?"

"Then you do still care for him?"

"Was there any doubt? I've loved him all my life, even when I thought he was only a figment of my imagination. Every man I ever met could never measure up to what I found while I was sleeping."

"'Tis fairly obvious, Katherine, you still love him. How could you not when you carry his child?"

"But, how in the world would I ever learn to trust him again if I were to go back?"

Ella patted Katherine's back with what comfort she could offer. "Only you can answer that mystery, Katherine, for that would have to come from within your heart."

"My heart is devastated beyond repair, I'm afraid," Katherine mumbled to herself so quietly that her words became lost in the breeze that softly floated by.

Far into the night, Katherine tried to stay awake, but, in the end, sleep finally took her gently into a restful slumber, and she had the sweetest dreams of Riorden. For in her dreams, Riorden still loved her with all his heart. She could be embraced in the comforting spell they wove together, and she could again become mesmerized by the bluest eyes she would ever find. Maybe it wasn't so bad to dream, after all.

Twenty-Four

*H*IS LUNGS WERE BURNING; *his leg muscles tight from run-ning. His boots crunched the dead, fallen leaves on the forest floor. Winter was fast approaching, and he was more de-termined than ever to continue his mission to find her afore the snow began to blanket the earth. He called out for her, over and over again. The only answer he ever received was the sound of his own voice resonating in the frigid air.*

His throat was raw from sounding out her name with no re-sponse. At last, he could run no farther, and he fell to the ground in hopeless despair, knowing she was lost to him for all time. Vigilant prayers to God had gone unanswered. He had even sunk so low that he pleaded for God to take him as well so he could be with her again. 'Twas a sin, he knew, but how could his life go on without her? His faith, along with their love, was destroyed.

Knowing he had erred, he wept blinding tears and knew not how to forgive himself. He might as well have killed her himself, along with their unborn child.

He heard it then, or was it his imagination, the sound of his name being whispered on the winter wind? A mist appeared all around him and gave him the slightest bit of hope. When he saw someone take shape and begin to come towards him, he rubbed his eyes and blinked several times. Knowing she was at last near, he reached for her.

"Katherine...Forgive me," he spoke, rising to his knees. She stood afore him, and yet, 'twas as though she stood not at all, but hovered inches above the ground. His beloved wife was a ghost, once more.

"You betrayed me," she announced, inside his head. God would not even grant him his deepest wish to hear her voice aloud. Had he truly ruined everything?

"Aye, Katherine...I am most sorry, for I knew not what I did, but I swear nothing happened between us," he pleaded for her to understand, but her eyes, those beautiful eyes he had come to love, only gazed down on him with unreserved disappointment.

"It's too late for meaningless apologies, and really, all that doesn't matter anymore, Riorden," she whispered. Even her voice sounded as despondent as his own tortured soul. "Time has taken me forward to where I'm supposed to be."

"You belong with me!" he cried out, desperate to hold on to her at all costs.

She shook her head. "I belong only to myself, and we will only be but shadows to one another forevermore."

"You can come back to me, and I will make all aright with us again. Just give me another chance to win your love."

She gave him a sad, thoughtful smile and began reaching out her hand to touch him. He waited, breathlessly, to feel her tender touch. But 'twas not to be, for when she drew near enough to caress his cheek, she changed her mind. He watched, in dis-

ONLY FOR YOU

may, whilst her hand dropped lifelessly to her side. His connection to her was fading with each moment they were in each other's presence. "You did have my love, Riorden. I can never come back for a second time."

"Go to Bamburgh and try once more," he urged.

She shook her head, yet again, and he watched a tear escape slowly down her cheek. "There is no reason for me to return to Bamburgh. Time will not grant us such a gift twice only for it to be thrown carelessly away again."

"I have failed you."

"We failed each other, Riorden, for we should have had more faith in what we had found between us. Our love transcended time itself and was something to be cherished. God does not grant such miracles without a purpose in mind."

"I shall never see you again..."

"I have complete faith we will one day find a way to each other, Riorden. Perhaps not in this lifetime, but do not lose hope that you'll never be with me again."

She began to fade from his vision, even whilst he tried to memorize her features. "I love you, Katherine. For all of ever will I love you."

"And always remember, I love you, my dearest Riorden. Only for you would I wait an eternity just to be able to love you once more," she said softly. She began to leave his sight but turned to face him one last time with a bright smile. "Make amends with your father, my love, for he has much he can tell you to ease your suffering...if you would but take the time to listen to him with an open heart."

"Katherine! Please stay with me!" he begged of her, but there was no longer any ghostly apparition for him to gaze upon. She was gone, and with her parting, she took what little he had left of his tormented and broken heart.

"Please stay with me!"

Riorden jerked awake and, with bleary eyes, surveyed his whereabouts. How and when had he managed to make his way to the Garrison Hall? 'Twas obvious no one had come to retrieve his sorry arse from the floor near the now cold hearth. But, it mattered not how he came to be here. 'Twas no more than he deserved.

His body protested the night spent on the hard stones as he rose and managed to gain his feet afore he stumbled towards the door. He slammed and bounced off the walls and through the arched Lion Tower. Out into the obtrusive sunlight, he continued his wavering stride, squinting as the brightness of the day hurt his head, making it pound most furiously. How could everything appear so normal when there was nothing normal about the life he now led?

'Twas obvious he was still drunk and in need of more spirits to dull his pain. He became aware he yet held a flagon in his hands and brought it to his lips, only to find it empty. Tossing it on the ground, he continued to stumble his way to the keep to find more whiskey, for ale or wine would in no way be potent enough to solve the misfortune of his sorry life.

For weeks they had searched for Katherine and had come up with nothing. Nothing! That was 'til that fateful day when he had ridden the river's edge and had espied her shoe. He had surmised how she may have possibly tumbled down the embankment after most likely falling from her horse. And he had leapt from Beast's back, only to find himself sitting there in the mud, scanning for further signs that she had survived. The swift flowing current had confirmed his worst fears she would in no way return to his side.

Nathaniel and Ulrick had found him still sitting there hours later. There were no words of comfort they could have offered him, for he had lost the one person who would ever complete him. He had given up hope that day that she would be able to return to him. Although he had not ever remembered consuming more than a few sips of wine or whiskey, he must have drunken far more than he realized, for he had been drunk ever since.

After that fateful day, his dreams had begun, dreams of her coming to him as a ghost. Night after night, he awaited sleep to overtake him, knowing that at least whilst he dreamt she could be at his side. Breathlessly, he waited each night for when he would pass out, just so he could envision her smiling up at him with her beautiful eyes and all the love she held for him reflected there, as well. He thought only on her words to him that she loved him. Any other message was of no consequence.

Riorden slammed the keep door and made his way into the great hall. "Whiskey!" he yelled, but there was no one to come and give in to his request with the exception of Marguerite, who was breaking her fast.

Quickly, she glanced about the room then went to do his bidding. She came to his side and held out her offering. He grabbed it without hesitation and took a small swig, feeling it burn his throat as it slid its way to his empty stomach.

"At least someone will obey me," Riorden muttered as he began to make his way towards the upper floor where he could retreat to his chamber.

"Riorden...let me help you," Marguerite offered softly. Was that worry in her eyes as she gazed at him, or pity? He could not tell, but the last thing he needed was any form of empathy coming from Marguerite, of all people.

"There is no help for me. Now, leave me alone."

He left her there and somehow managed the stairs. As he opened the door to his chamber, he was surprised to see Patrick inside, folding his garments into a neat pile.

"I have no need of you tidying up after me, boy," Riorden slurred, "or anything else for that matter."

"My lord?" Patrick squeaked with a hurt expression.

"I have no need of your services, Patrick." Riorden reiterated, as if the lad was hard of hearing. He made his way across the room to fall into his chair by the fire, which took the chill from the room. 'Twas too bad that 'twould in no way melt the ice that was once more forming around his aching heart.

Patrick brought bread and cheese to put down on a small table within his reach, in case he felt the desire to actually attempt to eat something. "Have I offended you, my lord?"

Riorden raised his blood shot eyes to the youth. For a moment he saw so much of Aiden and Amiria in his features that it took him by surprise. He had failed the boy, as well, and he knew Dristan would be disappointed in him for not training the lad properly.

"Perhaps 'tis best if you return to Berwyck. I fear I am not up to the task to be a proper master to you, Patrick," Riorden grumbled, taking another long pull of the fiery liquid.

"Ye canna mean that, my lord! Ye would send me home in disgrace? All would know that I had not performed my duties to ye!" Patrick's Scottish brogue was coming out, and Riorden now listened as the boy began cursing in Gaelic.

"Leave me, Patrick," Riorden ordered. "I wish to be alone."

"Seems to me, you have been alone long enough," Patrick proclaimed. He went to the door and, as if remembering himself, gave Riorden a low bow. "I take my leave of you then, my Lord de Deveraux."

Riorden barely noticed the door closing behind the lad as he leaned his head back in his chair. Closing his eyes, he prayed for his dreams to take him away and back to Katherine's side. 'Twas the only place that would bring him any form of comfort.

Twenty-Five

KATHERINE HALTED HER SLOW, forward steps to gaze up ahead, along the strand. It felt strange to be traveling in the light of day instead of hiding under the cover of darkness. She had lost count of the days or weeks they had been walking. Ella had taken such excellent care of her, and she was glad for the friendship they had formed between them.

Several times along their journey, they had hidden deep in the forest when there were signs that Katherine's pursuers still continued their vigilant search of her. It became evident that they should hurry to their destination where safety would be found under the protection of Dristan of Berwyck. Unfortunately, Katherine's feet didn't agree with the assumption that they needed to hasten their journey.

"Have you ever seen anything more spectacular than Berwyck Castle?" Katherine breathed in the fresh ocean air and, for the first time, felt some small measure of hope fill her heart that all would right itself soon. She just needed to get inside the gates. Dristan and Amiria would take care of the rest.

Ella began muttering before she crossed herself. "'Tis only a castle, Katherine. We have passed many such fortifications on our journey here."

Katherine was still impressed by the sheer size of the place. Situated high on a cliff with its rocky foundation, the keep rose majestically above the towers and other buildings within its guarded walls. High above, the standard of a fire breathing dragon flapped in the ocean breeze. They were almost there but would need to leave the beach and head inland just to reach the barbican gate before it closed for the night.

"Let's try to pick up our pace, shall we?" Katherine suggested.

"Ha! 'Tis not been me that has been slowing us down, but I would just as soon put off passing through the gates of such a fearsome foe as the Devil's Dragon," Ella declared cautiously. "Is there no other dwelling that may see to your needs, besides this one?"

Katherine laughed for the first time in weeks. "Come on, you scaredy-cat. I promise Dristan won't bite!"

"Aye, well, 'tis not the biting I am afraid of, but the burning, if you take my meaning."

"Come on, Ella! Let's be on our way." For the first time in a long while, Katherine felt a weight being lifted from her shoulders.

Katherine linked her arm with Ella's and they began making their way from the strand, following a narrow river. Crossing a bridge, they walked through the village where Katherine recognized familiar faces of villagers, who waved to her in greeting. Katherine kindly returned the gesture. Hawkers called out their wares, hoping she would purchase something, but she didn't have any money, so she left them disappointed.

She continued onward until she stood before the barbican gate, where her footsteps faltered. For the life of her, she couldn't seem to move, as memories of the last time she had past underneath its portcullis assaulted her senses. Briefly, she closed her eyes and relived when she had traveled in a beautiful carriage with her friends as Riorden rode by with a carefree smile and a wave in her direction. There had been such confidence in their plan to send her friends back to the future. How could she have known that months later everything she had come to cherish would fall apart so completely?

Raising her chin, she pressed forward and entered the outer bailey. She remembered everything about this place, and her eyes immediately went to the lists where she had spent so much time, running its perimeter. She was not surprised to see Dristan and his knights busily training. Since it was a daily activity, she knew this would be where she would find the lord and lady of the keep. They did not disappoint her.

Katherine tugged at Ella's arm, and she settled her friend on a lone stone bench. Leaving her there, she went to the sidelines to await a moment to make her presence known. Before long, Amiria noticed her and threw her helmet from her head as she ran to Katherine. From the worry she saw in Amiria's eyes, Katherine surmised Amiria knew something was wrong, since she had shown up here without Riorden.

She felt Amiria's arms encircle her, and it was as if the tears, which had somehow held her together through everything that had happened to her, finally broke free. She began sobbing uncontrollably in the younger woman's arms. Amiria started to pull away, but her hand grazed Katherine's stomach.

"You are with child?" Amiria whispered for Katherine's ears alone, so as not to embarrass her.

"Yes." It was the only word she could manage to get out through her tears until she saw Dristan approach. She dropped down into a curtsey. "My Lord Dristan," she sobbed.

"*Merde!* What has happened that you arrive here unescorted?" Dristan demanded. "And where the hell is Riorden?"

Katherine only began to cry harder.

"Not now, Dristan," Amiria said calmly. "Can you not see Katherine is distraught?"

"She is far more than distraught, wife! All and sundry can hear her caterwauling, clear to London and back." Dristan fumed, but then recovered himself upon seeing Katherine cringe. "No offense, Katherine." Though Dristan's tone was calmer, he ran his hand through his hair in a manner so reminiscent of the gesture Riorden performed when he was frustrated that she threw her hands over her face.

"Shh, you oaf! You are not helping, Dristan," Amiria scolded. "Men! They are so clueless sometimes."

Katherine peeked at Amiria through her fingers and gave a small smile. Her analogy of men was so twenty-first century she forgot for a moment she was stuck more than eight hundred years in the past. "I'm sorry to be such a burden to you, but I had nowhere else to go where I thought I would be safe."

"You are most welcome here, is that not right, Dristan?" Amiria gave Katherine a hug of reassurance.

Dristan gave her a small nod. "Our doors are always open to you and yours, Katherine."

"You are both too kind. I have much to tell you," Katherine stated and pointed to Ella, who stood, made her way to them, and gave a curtsey. Once the introductions were made, Katherine implored, "I hope Ella is welcome. If it wasn't for her, I'm afraid I'd be floating at the bottom of a river."

"What?" Dristan and Amiria stuttered at the same time.

"It's a long story, and one best told behind the privacy of closed doors," Katherine answered.

"Aye, of course," Amiria said, and they began making their way from the lists. She halted in the outer courtyard and turned back to Katherine with questioning eyes. "Where are your horses? Have our lads already seen them to the stables?"

Katherine looked sheepish and embarrassed. "I'm afraid we didn't ride here. We walked."

"Walked? But, that is nigh unto forty miles or more?" Dristan shook his head in disbelief and then noticed Katherine's bruised and battered feet. "By Saint Michael's Wings, where are your shoes, Katherine?" he bellowed and then continued his tirade in Norman French. She, of course, didn't understand a word he said, but clearly he was upset, not only with her, but with Riorden, as well.

Katherine shuffled her toes gingerly in the dirt. "As I said, it's a long story."

Dristan came to stand before her, looked her up and down, and suddenly scooped her up in his arms. "My apologies by being so forward, Katherine, but 'til our healer says you are recovered, you are not to do any more walking. Is that understood?"

"Of course, my lord," Katherine whispered and heard Amiria call out for Kenna to come to her solar. Serfs came running at her beckoning to carry out her orders to have hot water readied for a bath and fresh clothing brought to her.

They entered the keep, and Dristan continued carrying her up the spiral stairs. Her heart raced when he started taking her down the second floor passageway instead of going to the third where Amiria's solar was. He knew just where he planned on taking her, but she wasn't sure how she was going to handle being in the same room she had shared with Riorden but months ago.

If she had had the time to ponder matters, Katherine felt she would have fallen to the floor in a puddle of grief, once she was deposited inside their chamber. But she wasn't given the opportunity, for she was immediately instructed to sink her tired self into the warm, soothing water of the tub, where she was scrubbed clean. A MacLaren plaid was thrown around her body, keeping her warm once she had been dried off, and she was gently pushed down onto the feather mattress. Kenna set to work bandaging her feet, but it was the peaceful sound of Amiria's voice singing a Scottish ballad that was the last thing Katherine remembered before she fell into a deep and restful sleep.

TWENTY-SIX

KATHERINE AWOKE TO THE LOW LIGHT emitting from the hearth embers, telling her night had fallen. Feeling disorientated, her gaze fell on a lone woman, working on her stitchery by candlelight. She was squinting to view her work, and, from the frown placed on her young face, she didn't look pleased with the results.

"You know, you could light more candles to see better, Lady Lynet." Katherine voiced her worry for the girl's eyesight with a small smile.

"At last...you are awake." Lynet was clearly enthusiastic as she went about adding more light to the room. "I did not wish to disturb your slumber."

Katherine sat up in the bed and pulled the covers up to keep her warmer. "I don't think anything would have prevented me from sleeping the day away. It's been a long time since I've had the comfort of a bed beneath me."

"You have been asleep two days now."

"Two days?"

"Aye." Lynet came to sit on the edge of the bed. "You had us all very worried, Katherine. I may call you by your given name, may I not?"

Although she hadn't become as close to Lynet as she had her older sister Amiria, Katherine felt comfortable in her presence and smiled warmly. "Yes, of course you can. I feel like we're family."

She smiled brightly. "Then you must do the same."

Lynet silently went back to her needlework, giving Katherine time to ponder the young woman of nineteen before her. She was one of the most beautiful women Katherine had ever encountered; honey colored hair held in a long braid running down her back to her waist that most would envy, skin clear and smooth like the finest porcelain, and blue eyes that could rival a clear morning sky. She was a walking picture of elegance with her classical features. Lynet still had a look of innocence about her, but Katherine also knew she had inherited some of her father's Scottish stubbornness, a trait she shared with her sister Amiria.

Lynet looked up suddenly to stare at Katherine, as if she had been afraid to voice her worries. She bit her lip several times before she at last spoke her mind. "Lady Ella told us your tale...at least from her end of it, anyway. We are most grateful to her that she came upon you and was able to pull you from the riverbank to safety."

"I feel the same way. I could spend the rest of my days thanking her for her kindness and still it wouldn't be enough."

"She is quite secretive. 'Tis obvious she is a noblewoman, but she remains reluctant to tell us about herself," Lynet said. "Has she, mayhap, told you her tale?"

"I'm afraid not, although I'm curious to know why she was on a pilgrimage to Warkworth's Hermitage in the first place.

Somehow, I didn't feel it was right to pry the information from her, given how much she had been helping me. I figure she'd tell me her story if she felt inclined to do so," Katherine answered honestly.

Silence formed between them for several minutes until Lynet placed her needlework down in her lap. "I must speak my mind, Katherine, but do not wish to offend you."

Katherine gave a short, somewhat comfortable laugh. "Oh, I can only imagine what you're going to tell me, Lynet. You might as well speak your mind."

"I just canna imagine Riorden throwing away so carelessly the life the two of you had started together. 'Twas so perfect, and he has never acted so rashly afore. 'Tis highly out of his character and how I have come to know him all these years."

"Only Riorden can explain why he did what he did," Katherine sighed. "Personally, I didn't stick around long enough to hear whatever explanations he had to say. Somehow finding the two of them naked in bed together was almost more than I could handle."

"But, he loves you so," Lynet exclaimed with a dreamy eyed expression. "I am positive of it, along with the love you still bear for him. You do still love him, do you not?"

Katherine stared into the flames in the hearth. "I wish I could somehow learn to stop loving him, but it's just about as impossible as asking me to stop breathing. How can I not still care for him, especially with his child growing strong inside me?"

"We will send him a missive and—"

Katherine sat up quickly in the bed. "No!"

"But, he will come for you! Once he arrives, we can apprise him of the happenings at Warkworth, and Marguerite's part of ensuring his father's demise," Lynet reasoned. "Most likely she is the cause for your sudden flight from your home, as well, with those nasty villains chasing after you."

Katherine shook her head in doubt. "No, Lynet. Unless he comes to me of his own accord then there is no reason for me to send for him. He should realize this is the only place I would go. He would know Dristan would keep me and the baby safe."

"I still say we should send a runner to Warkworth," Lynet replied, clearly unsure of this course of action.

Katherine reached out and took Lynet's hand. "Please promise me that neither you, nor anyone else here at Berwyck, will send for Riorden. I don't want him coming here just to drag me home because he is the father of my child. It must be his choice, and one that is freely given, or else it doesn't mean anything. He needs to do so because he wants to, not because he feels obligated to see to my needs and those of our child."

"'Tis not right, nor the way things of this nature are done. Riorden protects what is his as any proper knight should."

Katherine fell back onto the pillows. "I don't want his protection. What I want of him is to somehow learn to trust him again. How can I do that if he's forced to retrieve his wife? I'd always doubt his sincerity that he'd never take another mistress. I don't need someone in my life who will continue to tell me lies." Katherine turned on her side to watch Lynet. "Promise me you won't send for him, I beg of you."

"I do not like it, but I give you my oath we shall keep you in our care and not send for him."

"Thank you," Katherine said in relief but continued to watch the young girl. "Well, now that we've discussed my troubles, what of your own? Has your handsome beau Ian seen fit to come grace you with his presence, or have you also given up on the man who holds your heart?"

"He is not my beau," Lynet murmured roughly and picked up her stitchery again. Katherine watched as she all but plunged the needle in and out with enough force to tear the delicate fabric.

"So he has not come for you," Katherine surmised.

"Nay, nor has he bothered to send even some form of a letter in five long years. I hate him!"

"It's been said there is a fine line between love and hate. I have the feeling, Lynet, you care as much for your Ian as I still do for my Riorden."

Lynet stopped her work and looked at her with dejected eyes that surely mirrored her own. "I know it does me no good to continue to care for him, but as you yourself just proclaimed, how do I dare not endure to have hope that someday he may return my love?"

"Long distance relationships rarely work, Lynet, and in your case he doesn't even come to see you so you can plead your cause. Perhaps it's time to move on with your life. I am sure Dristan and Amiria could find many eligible men who could make you happy."

"Bah! Dristan has paraded enough of them afore me for too many years, hoping against hope that one may catch my eye. But they are either too old, or too ambitious. They have all been fools and only see me as a means to get closer to my dowry and mayhap further their alliance in the king's eyes," Lynet wiped a stray tear from her eye and again began her work. "I would rather be alone or sent to a nunnery than be wed to a man of their kind."

"So you do still love the man," Katherine surmised, thinking how their stories were so similar, in so many ways.

"Aye," she whispered, "he is a most bonny man and is what every woman wishes for in a knight."

"Maybe you should send for him or write him a letter. Maybe he doesn't know how you feel," Katherine suggested.

"Oh, he knows how I feel, since I all but threw myself at his feet. He did not want me then, and 'tis obvious, he does not want me now." Lynet sighed.

Katherine stared at the girl, who she felt began to feel like a little sister to her, just as Brianna was. "Is there more to this story that you're not telling me? It seems like something is missing. You can tell me and it will stay between us."

Lynet put down her needlework again, but this time, when she gazed up into Katherine's face, there was so much grief reflected in her eyes that Katherine opened up her arms. Lynet all but fell into them and began crying. Katherine just held the girl and felt her sorrow. Suddenly, Katherine recognized her own sorrowful behavior, for it seemed that all she did was cry these days. Maybe Aiden was right when he asked where the lioness in her had gone. Perhaps it was time for her to start showing that fighting spirit that so intrigued Riorden in the first place.

Lynet finally gave a very lady like sniffle and sat up wiping at her eyes. "Oh my...what must you think of me?"

Katherine placed her hand on the girl's cheek. "I would think that you've held in your emotions way too long for them to build up like that. A person needs a good cry now and then. It wipes away all the pain of the past so you can pave out a way for a bright, new future."

"Speaking from experience, Katherine?" Lynet questioned with a small grin, the little imp.

"Something like that, although I never was very good at taking my own advice. So what did he do that he hasn't returned to Berwyck these many years? I thought this was for the most part his home."

"Aye, he was practically raised here and was the captain of Amiria's guard. That is where the problem lies," Lynet murmured with a heavy heart, "for he was in love with Amiria."

"That does pose a setback, doesn't it? Did she know?"

"Aye, I believe she did, along with Dristan. 'Tis why he left. Ian ensured that the woman he loved was wed properly, and then he was gone. Of course, he returned from London to help with taking back the castle when it became known 'twas once more under siege. But he has not returned since. He saved me that day from someone who would have ill-used me and gave me a kiss that I have remembered every waking hour since his lips touched mine. If I was not in love with him afore, that day was when he completely stole my heart. It has not been the same since."

"Somehow, I have the feeling he is just trying to get over his feelings for your sister. When you love someone so deeply, and you lose that love, it can take some people years until they are ready to move on," Katherine declared knowingly. "Trust me on this one. I've been in the same position and am not so sure I'm not exactly in the same place now."

Lynet seemed to ponder her words. "I would not even know where to dispatch a letter to find him. The last we heard, he was traveling in France, attending the tourneys there."

"We'll ask Amiria, discreetly of course. I'm sure your sister will be only too happy to help aid you in finding your soul mate."

"Maybe there is hope, after all," Lynet breathed, and, for the first time since they began discussing their problems, Lynet gave her a bright smile that lit up her whole face.

Hope...perhaps, Katherine would pray for a small measure of hope for herself, as well. She had the feeling she would need it, including a lot of patience in the months to come.

Twenty-Seven

RIORDEN WAVED AWAY THE EVER diligent servants, who continually tried to force him to eat. Leaving a tray near at hand, they left him brooding. 'Twas almost as if he could hear Katherine's voice telling them to take care of him, but he cared not for the attention. Nothing mattered anymore, except the spirits that dulled his inner turmoil and pain.

Bleary eyed, he refused to look at the chair across from where he slouched. Instead, he stared mindlessly into the flames of the fire, blazing in the hearth. Even the eyes of the lion head, carved in the hearth mantle, seemed to jeer at him for being a fool. Reaching over with a shaking limb, he took hold of the platter and let it go flying. He watched in satisfaction as the food smeared its way across the embodiment of his title. At least he did not have to look at it any longer.

A snarl of considerable outrage rang inside his head and interrupted his thoughts. He at last looked towards the chair he had been avoiding. Ever so briefly, the image of his father sitting there with a stern look of displeasure came afore his eyes, 'til he vanished. Even in his darkest hour, his sire would not deem it fit enough to have a conversation with his heir. So much for fatherly love! A few more drinks afore he would be numb again and could lose himself in the few fleeting memories he had of his wife. 'Twas the only thing he cared about anymore.

Riorden barely noticed when the door to the keep opened, nor did he comprehend that his brother came to sit across from him. They sat there in silence, 'til Gavin finally reached across and took the whiskey from his hand. The bottle was mostly full. Odd that he should feel so intoxicated with the small amount of spirits he had consumed.

"What are you doing, brother?" Gavin asked folding his arms across his chest to await his brother's answer.

"What does it look like I am doing? Drinking and sulking. What else should I be doing?"

"You have an estate to run. Or have you forgotten such a grave matter as the coming winter and seeing that enough supplies fill the cellars?"

"Others can attend to such things."

"You have never been one to overindulge in drinking, Riorden. Although I understand the cause, you do yourself harm to imbibe so liberally."

"That is just it, Gavin. I never remember drinking but a few sips, and yet I cannot seem to stop reaching for a bottle."

"You must needs get control of yourself, Riorden. You do Katherine's memory an injustice by neglecting those in your care," Gavin advised.

Riorden wiped at his eyes, trying to clear his vision. "What are you doing here? Do you not have your own keep to see to?" he asked, frustrated that Gavin deemed it necessary to bring up things he would rather not discuss. Though, he knew where this discussion was leading.

"Aiden sent me a missive. He felt, mayhap, I could put some sense into your thick skull, where everyone else had failed.

"You need not have bothered. As you can see, I am managing."

"God's Wounds! Have you perchance seen yourself lately, brother?" Gavin argued. "You appear as if King Henry's entire army trampled over you several times, and back again!"

A disturbing chortle erupted in Riorden's throat. "'Tis exactly how I feel, so why should I not look the same?"

"And exactly why is it Marguerite is still here, hovering over you like some lovesick cow?" Gavin fumed. "She should have been dispatched to Dunhaven Manor long ago?"

"She serves her purpose here," Riorden answered, although his words echoed shallow in his head as to his reasoning for keeping her at Warkworth.

"Are you insane?" Gavin bellowed.

Riorden looked upon his brother and was certain his grief was mirrored in his sibling's eyes. "Go home to your bride and live your life. Leave me to what is left of mine," he muttered.

Gavin leaned his elbows on his knees and put his head between his hands. Then he quickly stood, growling his irritation and knocking over the chair he had been sitting in. Raising his fist in the air, he turned towards the hearth. "Why do you not do something to ease his suffering?"

Riorden's brows knitted at Gavin's outburst. "Who the hell are you talking to, or have you lost your wits?"

"'Tis father, of course. Who else would I be talking to, since you do not listen to my council, or anyone else's, for that matter?"

"Bah! Our sire is dead, as is my wife. Although I am certain Katherine's soul has been lifted up through heaven's gates, I am equally convinced that our father shall be rotting in hell for all he has done to me!" Riorden spat.

He did not even see his brother move. Afore he knew what was happening, Gavin grabbed his tunic, yanked his unsteady form out of the chair, and slammed his fist into Riorden's face. Riorden was too sotted to make much of an effort to retaliate as he fell, uselessly, to the floor.

"Bloody Hell! You broke my nose!"

"I will do more than break your nose if you do not get your damn head out of your arse and get your act together, Riorden! Do not dare speak about father and wish such on his soul!" Gavin yelled, standing over him ready to do battle again. "You have become a disgrace to this house, our family, and Katherine's memory. 'Tis clear you were undeserving of her!"

"Do not tell me that. I loved her." Riorden made to rise, only to have Gavin push him back down onto the floor to make his point. Dazed, he stared at his younger brother.

"Sober up, Riorden, and put your household in order. Do not make me come back here again and find you in such dire straits," Gavin threatened then left the hall.

Riorden did not understand what was physically wrong with him that such a small amount of whiskey could make him feel so drunk. Perchance, if he could sleep this off, he would feel better come the morn. Rising, Riorden weaved his way towards the stairs so he could go rest in his chamber.

If he had been able to see clearly from his drugged state of mind, he would have glimpsed the ghost of his father, who lovingly put his arm around his son, as if protecting him and seeing to his safety.

The Great Hall at Berwyck Castle was quiet. The morning meal was long since over. The tables had already been scrubbed clean by hardworking servants. All the knights had broken their fast and had gone to the lists hours ago to begin the day's training. There was no resting for the guards in the service of the Devil's Dragon. Dristan demanded their best and would not be caught unawares by invading forces with guardsmen who were weak. He did everything in his power to protect and care for his people.

Taking advantage of the peace and solitude by the fire that was a rarity in an estate this size, Katherine set down the tiny garment she was attempting to stitch. She was determined to put together something made by her own two hands that would at the very least be passable. Lynet had been a Godsend, teaching her the fundamentals of this nasty business called sewing. Though it wasn't going to become a talent she would be proud of anytime soon, her unborn child deserved, at a minimum, one garment made by his, or her, own mother.

Katherine gathered a MacLaren plaid about her shoulders when a gust of wind blew across the chamber with the opening of the hall doors. Winter was fast approaching, and soon the ground would be covered in snow. She would be interested to see what a winter in England would be like, compared to those she had to bear when growing up in Michigan. She shivered with the thought of those relentless blizzards of her youth. The only good thing that came from storms of that magnitude was when the schools were shut down. As a child, she had loved nothing better than to hear on the radio such news. As an adult, she was thankful to leave the shoveling of snow to others and live in San Francisco where she only dealt with rain and the occasional bout of driver road rage.

As if to confirm where her memories had wandered, she finally noticed Fletcher, shaking off a slight dusting of snow from his broad shoulders. He was a handsome man, much like her husband. She was surprised when her heart did a little flip when Fletcher waved in her direction upon seeing her sitting near the hearth. Startled, or rather alarmed by where her next thoughts had momentarily wavered, the baby gave her a swift kick in protest, as if to remind her she was a married woman.

Placing her hand on her stomach, she gave it a small pat, as though telling the child within that all was well. Looking up, she had to promptly retract those thoughts as Fletcher swiftly began shortening the distance between them. My God, he was just so damn good looking, much like the rest of Dristan's guards. She may be married, but it never hurt to look. Touching was what would land you in trouble.

Trying to find something to keep her composed while her heart began to suddenly hammer away in her chest, she picked up the godforsaken bit of fabric. *What in hell was she thinking to even consider that stitching would have a calming effect?*

"May I?" Fletcher asked, indicating the vacant seat next to her.

"Y-yes...o-of course," she stammered shyly. *What other response could she have given him and still remain polite? Even her voice didn't sound like her own!*

"There is a nip in the air this day," he murmured, watching her face before he relaxed back into his chair and closed his eyes.

He sounded tired. He looked tired. That he should feel comfortable enough to let his guard down to actually rest in front of her said a lot. A lock of black hair fell rakishly across one eye, and she had to subdue the impulse to reach over and smooth it back from his forehead. He reminded her so much of Riorden that for just the briefest of instances she thought it was him until he opened his eyes. They were amber with golden flecks in the irises instead of the deepest blue she had come to cherish.

She gave a low, weary sigh but continued her observation of him from the corner of her eye while he extended his hands toward the fire to warm them. Apparently, his brief rest was at an end. Still...she continued to reminisce on how she had allowed Fletcher to lead her in a dance when she and Riorden were previously at Berwyck. It had been after they had had their first real disagreement, and an invisible barrier had grown between them that neither of them had been willing to let down or breach. She could still see herself standing there, pleading for Riorden to approach with her eyes and hoping against hope he would take Fletcher's place. Instead, he remained as stubborn as ever while she did her best to make him jealous.

It hadn't been a hard task to appear she was enjoying herself with Fletcher, nor to be flirting with him. He had treated her with respect, but there had been a twinkle in his eyes that he understood what she was about and had no problem in helping in her attempts to win Riorden's affection. They had formed a silent friendship during that dance, and she was glad for it. One could never have enough allies in one's life.

That night seemed as if it was ages ago, though the memory of it was forever ingrained in her soul, but not because of her brief time with Fletcher. How could she ever forget the night Riorden came for her, and they made love for the very first time? She would remember such a night for the rest of her days.

Even though she had been lost with thoughts of Riorden, Fletcher must have felt her blank stare upon him, since she noticed he had turned his attention back toward her. Hastily, she ducked her head and began poking the needle in and out of the cloth. She was surprised she didn't tear the fabric in her need to appear engrossed in the project before her.

Good Lord! Why did all of Dristan's guards have to look so much like Riorden? She thought she was doing a good job of appearing absorbed in her work until, in her haste to keep her mind off the gorgeous hunk of man-candy sitting next to her, she stabbed her finger instead of the cloth.

"Dammit!" she cursed, dropping her sewing into her lap and peering at the drop of blood beginning to form on her finger.

Fletcher reached over to capture her hand before she could protest. "Let me see," he urged, taking a piece of linen that appeared from who knows where.

"I'm sure, I'll be just fine, Sir Fletcher," Katherine exclaimed, trying to pull back her hand.

He was just as insistent and held her quaking limb firmly in place. "Let me be the judge of that."

His hands were warm and calloused from years of carrying a sword. Just like Riorden's. He took his time holding the cloth to her injured finger until the bleeding stopped. Even then he didn't let go of her hand while his thumb caressed its back. Her heart raced with his nearness, especially when his gaze slowly fell to hers. *Get a grip on yourself, you idiot. Just what do you think you're doing, allowing him to practically flirt with you? You're only infatuated with the man because he reminds you so much of your husband.*

Katherine attempted to find her voice. "Will I live, do you suppose?" she inquired, wondering where she found the nerve to tease him.

He cleared his throat, as if he finally remembered himself, and released her hand. She could tell it was done most reluctantly. "Aye...you will, unless you continue to be so careless.

Did you not have enough injuries to your fingers when you ran them against Riorden's blade?" he replied offhandedly.

That had the desired effect she needed to bring her back abruptly to reality. He might as well have taken a pail of ice cold water and tossed it over her head. Her memories of Riorden flashed across her mind, along with the reason she now sat here instead of at Warkworth. It must have registered on her face.

"Lady Katherine, I am most sorry. I did not mean to bring up such un-pleasantries." Fletcher offered his apology, and she could tell it was sincere.

"It's okay, Sir Fletcher. I try to remember the good times we had and forget about what brought me here."

"Do you wish to talk about it?" Fletcher urged. "I have been told, I listen well."

"Confession good for the soul, is it?" she said with a small smile.

"Would you rather I fetch Father Donovan?"

She reached over and patted his hand before realizing she shouldn't have touched him. This wasn't the twenty-first century, and a person just didn't go around being as bold as she had been, whether she was pregnant or not. "Thanks, but I'll pass. Besides, I'd rather not talk about Riorden right now. I'm sure he'll be here sooner or later to fetch me home."

"He should have been here long afore now," Fletcher grumbled. "But, come...I forget my purpose, and that was to take you outside for some fresh air."

"I'm really not sure I'm in the mood."

"'Tis Dristan and Amiria's orders, my lady. I was to retrieve you posthaste and escort you about the grounds," Fletcher stated and stood holding out his hand. "Even their healer Kenna says 'tis not good for you to be cooped up inside for so long."

She hesitated before reaching out as he pulled her up next to him. "I don't know that this is a good idea, Sir Fletcher." She made the mistake of looking up into his eyes again where she beheld the fleeting glimpse of yearning hidden in their golden depths.

"I promise to behave myself and be nothing but the utmost courteous of knights." He made a very formal bow to her, and she repressed the urge to giggle like some young schoolgirl.

"I have your word, then?" she asked, not wanting to put either of them into a position they would later regret.

"Aye, you have it," he said simply.

Her hand was placed in the crook of his elbow as they made their way to the door. Before she could even ask for a servant to fetch a cloak for her, one was provided by a serf, who just as quickly disappeared. She settled the hood about her head, still hesitant to be alone with the man next to her.

He began reaching for the door before she stopped him with a slight tug on his arm. His brow rose, and she tried to formulate inside her head how to phrase her words to him. "I still love him with all my heart," she blurted out, wrapping her arm around herself as if to protect herself from the hurt that pierced her heart every day since Riorden's rejection.

"Aye, I know." He reached out and tucked a piece of her hair into the hood.

"I won't betray him. I have faith he'll come to his senses and return for me, and our baby. When he does, I'm willing to forgive him for what he has done."

Fletcher pulled his cape closer around his shoulders before taking her hand once more and bringing it briefly to his lips. "He is lucky to have you as his wife, Lady Katherine."

"I just don't want any misunderstandings between us, or for you to think the mild flirting that went on between us before at

Berwyck would go any further than it has. I'm sorry if I've misled you."

"You have not done anything to give me such an impression," he murmured.

"Then you're good with us just being friends?" she asked, hoping she hadn't insulted him.

"Aye, I will do my best to guard my heart against your most beautiful charms, my lady."

Satisfied that her attention to him would not be misunderstood, she took his arm as he led her about the inner and outer baileys to enjoy what was left of the day. With the snow beginning to fall, her only worry was Riorden would be challenged by the weather to reach her side. She refused to think of any other alternative than having her happily-ever-after ending with the man of her dreams.

Twenty-Eight

*M*ARGUERITE WAS AFRAID TO MOVE...*afraid to even take one step. Gasping for breath in indecision on how to solve her dilemma, she looked all around, but there was no escape. She was completely surrounded.*

The inferno was overwhelming as the flames of hell came ever closer to where she stood. Soon she would have nowhere to turn, and the fire would be licking at her toes. Everywhere she gazed was consumed in an orange blaze of heat, and she knew she must have died and gone to the underworld!

She cried out, "Riorden," the name of the one she loved, and yet he came not to save her. Then she began to fervently pray for her soul and the forgiveness of those she had wronged in her life. Visions of Everard flashed in her mind, for she had erred with him more than any other. Warin's face came next, and she came to realize that he had loved her, too, at least as much as he was capable of loving just one woman.

She attempted to conjure up Riorden's handsome face, but it would not come to her mind. She tried even harder, yet the more she attempted to envision his visage, only Everard's image came afore her thoughts. 'Twas as if the forces of evil refused to grant her request to see the one picture of the man she had loved with all her heart. She had failed herself, to get him to love her once more, and she cursed herself for not trying harder. He had been hers. He should have been again, and would have, if it had not been for the memory of his dead wife haunting him. At least, he knew not what part she had played in his wife's disappearance and death. If he ever became privy to such knowledge, there would be no corner on this earth where she would be able to hide from his wrath.

Death! My God, I am dead, *she thought. For the first time in her life, she was scared for her immortal soul. She began to shudder in her grief that shook her to her very core. She became hysterical as the fire inched its way ever closer 'til her gown began to disintegrate, and she could feel her skin begin to burn. A demon of gigantic proportions took shape whilst she cried out. She could not run, nor could she hide. Satan's clawed hand pierced her arm and began dragging her down into a deep, bottomless pit with other doomed souls whilst her screams rent the air. Hell's demon king had at last caught her in his grip and brought her to his realm.*

Marguerite arose from her bed and she searched the dark corners of the room, as if the Devil were truly coming to claim her. She sighed in relief at being utterly alone and went to the hearth to place a log on the fire. Taking a peek out the window, she realized that the new day had dawned dark and gloomy. She closed the wooden shutter to keep out the snow that had already blanketed the earth.

For months, she had been plying Riorden with drink, hoping that she would be able to get him in her bed again. So far, the closest she ever got to him was when she replenished his latest bottle. He continued to keep himself hidden away in his chamber or solar so the opportunity to sneak into his chamber never presented itself. 'Twas hard to get past a door that was bolted.

If she could only get with child, he would feel obligated to wed with her, she thought. She was fast running out of the potion Warin had given to her. Mayhap, 'twas time for her to use the last of the precious concoction and be damned with the consequences of what harm she may do him. She was running out of patience and wanted him warming her bed afore spring.

She had just taken a sip of wine that had been left for her pleasure when a cold chill swept into the room.

"Do not get too comfortable, my dear," Everard's voice came into her head. "I am not done with you for the night."

"'Tis morn, Everard, so go haunt someone else for a change. I have had enough of you to last my lifetime," Marguerite muttered. She heard his laughter filling her head 'til she put her hands over her ears, not that such a motion ever did any good other times he felt the need to torment her.

"But, the night is so young, Marguerite. Besides, you robbed me of years to spend with my family. 'Tis the least I can do for them to never give you a moment's peace, whether you are awake or whilst you slumber."

"Soon, I will be gone from here, and you will not be able to follow me. Riorden will be with me, and he will protect me. I never should have married you, you old goat!" she spat.

"You vile bitch!" Everard bellowed. "You will stay away from my son. You have done enough damage to ruin what little happiness he had found. Trust me, when I tell you, Marguerite...you will pay for all you have done in your miserable life."

"Bah! You cannot harm me if I am gone from Warkwoth. When I am away from here, after I have found the gold you have hidden from me, you can haunt this castle for all of your immortal life, and good riddance to you Everard de Deveraux," Marguerite yelled in return.

His frightening laughter filled her head whilst chills began to race down her spine.

"You can search these grounds 'til you take your last dying breath, and still you will not find what you so eagerly search for." Everard taunted. Then his tone turned deadly serious. "Heed my words to leave Riorden alone. I have warned you, Marguerite. I will not do so again."

"Riorden *will* be mine again. I swear by all that is holy, he will be mine again," she vowed, shaking her fist in the air to prove her point.

"I hope you enjoy Hell, my sweet, for 'tis coming for you."

A blast of cold air passed through Marguerite, clear down to her bones. 'Twas as if her fate had been sealed with her vow. She could stand her chamber no more, for the walls seemingly closed in on her. She quickly threw on her garments and fled in search of the one man who would save her sanity. No matter what his ghostly sire threatened, Riorden would love her once more, even if that meant dragging the man afore the priest in chains.

Twenty-Nine

R IORDEN YANKED THE NEARBY BOTTLE off the table in his solar, giving it a shake. 'Twas full! He pressed his lips around the rim and pulled at the cork firmly with his teeth. With the sound of a pop as 'twas freed, he spat the stopper from his lips and watched as it sailed across the chamber to land against the wall. He took a short sip of the whiskey and felt the relief the fiery brew brought him. 'Twas the only thing that took away the nightmare he now lived and gave the respite he stood in need of. The liquor burned its way down his throat and settled in his empty stomach. It rumbled at him in protest for the abuse, but Riorden cared not. A few more swigs of the heady amber brew, and he would soon be numb again to anything around him.

His head fell back against the top of the chair he sat in by his fire. With sightless, bloodshot eyes, he stared up at the ceiling, not caring what day 'twas, or if there were duties in need of tending. He only knew winter was here, and there was food provided down below for those who wished to partake of it. Had it really been four long months since he had lost his beloved Katherine? If she had yet lived, she would be well along with his child by now. How he missed her and the way she made him feel with her presence in his life.

Life! His life was meaningless now without her. Nothing had improved since her death, nor was it likely to. Riorden had been living in a dull haze. As far as he was concerned, he could just stay there 'til God in his mercy took his own sorry life too.

Somewhere in the recesses of his mind, he registered comforting hands that began kneading the knots that had formed on his neck and shoulders. It had been far too long since he had given in to any form of kindness, and he forgot himself as a lone moan of pleasure passed his lips.

"Does that feel good, Riorden?" Marguerite leaned down to whisper seductively in his ear. "I can make you feel better, my love, if you just allow me to show you how good it can be between us."

Riorden's mouth was dry, and he reached for the ever present flask in his hand. He was trying to form some kind of a coherent thought, but, for the life of him, he could not remember why Marguerite was in his solar. Afore he could reply, the door opened, and he turned his attention to the intruder. 'Twas Aiden, and he looked none too happy to see him, not that it mattered. He felt Marguerite take his hand and kiss its back afore she went to stand behind his chair.

"What is it, Aiden?" Riorden managed to gasp whilst Marguerite began playing with his hair. It reminded him too much of Katherine, and he swatted her limb away, as he would a tiresome bug.

"May we speak privately, Riorden?" Aiden requested.

Marguerite took a step forwards. "He is Lord de Deveraux to you. Do you not know your place in his household?" she snapped.

Aiden's brow rose in apparent amusement at her words. He took a step forwards, and she wisely retreated again behind the chair. Riorden only smirked whilst he watched this battle of wills.

"You must be mistaken, Countess, if you think I am his vassal," Aiden replied snidely. "I am no more than a guest in Riorden's household. Much like yourself, I might add."

"I am more than a guest!" she declared, stomping her foot.

"If you say so, Countess. In either case, Riorden and I do not stand in need of titles to have speech between us."

Riorden raised his hand when he saw Marguerite's face turning red with rage. "Enough, the both of you. I cannot stand listening to you sparing at one another. Leave us, Marguerite," he commanded, although he assumed his words lost some of their importance when they slurred together.

She leaned down to whisper in his ear. "I will return shortly in case you have need of me."

He waved her off, and she left the chamber without any further comments to Aiden, although 'twas clear she would rant at the man if given the chance. "What do you want to have speech about, Aiden," Riorden asked, taking another pull of whiskey. Aiden began pacing the chamber 'til Riorden was getting dizzy watching him. "Will you sit? You are making my head spin trying to keep up with you."

Aiden angrily came to him, ripping the bottle from Riorden's grasp. It went flying across the room and shattered into a thousand pieces as it hit the wall. Riorden watched in fascination as the brown liquid slowly trickled down the stones to leak into a puddle on the floor.

"What did you do that for?" Riorden bellowed. "'Twas nigh unto a full bottle!"

"What the hell are you doing to yourself, Riorden?" Aiden yelled, shaking his fist at him. "Do you think Katherine looks down from heaven upon you and is pleased that you have become a drunken fool?"

"Do not mention her name to me. I drink so I can forget."

"Aye, you wish to forget, but you do yourself, and her memory, an injustice by indulging in spirits! When was the last time you had something to eat?"

Riorden raked his hands through his hair. "Who can eat? Get me another bottle."

"Get it yourself if you want it. I will not stand here and watch you throw your life away by drowning out your problems," Aiden said and sat down in a chair opposite Riorden. "And speaking of problems, why do you keep her close to your side? I would think that she, of all people, would no longer be welcomed here at Warkworth!"

"You mean Marguerite?" Riorden said, trying to focus his thoughts on the conversation. His brow furrowed in concentration, but it only confused him the more he thought on the woman. "Why should she not be here? 'Tis her home, is it not?"

Aiden stared at him with his mouth hanging open then snapped it shut. He stood in disgust. "The next thing you shall tell me is the two of you plan to wed," he jested, waiting for a reply. None came, and Aiden began his pacing again. "God's Wounds! Riorden, tell me you will not wed the wench."

"Why ever should I not wed with her? She is a comely enough woman, who I once loved. Even the king desired our union," Riorden exclaimed. "Besides, it matters not who I wed with, be it Marguerite, or another. Without Katherine, my life is nothing."

"Your life is what you make of it, Riorden. But to wed with Marguerite would be an even worse betrayal to Katherine's memory than what has already occurred. Marguerite is like an evil spider, spinning her web around your thoughts. Why can you not see this for yourself?"

"Bah! She is but a woman. She will soon learn her place in my household."

"She has already taken over running the place, as if she is your wife, instead of being where she belongs in her dower house. Do you not care at all what Katherine would think of such a happening?"

Riorden's hands clenched in a tight fist. "I told you not to mention her name to me ever again, Aiden. You have been a friend to me these many years, but I will break our brotherhood forevermore if you do not leave me in peace," he roared between clenched teeth.

Aiden threw up his hands in disgust. "I wash my hands of you, then. Since you will not heed my council, or anyone else's, I will not idly stand by and watch your demise in the bottom of a bottle, nor watch you wed that bitter bitch."

"Then go! No one ordered you must needs stay and watch over me."

"I will leave come the morn for Berwyck," Aiden said, heading to the door, "and I take Patrick with me. He will be better off in Dristan's care than here with you."

Riorden flinched as the wooden door ricocheted off the wall and closed with a loud bang. It made his head pound fiercely, but 'twas of no matter. Soon the door opened again, and he reached out his hand as another bottle was magically placed in his palm. Marguerite's smiling form came to sit down next to him as the whiskey began to do its job. At least there was one person he could rely on.

THIRTY

KATHERINE LISTENED TO THE SOUND of the many parish-
ioners while they uttered a reverent amen at the conclusion of Father Donovan's evening mass. She lifted her head with
a heavy heart and put on a brave face for those who sat closest
to her. A hand was held out to assist her from the bench she
had been perched on longer than she would have liked. She
gratefully took the proffered limb and felt her hand tucked securely into place at the elbow of Sir Fletcher, who gave her a
kind smile.

She had been enjoying his company, the handsome devil with
his sparkling amber eyes, even though she knew she shouldn't.
Katherine assumed he most likely had women throwing themselves at his feet on a regular basis. She could understand why,
for he always comported himself as a gentleman and a most
chivalrous knight. What was there not to like about the man?
She herself might have fallen under his spell if her heart hadn't
already been stolen by another, who possessed the same unnerving qualities.

Sir Fletcher had been extremely courteous and attentive to her these many months, ensuring her comfort was seen to whenever she was in his sight, and time permitted him to do so. Being captain of the guard was a demanding job, however, and Katherine had come to know that free time was not something given if not earned. Hence, so as to gain that which was most cherished, the guardsman took full advantage of the opportunity, whenever it presented itself, to impress while under Dristan's watchful gaze.

She placed her hand on the lower portion of her back, hoping for a little relief that some of the pain found there might lessen. The nagging ache persisted, and sitting for two hours hadn't done it any good. She refused to be cooped up in her chamber until her time came, but maybe sitting on a hard bench for such a long length of time was over doing it a little.

"Are you unwell, Lady Katherine?" Fletcher asked quietly.

"Just stiff from sitting too long," she replied, stepping aside to allow those able to move faster than she to go ahead of her. The sharpness of the frigid winter wind blew in through the opening and closing of the chapel door, causing Katherine to quickly grab the plaid Amiria had given her and wrap the fabric around her shoulders. Shivering from the cold, she mentally cursed, wondering if she would ever feel the warmth from the sun again.

The church became eerily deserted until only a few people remained. Fletcher came to stand between her and the door to keep the freezing weather from reaching her. Her cloak rested on his arm until, with a flourish, he held it up so he could assist her with donning the garment, as if she were not capable of doing so by herself. She knew better than to argue with him. After all, he was being a gentleman. By now, she should be used to the chivalrous nature of these honorable knights found here in the twelfth century.

Her cape floated behind her until it settled on her shoulders, enveloping her in a cocoon of warmth from the heavy wool. He reached out for the hood, bringing the fabric over her head. It was a thoughtful gesture, yet Katherine wondered if he was thinking more of their association than that of being friends. She had tried to keep her guard up and hoped she hadn't given him any signs she was interested in him. She would hate to hurt this caring man with a gentle heart. He was pleasant company, but she couldn't offer him anything more than friendship, and she had thought he understood the boundaries they had previously set in place.

Afraid to find her musings were true, Katherine finally raised her eyes to his, and her worst fears must have shown clearly on her face. His own features fell briskly and confirmed his feelings for her. She watched him take a deep breath of remorse.

"He is a fool," he whispered, reaching out to tuck a stray lock of hair inside her hood. His hand lingered momentarily next to her cheek before he remembered himself and placed both his hands behind his back. "Any man with common sense would realize what a treasure you are and thank the stars above he had you to love."

"You are very kind, Sir Fletcher." She gave him a soft smile, for really what more was there to say. After all these months of waiting for Riorden to come to his senses and return here to Berwyck for her, she had given up any sense of hope. It was only now, sitting here inside this sanctuary with its calm serenity that Katherine had come to a decision.

The baby made its presence known by giving her a swift kick in her side, causing her to gasp aloud. It was almost as if he, or she, protested what direction Katherine's thoughts were beginning to take her. She gave a little push on her stomach and felt the tiny foot that had been kicking her recede back inside her womb. There wasn't much room left for the little tyke to grow at this late stage in her pregnancy.

Her gesture that she was uncomfortable wasn't lost on Fletcher, and he offered her his arm, again. She took it, although they moved no closer to the door. She could see his hesitation before he at last spoke, although his gaze didn't focus on her, as if he was afraid to physically watch what her answer would be.

"I would ask for you, if we could obtain your freedom with the king's leave, but I fear you would only decline such an offering, no matter that it had been sincerely given," he suggested.

"I'm so sorry, Fletcher." Considering their conversation, she felt it only right to use his given name. He looked pleased that she did so, regardless of her answer.

"As am I, Katherine, yet I had to try."

"I can't help it if I still love him with all my heart. I always have, for as long as I can remember, and until I take my last dying breath, I always will."

"Such loyalty is rare and is to be commended," he murmured until he gave her a devil-may-care look. "Riorden is lucky to have such a devoted wife in spite of all that has torn you apart."

He gave her no further time to reply, and they at last made their way out of the church. The weather had worsened since they had entered the chapel, and she watched the snow swirling all around them. She took a hesitant step, but, despite her care, she suddenly slipped across a patch of ice. Her equilibrium off balance due to the size of the baby, she lost her footing and cried out as she felt herself begin to fall. Without any hesitation on his part, she was scooped up in the strong arms of her ever present protector. Fletcher held her close, as if she was the most precious treasure he had ever carried. She indulged herself for the briefest instant, relishing the security he offered. She didn't realize how much she had been craving the feeling of being taken care of until that very moment. She hadn't felt this safe since before she left Warkworth.

"Thank you," Katherine whispered, almost shyly as he brought her closer into his warmth.

"'Tis my pleasure, my lady," Fletcher replied with twinkling eyes.

She gave a laugh, watching his carefree expression, for it was obvious he was happy her steps had faltered. The baby kicked again, and his eyes widened in surprise when he felt it, too. His eyes lowered to hers, and for one stolen moment, she wished she could feel differently where Fletcher was concerned. He would be so easy to love.

Fletcher carried her with a confident stride across the icy patches of ground until they entered the warmth of the keep. As the door closed behind them, he slowly set her down upon her feet. He lingered close to her in spite of the fact her stomach held them at a distance. She felt that some sort of dialog was necessary between them, for this may be the last time they spoke. She placed her hand softly on his cheek, and he covered it with his own.

"You're a good man, Fletcher. If things were different, I may have taken you up on your most gracious offer."

He gave her a small bow. "And you are a good woman, Katherine. I pray for your sake that Riorden returns for you and your child."

"You'll make a good husband to your own fair lady, someday," she whispered. Taking her cloak off, she handed the garment to a servant who came to retrieve it. "Where are Lord

Dristan and his lady?" she asked before the serf could disappear.

"They went up to 'is solar, milady."

"Thank you," Katherine said and watched the maid bob a curtsey. "If you would excuse me, Fletcher, I'd like to have a word with Dristan and Amiria."

"But, of course." He gave her a nod, even as his name was called from the guardsmen who had gathered near the hearth with a tankard of ale. "Do you need assistance with the stairs?"

She watched his eyes narrow when he heard the heckling of his comrades-in-arms, and a small laugh escaped her lips. His attention instantly returned to her, and she had the distinct feeling those men would pay for their comments the next time they stood across from Fletcher in the lists.

"I'll be fine, Fletcher," she said with a knowing smirk. "You best go put those men in their place."

"Rightly so."

Katherine watched him take his leave of her, and she crossed the floor of the Great Hall. She stared approvingly at the MacLaren tapestries that hung on the walls. Dristan's crest of a fire breathing dragon had also been portrayed in a place of honor, and she had the feeling Lynet's skill had something to do with that.

She slowly made her way up the stairs, resting when she came to the second floor that housed her chambers. The steep steps became harder and harder for her to climb and, at times, became too much for her, carrying this extra weight in front of her. She gazed upward in fascination as she saw the circular turret going forever upward. *One more floor to go*, she thought and began her progress again.

Slightly out of breath with thoughts of how an elevator could be so welcome the next time she had to go up three floors, her feet shuffled slightly as she made her way down the passageway. She tapped her knuckles lightly on the door of Dristan's solar and heard his call to enter.

She halted in her steps when she swung the door open. It was clear this was a family meeting and perhaps they were discussing something private between themselves, or were saying additional prayers, since a sister of the cloth was present. Or so she thought until she noticed Ella.

"Oh, I'm sorry. I didn't mean to interrupt. I can come back later," Katherine said, embarrassed that she had intruded, and turned to leave.

Amiria came and took her hand then led her to a comfortable chair near the fire. "You are most welcome, Katherine, and are not intruding. This is my sister Sabina, whom you have not as yet met. She came from Haversham Abbey just this eve, although she could have chosen a better day for travel."

"I felt compelled to come home, and, with Mother Superior's blessing, I came with all due haste," Sabina proclaimed. "'Tis a pleasure to meet you, Lady Katherine. I have heard much about you and of your...err...travels."

"Sister," Katherine acknowledged the young woman with a raised brow. Though she was surprised that they would divulge her secret.

Sister Sabina reached over to pat her hand. "You have nothing to fear," Sabina began, as if reading Katherine's thoughts. "We are all family here. You are safe, for they only thought of you and your troubles when they confided in me."

"I see."

Amiria leaned over and took Katherine's hand. "I pray you are not upset with us?"

Katherine shook her head. "No, but that is just it, and why I am here. I have come to a decision. I'd like to go home."

Dristan stood and folded his arms across his chest, nodding in approval. "I must say, 'tis about time. A wife should be with her husband, especially when you are about to give...umm..."

"Give birth?" Katherine finished his sentence and noticed his embarrassment to be discussing such a private matter that was generally not talked about with anyone other than one's spouse.

"Aye, give birth," Dristan finished, still looking ill at ease. "I will take you there myself, for 'tis more than time you should be at home."

Katherine held up her hand. "No, you mistake my meaning, my lord. I mean, I want to go...*home.*"

"You mean to Warkworth?" Ella asked.

Katherine only shook her head. "No. I mean my real home."

Silence descended upon the room, and Katherine's heart felt heavy, knowing she would never again see these people who had become as dear to her as any family member could be.

"You cannot be serious, Katherine," Lynet suddenly cried out, clearly distressed. "You were meant to be together. Do not give up on him, as yet."

"Just wait for him a little longer," Amiria urged. "You have both been through so much to be brought together. I know he will come for you, Katherine, given enough time."

"He's had more than ample time, Amiria. How much more am I supposed to give him?"

"But, what of your dear friend Brianna?" Ella said. "May-hap, we should send for her afore you act so rashly?"

Katherine only shook her head, again. "Please, don't. She's happily married to Gavin now, and I wouldn't want to spoil what they have together. Besides, it would change nothing. Her place is here now, in the past with her husband. Her path doesn't lie in the future anymore."

"Neither does yours, Katherine," Dristan said gruffly.

"I'm afraid I can't agree with you, my lord. I just want to go home. I need to go home to my mother," Katherine reiterated. "Please, will you take me to Bamburgh tomorrow? I just can't stand being here any longer, knowing he is with her. It continues to break my heart."

Her resolve to remain strong quickly faded as tears rushed down her face. She felt herself enveloped in Dristan's arms.

"I shall take you, if that is your wish, Katherine," he muttered, more or less against his will.

She nodded, wiping her eyes, and made for the door. "Thank you, Dristan, and all of you for your kindness these many months. I'll cherish this time we have spent getting to know each other all of my days."

"You know you are always welcome here, Katherine," Amiria said kindly.

Katherine nodded. "If you'll excuse me, I think I'll go lie down. I'm a bit tired."

"Katherine, wait a moment, if you please," Ella said as she took her arm and pulled her to one of the solar corners for a private word.

"You can't change my mind, Ella. It's time I go home."

"I won't try to change your plans, honey." Ella looked toward the others, but the family was engrossed in their own heated discussion. "I only wanted to give you a bit of advice."

"And what is that?" Katherine asked, curious about what her friend would tell her.

"My advice is that a person should be careful where he or she puts their stupid feet, Katherine. Even America has time gates where you may end up where you don't belong."

Katherine's mouth hung open after listening to Ella's brief speech...her very modern speech.

"You mean you're from..."

Ella only smiled. "I had my reasons, much like your own, for staying here and not going home. Perhaps, you should sleep on your decision before you do something you'll regret. Time Travel doesn't always work the way we want it to, and you should trust me on that one. If you go forward, you may not be able to return to your place in the past, where you should've stayed put in the first place."

"I can't believe we spent all that time traveling together and you never told me you, too, were from the future," Katherine stated with a shake of her head.

"I'm sorry I didn't confide in you sooner, my friend," Ella replied with a sheepish smile. "It's just been such a long time with me trying to remember to speak like a proper medieval woman, I sometimes forget that I'm just a stranger here in an unbelievable situation I can't control. I never thought there were others who have also traveled through time to be with those they loved."

Before Katherine could form any kind of response, since she was too stunned to mutter even one syllable, Ella gave her a brief hug and returned to the others, where silence crackled with tension between them.

Emotionally exhausted from having conveyed her decision to these dear friends and amazed if somewhat baffled about Ella, she turned from the now solemn group and reached for the door handle. Before she could grasp it, the wooden door swung opened, and Katherine stepped quickly back to avoid getting hit.

"By Saint Michael's Wings! Katherine?"

Freezing cold arms embraced Katherine in a firm hug, as if the knight would never let her go. He then began sputtering away in Gaelic, heaven only knew what.

"Hello, Aiden." Caught off guard, Katherine didn't know what to say, knowing he had just come from Warkworth and had most recently seen Riorden.

"My God, Katherine," Aiden exclaimed with excitement. "You have no idea how happy I am to see you. I have news of Riorden and—"

She held up her hand to stop the words that surely would break her heart yet again. "It's good to see you...but we'll have to talk later. I'm about to go rest," she patted her stomach for good measure.

"Aye. Of course." The young man seemed strangely flummoxed as she left the room.

Aiden's sudden appearance was too much to think on right now. Although Katherine knew he was about to offer her news of the goings on at Warkworth, she was unable to bring herself to stay and listen, much less inquire after her husband. Anyway, she had made up her mind to return to her own time, so there was little point.

As soon as the door closed quietly behind her, conversations erupted inside the solar. She smiled, listening to the siblings squabble, but didn't give it another thought as they chirped away in a tongue completely foreign to her. She made her way to her chamber, ready to leave everything behind her, knowing her time here in the twelfth century was almost over.

She would have been panic-stricken had she observed the lone rider who practically flew through the gates of Berwyck a short while later.

Thirty-One

MARGUERITE WRAPPED HER SILKEN LIMBS around Riorden's neck 'til her fingers pushed inside his shirt. She cared not that the man was in a daze and had called her Katherine more often than not. All she cared about was word from the king, granting them permission to wed. Then, and only then, would she feel he was truly hers once more.

There was not much of a response from him. There never was. She had attempted to crawl into his bed on numerous occasions, but even that course had been barred against her. It seemed the only use he had of her was to replenish his ever present bottle of whatever he chose to drink that hour. She had begun alternating the few drops of potion she had put into his drink, learning that only one drop was generally enough. She had sent another missive for Warin to bring her more but had yet to have any word from the lout.

She was thankful, however, that Riorden had never drunk the wine she had left for him at her dower house. She had stupidly put several large drops in the decanter and knew if he had tasted of it, he would have been slumped over dead, much like his sire had died. It had been a close call.

Everard had been silent lately, which was of great concern to her. She didn't understand why he left her alone, but her slumber of late had been so peaceful. At least she was able to take advantage of sleeping the night away as she had not done in some time.

Her fingers ran lightly across Riorden's chest and she closed her eyes, thinking how fine 'twould be to at last see him naked once more. It had been so long since that fateful day when all her plans had finally worked in her favor. Katherine was dead, Everard was leaving her alone, and Riorden would soon be her husband. Life could not get much better than that.

She began placing loving kisses on his neck, hoping that, for once, he might take advantage of what she willingly offered him. To her dismay, he waved annoyingly at her, promptly laid his head down on the table, and snored.

A snicker filled the Great Hall, or so it seemed to Marguerite's ears, as two of his knights turned from her sight and went back to drinking their fill at the hearth. At least she did not have to see the knowing leer in Aiden's eyes when she was all but rejected. As far as she was concerned, they were well rid of the annoying Scotsman.

She pulled up her chair next to Riorden's and draped her arm around his shoulder. He looked so peaceful and carefree as he slept, as if nothing troubled him. That she was the cause for all his misery, never crossed her mind as she laid her head down on his shoulder and stroked his hair.

Marguerite was enjoying the moment of acting the wife, giving her husband comfort 'til there was a commotion at the keep's door. She could feel a chill as the cold winter wind came whipping through the vestibule and made its way into the hall.

The door slammed shut, and the noise echoed throughout the keep. A shiver went through her, as if death were breathing down her neck.

"Katie!" a woman's voice sang out.

"Come out you pansy! We've come for a visit," another called.

Marguerite raised her head, and she saw two women taking off their snow covered cloaks. Her mouth hung open as she stared at their strange garments. Never had she seen clothing such as theirs, and she wondered from whence they hailed.

"Lady Juliana! Lady Emily!" Ulrick announced, coming quickly to their side.

"We are so surprised to see you here," Nathaniel chimed in. "Are Danior and Tiernan with you, as well?"

"I'm afraid not," Juliana answered as she wiped the snow from her hair. "We...ah...had a little mishap, if you take my meaning."

"Yea...seems like Bamburgh isn't the only place where one should be careful where one steps," Emily added, and both women burst into laughter. "Where's Katie?"

Marguerite's brows drew together, not liking where this conversation was leading, and yet she could not for the life of her move, nor help herself, as her arm tightened around Riorden's shoulder. 'Twas as if she was already losing her claim to him with the presence of these two strangers.

Nathaniel cleared his throat. "I am afraid, Lady Katherine is no longer with us."

"Where'd she go," Juliana asked. Emily tugged at her sleeve.

"Jesus, Mary, and Joseph," Emily cursed.

Marguerite, hearing these strange women's accent, began crossing herself but still listened with interest, trying to comprehend who these women were.

"Emily, how many times have you told us to watch what we say, or are you forgetting your own rules about the fabric of time issue," Juliana whispered between clenched teeth. She then proceeded to put a forced smile on her face afore turning her attention back to the knights standing afore her, who shifted uneasily upon their feet. "So, where's Katie?"

"Jewels, we have a problem," Emily muttered, giving the other woman a poke.

"What? Geez, Em, can't you hold your horses for a sec so we can find out where Katie is?"

Marguerite rose from her chair in irritation as the woman called Emily pointed in her direction.

"Who the hell is that?" Emily inquired with knitted brows.

Marguerite raised her chin a notch. "I am Countess de Deveraux and soon to be Riorden's wife! Who are you to come barging into my home unannounced?"

Emily began closing the distance between them.

"Emily...wait!" Juliana yelled.

"Bullshit!" Emily bellowed.

Marguerite was unable to move fast enough as that evil woman's fist slammed into her eye. An unladylike scream was forced from her lips when she fell over backwards whilst her head felt as if it had been knocked off her shoulders. The irrational woman then had the nerve to stand over her, clenching her fist, as if she was unsure if she should continue her assault.

"You keep your God damn hands off my friend's husband. Do I make myself clear?" Emily threatened.

"I am not afraid of you," Marguerite answered with clenched teeth.

"Ha! You should be," Emily declared knowingly.

Marguerite watched Ulrick pull Emily away from her as the woman sputtered curses. She had never heard a woman use such profanity openly in the company of men. Nathaniel came and assisted Juliana to a chair near the hearth, and still no one offered to help her from the floor. She picked herself up from where she had fallen and made to sit back down in her chair at Riorden's side. She changed her mind when Emily cleared her throat, waving her fist in her direction again. Mayhap, for the time being, she would let this stranger have her way. She took a small sip of her wine and heard the conversation of Katherine's death swirling about the four people who hovered around the fire.

"We searched everywhere for Lady Katherine," Ulrick was saying, "but her body was never found."

Startled gasps escaped the two women, who looked at the knights in total disbelief, causing Marguerite to hold back a satisfying grin that the rival for Riorden's heart was now out of the way.

"But that's impossible, Jewels," Emily began with a furrowed brow.

"Not now, Em," Juliana firmly said.

"But we have—"

Juliana held up her hand, all but cutting off Emily's words. "I said, not *now*," she repeated sharply. With a severe expression on her visage, she gave a nod of her head in Marguerite's direction. The two strangers then proceeded to look upon each other 'til their cheerful laughter rang out. 'Twas not long afore their common sense returned, and they clamped their hands over their mouths to cover their mirth.

Marguerite folded her arms across her chest in indignation, wondering at the jest they made that must surely be about her, not that she cared what these strangers thought of her. Ulrick and Nathaniel's expression's showed their dismay that these women would find humor in their friend's demise.

"My ladies," Nathaniel interjected 'til Juliana held up her hand once more.

"Emily and I didn't mean to appear disrespectful," Juliana murmured with a strange smile on her face, "but are you perhaps trying to tell us that Katie is dead?"

"Aye, she passed on several months ago, but we continue to pray for her soul to rest in peace," Nathaniel declared in a solemn whisper of reverence. He made the sign of the cross and then lifted his eyes upwards in a brief moment of prayer.

Ulrick peered in confusion at the two women afore he leaned forwards, and Marguerite strained to hear his words. "Riorden has not been the same since and blames himself for her death, and that of their unborn child."

"Aye, Ulrick speaks the truth. Riorden is never without a bottle of spirits in his hand that continues to be replenished by the Countess," Nathaniel answered, as if the current state of Riorden's health was grave. Marguerite should not have been surprised when all four heads swiveled in her direction.

Juliana had a grave expression on her features. "Are you trying to tell me that Riorden has become an alcoholic?"

Marguerites brows furrowed at the strange words coming from this lady's mouth. She didn't understand half of them. Apparently, she was not the only one, as Ulrick and Nathaniel looked just as confused.

Emily began to clarify. "You know...he drinks too much, day in and day out."

"Aye," Nathaniel answered as he stared at Marguerite with hatred in his eyes. "We have attempted to reason with him, but he has lost his will to live without Lady Katherine at his side."

"I see," Juliana said. "Excuse me for a moment."

She made her way towards Marguerite, who watched in puzzlement as Juliana picked up the bottle Riorden had been drinking from. Juliana lifted the cork and sniffed the contents then turned her glaring green eyes upon her.

"Damn you for what you've been doing to him! You're lucky you haven't killed him!" Juliana swore at Marguerite afore she turned away, turning her attention to those near the fire. "It's not the booze he's become addicted to. She's been drugging him."

Marguerite stammered her retort. "How d-dare y-you...a-assume...*I* would do such to the man I love?"

Juliana's emerald eyes flashed with fury. "Honey, you don't know the first thing about love."

Marguerite sputtered, trying to justify herself as her ruse was quickly unraveling right afore her. Ulrick and Nathaniel looked as if they were about to lead her away in chains, but she was spared the humiliation, as their attention was drawn to the woman named Julianna, who picked up two buckets set by the hearth and went outside. She returned shortly with them filled halfway full of snow.

"Where's the kitchen?" she asked, and Ulrick pointed her in the correct direction. "Emily, come with me."

They were not gone long, and when they returned to the hall, they each carefully tried not to slosh the water that was filled nigh to the brim of the buckets they carried. The women crossed the floor to Riorden then stood behind him whilst he still slept on, with a soft snore.

"Ready?" Juliana asked Emily.

"You betcha!"

"Get ready to jump back. He's not gonna like this. One, two, three!" Juliana said, and they let the freezing water sail through the air to drench Riorden to the bone.

Marguerite did not think the man could move so fast, considering how drugged he was, but he roared like the lion he was, reaching for his sword that was fortunately not to be found at his side. His stance wavered from the drink and potion she had been feeding him 'til he slipped back down, into his chair. Marguerite made to come to his aid but stopped short of her target.

"I think you've done enough, Countess. If you value what little patience I have, you will get yourself out of my sight, or I won't be able to stop my friend there from most likely ripping the hair right out of your skull," Juliana warned.

"How dare you speak to me like this? You'll answer to Riorden for this insult," Marguerite swore.

Emily grabbed a dirk that had been lying on the table. "Oh, I don't think we'll be thrown out anytime soon, especially when Riorden learns what we know. If you were smart, which I doubt you are, you'd take Juliana's advice and go to your chamber. We'll take care of Riorden now."

Marguerite could only stammer, trying to form some kind of a response. 'Twas the first time she was ever at a loss for words. Reluctantly, she began to make her way to the stairs.

"Sober him up, and fast," Juliana ordered the two men. "If you have to go dunk him in a horse trough, then do it."

"But, my lady, he will be mad as hell when he wakes from his stupor. 'Tis the only thing that dulls the pain of knowing his wife is dead," Ulrick proclaimed, as he and Nathaniel each took one of Riorden's arms and draped them around their shoulders.

Juliana and Emily gave them a knowing look and began to smile.

"Dead?" Emily giggled." Katie's not dead, and we have the proof."

"And it's long past time Lord Riorden went to fetch his wife," Juliana answered.

Marguerite's eyes widened in shock as she hurriedly made her way to her room. Knowing all her plans were falling apart, she slammed the door. *How can Katherine not be dead?* She had paid a large sum of coins to ensure the woman no longer graced this earth. Yet, she had a bigger problem that must needs be solved. Once Riorden was no longer indulging in the spirits she provided him, she would be sent posthaste to Dunhaven, without a backwards glance.

She began to pace. Suddenly, she shuddered, for with her fear of losing Riorden, his father made his presence known again and proceeded to renew his efforts in his revenge. Everard's laughter would fill her head for the remainder of this night, and many more to come.

THIRTY-TWO

RIORDEN WAS ABOUT TO ENTER his solar when he heard the laughter of the two ladies inside. He had been astonished to learn they had traveled, yet again, back in time. And that 'twas no more of their own choosing this time than it had been the last. At least he finally had a clear head on his shoulders, although it had taken almost a whole fortnight to come out of the daze he had been in. He knew 'twould be a long time 'til he felt once more in control of himself.

He was actually surprised that Ulrick and Nathaniel were yet alive. He had lost count the number of threats he had made against them since that first night when his head had been dunked in a frigid water barrel by the two knights. His teeth still ached, he swore, from spitting out large chunks of ice that managed to find their way into his mouth when he bellowed out his frustration.

He grimaced, thinking that he had sunk so low as to fill himself with drink, as he had. Yet, he wondered, not for the first time in the past few days, what Marguerite had been putting in his wine and whiskey. As he opened the door, it appeared the women were soundly trouncing his knights in another round of cards. They looked most pleased with themselves at their accomplishment.

Emily was the first to smile brightly at him. "We're playing Euchre. Would you care to learn the game, Riorden?"

He shook his head, never having heard of such a thing as a game called Euchre, but the women were enjoying themselves, and he was glad of it. However, he had more important things that needed discussing than the rules of a game of chance.

Juliana rose from the table and made herself comfortable in front of the hearth. "I think Lord Riorden has questions that only we can answer. Are you ready to learn the truth of the matter of why we have, most likely, been sent here?" she asked hesitantly.

The others joined her and awaited his seating. But he remained standing at the door, not sure where to start. He watched as Juliana motioned to his chair, as if he had no idea where he should sit. *Merde,* he was a mess of confusing thoughts!

"Why are you here?" Riorden at last managed to form a few brief words on his lips. They were raspy, at best, proving even to his own ears that he had been drugged.

Juliana and Emily exchanged glances afore Emily finally answered him. "To make things right, of course."

Riorden ran his hand over the stubble on his chin. "Nothing can make up for my mistakes, for my losing Katherine. You cannot make any of that right."

Juliana leaned over and took his hand. "Yes, we can, my lord. If Katie were sitting here with you now, she would tell you everything happens for a reason. We may not comprehend the why of it, but sometimes these things take years for us to understand. Only God above knows for sure why He puts us through the trials in our lives as He does. It's been said, He does it to make us stronger."

"You cannot possibly under–" Riorden began to protest. She held up her hand when he was about to renounce her words. His lips snapped shut as she continued.

"While I won't try to guess the ins and outs of what you have gone through, I will tell you that there is no reason for you to be grieving. Katie is alive, and for that we're very thankful."

"Do not jest with me, Lady Juliana, for I cannot bear it," Riorden whispered.

Emily reached for a satchel she had sitting on the floor next to her. "Ulrick and Nathaniel have kindly filled us in on how you believed that Katie drowned in the river, but that's a false-hood. We have the proof of it here."

Reaching into her bag, she pulled out a fairly large piece of parchment, though none that was from this day in age. She handed it to him, and he noticed some strange kind of clasp on it. He looked on her, not sure what he should do with it.

"Oh...sorry," Emily said, knowing she had embarrassed him. "I sometimes forget where I'm at, and that you've never seen anything like this."

She leaned over and pushed the two metal pieces upwards. Taking the edge of the parchment, she pulled on a flap as the metal went through a small hole.

"It's called an envelope, but the proof you seek is inside," Emily declared with a knowing smile. "Go ahead, Riorden. Take a look at your future and know that your heart's desire is still attainable if you just go and get your wife."

"This is how Em and I knew the four of you had lived a full, rich life," Juliana added with a smile of her own.

With trembling limbs, he took out the thick parchment. There was another sheer film of something almost see through. He pulled back this layer and almost dropped the portrait he held in his hands. Tears formed in his eyes as he stared at it in disbelief.

'Twas a family portrait of their children, along with Gavin and Brianna's. They were all older than they were now. As his eyes focused on the right side of the picture, he gazed lovingly at the perfect image of Katherine sitting on a bench with a daughter. The young woman had a long braid of tawny colored hair, filled with different colored flowers. Another small girl sat at his wife's feet, and a young puppy was lying next to her with a curled tail. She looked as if she would be a handful, and the little imp had his dark black hair and sparkling blue eyes. But 'twas the son, standing next to him in his image, with the exception of his hair, that almost was his undoing. The young man also had his mother's coloring, but there was no mistaking this was his son. The son she was carrying right now.

Riorden lightly skimmed the image of Katherine's face, lovingly set with a perfect smile, with his fingers. His eyes widened in surprise as her favorite scent filled his nostrils, and he inhaled deeply the fragrance she called Japanese cherry blossoms. Aquamarine eyes twinkled back at him as if they shared a lover's secret, and 'twas the first time in months that he had the smallest measure of hope. Looking at his wife's two lady friends, who were doing their best to hold back their tears, he knew within his heart that they had enjoyed the same experience as he just did. His beloved Katherine was indeed alive!

He handed the portrait to Ulrick and Nathaniel, and they, too, gasped in surprise. After their quick examination of the picture, Emily put it back away. 'Twas not something to be left lying about for prying eyes.

"It was given to us by a man named Simon Armstrong who helped us while we were in twenty-first century Bamburgh. He's also the person who assisted with certain delicate matters relating to our very twelfth century husbands," Emily said softly.

"Hopefully you remember Em's love of history," Juliana began. "We had moved to England recently and were doing a bit of research when we stumbled across an article stating it was thought your father had been poisoned, although there had been no proof as to who might have done such a deed."

"Mostly, everything we found showed that your father had no enemies, and, since Warkworth was relatively small, we couldn't find any reason why someone would want him dead," Emily added.

"Where is she?" Riorden whispered, ignoring for now the news of his sire's death.

"Where do you think she would go?" Juliana and Emily asked at the same time.

Nathaniel rose from his chair. "There really is not any question where she would go, since she is only familiar with two estates.

"You mean to tell me she's been at Berwyck all this time, and Dristan did not even have the decency to let me know?" Riorden yelled.

His solar door suddenly burst open as Aiden came stumbling in, still covered with snow. "Riorden, Katherine's alive!" he exclaimed, and then came to notice who occupied the room. "Emily? Juliana? What the devil is going on here?"

Emily hurled herself into his arms. "Hi ya, brother? How's it going?"

"You are going to be the death of me, lassie, but 'tis good to see you," Aiden answered. He looked at Riorden with a raised brow. "Why do I have the feeling I have just told you old news?"

"I have just learned of it, myself," Riorden grumbled, "but first let me apologize for my actions afore you left."

"You can make it up to me," Aiden said with a smirk. "I would think you need to get yourself to Berwyck and retrieve your wife afore she gives birth."

"You have seen her then, and she is well?" Riorden prodded expectantly.

"Aye, she is more than well, from what I could see. To be honest, I did not stay around long enough to have much speech with her, or anyone else for that matter. I turned right around and headed back so I could let you know she yet lived. I was overly delayed due to the horrendous weather we have been having."

"I must needs get to Berwyck, right away," Riorden declared, heading for the door. His footsteps halted suddenly at Juliana's next words.

"She won't be there, my lord."

"Why the hell not?" he roared.

Juliana came to stand afore him and placed her hand gently on his arm. "If I know my sister of my heart, and I think I do pretty well, then she has been waiting for you to come for her. She isn't one to not give someone she loves a second chance. Some may think it's a fault of hers, but, personally, I think she's just more tenderhearted than the rest of us. She is a firm believer that true love will win out if freely given. Since she will know that Aiden will ride to get you, there is only one place she will go, and that's to Bamburgh to return to her own time. She will have felt that all hope is lost, because you never came for her of your own choice."

"But, I thought she was dead!"

"Yes, but she doesn't know that, now does she?" Emily answered softly.

He gave the ladies a bow. "I can never repay what you have returned to me."

Juliana only smiled. "Just hurry and go get your wife before she makes the stupidest mistake of her life."

He made for the door and practically ran into Gavin and his lady. "I must hurry, but I believe there are those within who would love to have speech with Brianna," Riorden said, and they witnessed his smile for the first time in months.

Squeals of delight emitted from his solar at the reunion he could only imagine between the women, who were more like sisters than just friends. Riorden rushed to his chamber and threw only a few things in a satchel that he felt he would need. Running to the stables, he began to pray in earnest he wasn't too late to bring his lady home, where she belonged.

THIRTY-THREE

P LEASE DON'T FOLLOW ME, DRISTAN," Katherine announced gently. "This is something I think must be done
alone, and I don't think the time gate is going to open with you
two hovering over me like you have all this time."

"'Tis not seemly to leave you alone and unescorted," Dristan
grumbled.

"I do not care for this either, Katherine, not that you would
heed my council," Fletcher added with furrowed brows. "I know
you said you are independent in this future of yours, but I
would feel better if you would, at the very least, allow one of us
to be close at hand in the event you have need of us. I do not
like this idea of Time, as you say, taking you back, without us
seeing that 'tis done safely."

"You dolt," Dristan muttered with a slap on Fletcher's back,
"how can she be traveling through time safely? It does not
make sense, given her early description of being hit with a hard
enough force to knock her over."

"Gentlemen, please stop! Really, I'll be just fine." Katherine raised her hands and placed each on the two knights who appeared ready to have a wrestling match right in front of her. "It doesn't matter what you two think or say. I've made up my mind, and that's all there is to it. Both of you stay where you are. If in an hour's time the gate doesn't open, I'll come back here so you can see for yourself that I'm still around. Hopefully, it won't come to that, and I'll just get swallowed up and thrown back to the future."

She watched the uneasiness come across their features. And she did what she had done for the past several days, each time they had had this conversation, when she attempted to return to her own time. She hugged Dristan first and then turned to Fletcher. This time, it felt so very different, as though she really was saying goodbye to him for the very last time.

Fletcher held open his arms, and she willingly went into them, even though it was so reminiscent of her encounters with Riorden that she could hardly bear it when he wrapped his arms around her in a fierce hug. He had been such a support to her these last few months, and she didn't know how she would have survived without his friendship. He held on to her longer than he should have, she supposed, but what could she say to him that they hadn't already discussed before?

"Please do not go, Katherine. Stay here with me," Fletcher urged. "I will do my best to make you forget him."

A startled gasp escaped her as her emotions began to get the best of her. It was the last thing she expected to hear from him and was a clear indication he cared for her far more than he should. "I wish I could, Fletcher, but I just can't. It's not you...honestly...you're a wonderful man, but I'll never be able to forget him. I know in my heart that I could never love another the way I've loved him. He's a part of me, you see, my soulmate. He's the other half of me, and a love like that only comes around once in a life time. It certainly wouldn't be fair of me to stay with you, knowing I could never offer you even the smallest measure of what I have felt for Riorden. I care for you, Fletcher, but not in the manner you wish me to. I'm so very sorry."

"There is nothing for you to apologize over, Katherine."

Katherine looked around to see if Dristan watched them but saw he had moved to a nearby window, thereby giving them what privacy he could. Her attention returning to Fletcher, she reached up, placing both her hands upon his cheeks, and urged him to lower his head. She placed but the briefest kiss upon his lips before she released him again, much to his disappointment.

"Katherine, I lo—"

She swiftly halted his heartfelt declaration with her fingers upon his lips. "Please...don't say it. You have been a dear friend to me, but you and I both know, I am not the one for you. Find your sweet lady, Fletcher," she prompted, watching the shadows of sorrow swim across his amber eyes. "She's out there somewhere, waiting for you to discover her. All you need to do is go and follow your heart."

With another hasty kiss upon his cheek, she went to Dristan and repeated the gesture. With one last look, she whispered a soft goodbye and left them standing in the middle of Dristan's chamber, looking like two lost little school boys who hadn't gotten their way. The image made her smile, for it wasn't a bad way to remember two people she had come to care for.

She walked steadily down the passageway and momentarily hesitated at her...rather, their chamber...his door. She gazed at the familiar wooden door, and with a firm hand, entered one last time to peek inside a room that had meant so much to her. Her breath caught, and fresh tears threatened to spill from her eyes. Flashes of memories echoed in her mind as she began re-membering everything that had happened in this room, espe-cially the first time they saw one another as ghosts. Her eyes darted to the wall, and her face became flushed as she recalled how he had taken her right then and there. It had been one of the most erotic encounters of her entire life and one she would treasure for all of her days.

Katherine wanted to leave something behind for him but could think of nothing she had with her that would be of any significance. He had already taken her heart. She had nothing left to give him, or anyone other than her unborn child. She turned from the room as unhappiness enveloped her soul. She was ready at last to go home.

With a deep breath, she again made her way down the torch lit corridor. She came upon the turret that she needed to go in-to but had the same feeling come over her as when they were attempting to get her friends back to present day England. She must go up the steps to return, for to go down would only hurt-le her farther into the past.

Katherine made her way down a different set of stairs and backtracked to the tower. She stared up the stone stairwell as if willing the portal to open at her command. But there was noth-ing unusual happening. The stairs remained normal stairs. The walls remained sturdy with a few cobwebs hanging from the torches lighting the way. She sat down on the first step, praying for Time to take her back, but only silence met her ears. As in the previous days when she had willed the time portal to open, nothing happened to make Katherine think she was ever going to be transported to any place or to any other time period at all.

She wasn't sure how long she sat there, whispering to God or the time travel faeries to take her back home. No matter how much she pleaded, her prayers went unanswered. She was so tired, and, as her tears began to fill her eyes, she rested her forehead on one of the stairs above her, praying for a miracle to save her.

Riorden opened the door to Bamburgh's Great Hall, expecting to see it filled with courtiers. He was pleasantly surprised to see only a few knights and their ladies waiting about. He began to wonder if the king was even in residence when he heard his name being called from across the room. His eyes narrowed whilst a knight made his way to his side.

"Ho, Riorden!" Came the cheery call. Yet Riorden only thought of a young girl at Berwyck, pining away for this very same knight, who now casually crossed the room without a care in the world. His fist clenched and landed squarely on the man's chin, and Ian went stumbling backwards. He kept his feet, unfortunately, and Riorden thought he was out of shape if the man had not come up close and personal with the floor.

"What the hell is the matter with you, Riorden?" Ian asked, rubbing his jaw.

"That is for Lynet!" Riorden bellowed, closing the space between them and grabbing Ian by the scruff of his tunic. He was just about to let his fist fly with a second blow, when he heard his name called, yet again. He was surprised to see Fletcher angrily making his own way into the hall. Thinking he, too, was about to place his own mark on Ian's visage, Riorden smirked with a knowing gaze at Ian, who still stood, muttering away about the welcome he was receiving.

Riorden should not have looked away, for the next thing he knew, he was yanked away from the grasp he had on Ian. He was about to make his protest known, when lo and behold,

Fletcher's fist made contact with his eye. Ian began to laugh, but Riorden found this not at all amusing.

"What the hell was that for?" Riorden demanded.

"That is for making your wife shed more tears than she should, considering her condition, you imbecile!" Fletcher announced. "Why have not come for her?"

"What business is it of yours?" Riorden bellowed, advancing on Fletcher.

"I am making it my business!" Fletcher yelled as Riorden made a grab at him. They stood nose to nose, their tempers flaring.

"Enough!" Dristan shouted as he entered the room.

Riorden quickly dropped his hands that were near to clenching Fletcher's neck.

Dristan approached the group, looked Ian up and down, and then turned his attention to Riorden "'Twould be in your best interest, my friend, to quickly go and retrieve your wife afore you cannot follow where she plans to go."

"She's at the entrance to the tower?"

"Aye," Dristan replied, "and you had best hurry."

"Did Aiden not tell you, I thought she had drowned in the river?" Riorden asked.

"Aye, he did," Dristan replied.

"And does she know this, as well?"

"Aye, she does."

Riorden shook his head. "Then, why does she still want to return to her time?"

"I believe she does not feel as though she has an alternative," Dristan answered with honesty. "If you do not hurry, you will lose the opportunity to convince her to stay."

'Twas all the encouragement Riorden needed. His boots echoed down the passageways as he made his way towards the tower where her friends had disappeared through the time portal, but a few months afore. All he heard was the pounding of his heart as he raced to be in time. All he saw was her beautiful face, her warm smile, her blessed soul as his focus on his quest intensified, and he pushed himself harder to find her. All thoughts were gone from his mind, save one. He rounded the corner and slowed his steps when he at last espied the one person he feared never to see again this side of the veil.

Riorden's eyes drank in the mere sight of the woman who had crossed time for him. She had to be uncomfortable, lying as she was on the stone stairs, and he worried for her welfare, along with the babe's. Riorden vowed then and there that he would do all in his power to prove his love of her and make her stay with him. But her whispered words, spoken from the depths of her soul, nearly broke his heart all over again as he listened to her plea.

"Please, God! Why won't you let Time take me back home to where I belong?" Katherine cried softly.

Riorden lowered himself quietly to sit beside his wife, although he dared not touch her. He leaned in close to her and whispered gently, "'Twill not open, my love, because God knows you already *are* where you belong."

He saw her flinch upon hearing his voice. Quickly, he rose and offered up his own silent prayers that he was not too late to prove to her he was still worthy of her love.

Thirty-Four

Katherine tried to catch her breath as every imaginable emotion raged inside her torn and broken heart. Happiness that he had at last come for her was overshadowed by a fear of losing him again. Anger boiled to almost overflowing that he had cost them so much until she let out her breath to calm the words that nearly burst unhindered from her lips. Words that, if spoken, would always separate their souls and split them forever apart.

She raised her head where it had been placed on the hard step, but she didn't turn to face him. She was afraid that once she gazed into those hypnotic eyes, she would be lost. There was still so much that needed to be said before she could even begin to forgive him, and yet, a part of her still desperately wanted to go home. She was terrified to be hurt again, terrified to believe in him, and worse yet, terrified to let him see how much she still loved him with every beat of her heart.

Looking up into the stairwell, she silently begged for God or Time to take her this very instant so she wouldn't have to make such a life altering decision for herself. It would be so easy if they just took her now, before she gazed again at his features. But Time wasn't listening to her request and, apparently, neither was God.

Katherine tried to take a deep gulp of air to calm herself, yet, she could feel everything about him with his presence so very near. She could tell he was quietly waiting for her to make some effort to speak with him. She held her silence, trying frantically to wrap her head around what to say. She could even hear him breathing, and the will to throw herself into his comforting arms was almost her undoing. She withheld the impulse and clenched her fists at her sides, as if that in itself would stop the little currents that were racing up her arms, now that he was so very close. That magnetism was what had brought them together originally. At the moment, she felt as if she were cursed that he could still have such an effect on her, especially considering everything he had put her through. She wished she had more of a backbone, along with the ability to harden her heart against her feelings. Unfortunately, such capability was completely impossible and hopeless, for she still loved him that much.

She at last sat up and rested her back against the stone wall. Closing her eyes, she steeled her voice to remain steady before she made some form of a reply. Her limbs trembled beneath her gown, as she tried to remain calm.

"I don't belong here, Riorden," she said slowly. "What makes you think I do?"

"You belong with me, Katherine," he replied firmly.

"Do I?"

"Aye!"

"I don't belong to you or with you, Riorden. You gave up that right when I found you in bed with your lover."

"I had been drugged and thought you were dead these many months. 'Tis why I never came for you. If I had known you yet lived, nothing would have kept me from reaching you so I could explain and beg your forgiveness."

She finally turned to look up at him. It was worse than she thought, for he was standing far closer than she realized. Their eyes held one another, almost as if Time itself were pulling their souls together as they were meant to be.

Riorden looked as if he had been to hell and back. He'd lost a lot of weight and one eye was badly bruised. Katherine wondered who had caused the injury to her husband although it wouldn't be hard to guess at the culprit. She continued to study him, and, although one eye was beginning to blacken to a lovely shade of purple, she could see there were dark circles underneath those magnificent eyes of his, giving truth to his words that he had been ill. It saddened her that they appeared so very dull, far from the normal brilliance she was used to seeing reflected in their depths.

"And do you honestly think everything will be all right between us, just because you tell me she drugged you, and you're now saying I'm sorry? I didn't realize I came off as that big of a fool." Her voice sounded strained from the turmoil she felt, roiling in her mind.

"I am the one who was the fool for not listening to your words of warning about her," Riorden confessed. "I had so many haunting memories at Warkworth, and being there again, immersed in surroundings that brought all those painful events to the fore, caused me such anguish, I turned to anger too quickly. 'Twas not my intent to hurt you, Katherine."

"Well, you did, and it's not something that's so easily forgiven, or forgotten."

He lowered his head, as if dejected. "Aye, I know, but I would spend all of my days trying to make it up to you, if you but gave me the chance."

"Why should I, Riorden?" Katherine asked, knowing she was about to lose her resolve to remain strong and burst into uncontrollable tears.

"Because, I love you," he answered simply.

"Maybe, that's not enough anymore. What am I supposed to do? Should I just let you waltz back into my life, and our child's, so you can hurt me again? I'm afraid, I'm not that strong, nor is my heart, to survive going through another such emotional beating."

Katherine made to stand, and he reached out for her elbow to steady her. She gasped unexpectedly at his touch. That unmistakable sensation was there again as she looked into his eyes, and she knew he had felt it, too. Those damn, little currents pulsed through her and reminded her heart of what she had known from the very start. They were meant to be with each other, for only when they were together, could they be completely whole. Riorden had always belonged to her. And throughout all time, their souls would be forever bound by invisible ties that others could not see.

She realized, he hadn't let go of her. In fact, both his hands somehow had managed to make their way to her waist, what little of it that could be found with the baby between them. Katherine noticed her own hands had found their way to his muscled arms, and her thumbs were automatically rubbing the fabric of his tunic. God only knew how much she had missed this man.

"'Til a se'nnight ago, I never thought to see or touch you again," he whispered with so much agony in his voice, it became pretty obvious that thinking her dead had affected him more than he was letting on. "Even if you do not stay, I am forever thankful you yet live."

Katherine felt some of the pain he must have gone through. "I'm sorry you were under the impression I was dead. I would have been, if not for a friend. It still changes nothing, Riorden. How would I ever know I could trust you, that you wouldn't break my spirit again?"

Her eyes rose to meet his, and, once more, that spark between them ignited in her soul. Hesitantly, he reached out and cupped her face, running his thumbs along her cheekbones. His fingers skimmed through her hair until he ever so gently pushed her head down onto his chest. She wrapped her arms around his waist and waited, for what, she knew not. He took a deep breath and began stroking her hair.

"If you but listen hard enough, you will know, Katherine," Riorden said softly.

"Know what?" she asked with a fair amount of curiosity.

She raised her head, and he took her chin between his fingers and stared at her, as if memorizing her every feature. "You will know that when you hear my heart sing, it will sing for you alone, throughout all time, unto eternity. If you stay here with me, I will prove my love for you all of our days 'til I draw my last dying breath, my dear sweet wife. If you go back from whence you came, then nothing, and I mean nothing, will keep me from your side ever again. I will follow wherever you go, Katherine, even if I must needs sacrifice my life here to go to this future world of yours. Forever will I find you, and our souls shall always be together."

"Oh, Riorden," Katherine gasped as a tear escaped down her cheek. He wiped it away and took her hand, bringing it to his lips. She could tell he was about to speak when suddenly the turret lit up and the ground shook beneath their feet. Riorden grasped her arms firmly, yet took a step back so he could watch her.

"It appears Time is giving you your opportunity to choose your fate and but awaits your decision, Katherine," he said gravely.

"I don't know what to do," she murmured, looking between the turret and the man who had so much hope in his eyes.

"I will follow you, if I must, to keep you at my side."

Katherine watched as the twinkling lights began dancing inside the time gate as if beckoning her to return to her future life. This was the chance she had been waiting for, and yet, every fiber in her being told her she would be giving up far more than her life here if she were to step inside the welcoming light.

"Choose, Katherine, and quickly afore you no longer have an option, if 'tis your wish to go home."

"I *do* want to go home..." she whispered, feeling his body react to her words, but his mind really not understanding her meaning. "I want to go home...with you...to Warkworth."

"God, how I love you, Katherine," Riorden proclaimed and crushed her to him in a powerful embrace.

"I love you, too, Riorden, with all my heart," Katherine replied. Even the baby must have approved, as she felt a fierce kick. Their arms tightened around each other, and the world once more seemed to right itself as if everything was as it was meant to be.

Time heard her decision, along with their declaration, and with a strange sound ringing in their ears, the lights quickly diminished, as if they had never been there at all. Suddenly, they were once more immersed in the dimness of Bamburgh's passageway.

Katherine reached her hands up to pull her husband's head down so she could receive his kiss. She must have made the right decision, since her heart was filled to overflowing with joy. At a loss for words, she placed her head against his chest and listened to his heart sing. She could have sworn its steady beat was calling out her name.

THIRTY-FIVE

Y OU HAVE GROWN, WIFE, since last we met," Riorden
teased as he caressed her stomach. His fingers made several circles as he felt the babe kick. He was ever amazed as the
heel of a foot appeared, and his wife gave a gentle push 'til the
tiny limb receded back into its safe cocoon. She had never
looked more beautiful than she did carrying his child.

Katherine gave a small laugh and reached out, tracing her
fingers lightly under his eyes. "And you haven't been taking
very good care of yourself, sweetheart. I can see I have my work
cut out for me to get you back into shape. Dristan must be appalled to witness you looking so unhealthy. Does your eye hurt
much?"

"'Tis no more than I deserve, although I am still bemused on
what overcame Fletcher."

"Hmmm," was her only reply, and he watched her reach over
to their repast to place another piece of cheese between his lips.
He chewed more to appease her than because he was hungry for
anything other than her. Looking at the size of the child she

carried, they would not be waiting much longer afore its birth. He said a silent word of thanks that he could satisfy his desire coursing through him for this woman...his woman...for the rest of their lives, and into eternity.

"You will make me fat and unfit to heft my sword—" he began.

She cut off his words by laughing at him with a raised brow. "I don't remember you ever having a problem before with your...*sword*, my lord."

He stared at her with a devilish grin at the implication of her words. "Your quip is not lost on me, you little minx."

"I'm glad to see you haven't misplaced your sense of humor." She patted her belly. "Besides, I would think the proof of your prowess with your blade is here for all to see."

"My, you are a bold one today, are you not?" He laughed at her jest and brought her close to his side. His hand again began caressing the babe she protected within her. "He grows strong inside you, my love."

"He? It could be a girl, you know," she smirked.

"'Tis not," Riorden replied confidently.

"Well, unless you know something that I don't, we won't know for sure until after the baby is born." He didn't give a retort as she expected, and she looked at him with wide eyes. "What do you know that you're not telling me?"

"Let me just say that there are two ladies, who are anxiously awaiting your return to Warkworth." Smiling, he waited for his words to take meaning inside her head.

"Riorden, you buffoon! Are you trying to tell me Juliana and Emily are at Warkworth?" she slapped at him playfully 'til she settled herself against his side again. "Why didn't you tell me?"

He leaned down and kissed her lips. "My apologies, *ma cherie*. I was slightly preoccupied, making up for lost time with a small measure of help from you, no less. I only pray we did not hurt the babe with our play."

"The baby is fine, Riorden." She ran her hand along her stomach. "A son," she marveled with wonder. "We should think of a name."

"We have plenty of time to pick one out, do we not?"

"I would think a few weeks, more or less." She shrugged her shoulders. "It's not like I have any choice when I will go into labor, you know. It's all up to the baby." She laughed at him when his expression turned to one of alarm. "Will they still be there, do you think?" Katherine uttered in concern.

"I am positive they only await your return, my love. They were most anxious to see you, as you can well imagine. They brought the proof for me to witness that you yet lived, and I am most grateful for it. I think you will be pleasantly surprised when you feast your eyes upon it for yourself," Riorden exclaimed with a smile.

"I can't wait to see them."

Riorden placed a kiss on the top of her head as he sighed contentedly. "I am positive they have missed you as much as you have missed them, Katherine. Gavin and Brianna have also arrived, and I believe they plan to stay 'til after the birth of our child."

"Then we'll all be together again! Isn't that exciting?"

"'Tis indeed, my sweet."

Silence filled the air, as if all their unsolved troubles were standing between them again.

"Riorden?" her voice was precarious as she whispered his name.

"Aye, Katherine?"

"We still have much to discuss so we can put this behind us and move forward with our life together."

"Aye, I know." He brought her closer, and he felt his child kick inside her. "But know you this, Katherine. Marguerite will be sent immediately to her dower house. I will send Ulrick and Nathaniel as escort," he assured her.

"You won't go yourself?" she inquired hesitantly.

He chuckled, not that this was a laughing matter. "Nay! My place is here with you. I would not want to miss out on the birth of my heir now, would I?"

"Not if you are wise, darling."

"I am sure you will tire of having me underfoot. I plan on keeping you in my sight so you do not become misplaced again," Riorden jested.

"I like the sound of that. Maybe we can just bolt ourselves in our chamber and say to heck with the rest of the world," Katherine suggested with a giggle.

"If this is what my lady wishes, than I shall endeavor to make it so."

Katherine sat up and pushed him down onto the bed. A wicked gleam entered her eyes as she straddled him and carefully leaned down to give him a kiss. He saw her dilemma when she realized she could not get anywhere near his face. He gave a laugh as he felt his son kick between them yet again, almost as if telling his parents they should behave themselves.

She gave a heavy sigh, and instead of trying, he assumed, to kiss him, a sparkling gleam came into her eyes. She wiggled her very fetching bottom on his thighs and teased him with a come hither look. "We may have our child in the way a little, but I think we have a lot of time to make up. How about we start now?"

"As my lady commands," Riorden agreed, and they spent the next several hours proving just how much they had missed one another. 'Twas not a bad way to spend the night.

Katherine pulled her cloak around her shoulders as she entered the Great Hall. Once again she was leaving Bamburgh behind, only this time, she had a confidence about her that she had not had the last time she graced these walls. She glanced across the room and saw the handsome group of men all turn in her direction. They were all so similar, it was uncanny...well...except one, who stood out from the group. She didn't have a clue how they knew this gentleman, but he was obviously on friendly terms with Riorden, Dristan, and Fletcher, since they appeared to be carrying on a pleasant conversation.

She halted her stride momentarily when she felt a low dull pain in her back and she reached behind to try kneading the discomfort away. She let out her breath and continued her stride forward through the chamber. The front door to the hall suddenly blew open with a gust of snow following a group of three men as they entered, shutting the great door quickly behind them. Two were clearly brothers, and it wasn't hard to miss hearing their jovial demeanor in one of their voices.

"Aye, Taegan, you still make me laugh at your jest, after all these years. I am telling you, brother, the whole garrison took a turn at her. You were not the only one to bed her. Why do you not believe my words," the man laughed boisterously, slapping his brother on the back, who only gave as well as he got with a good shove. Katherine observed the two rough house for a few moments and likened the brothers to huge massive tree trunks with their barrel chests. She wouldn't want to meet these two in some darkened alley. They saw her approach and halted their play abruptly, giving her a courtly bow.

"My lady," they said in unison and elbowed one another in the ribs with a muffled oaf.

Riorden took her hand and placed it protectively in the crook of his arm. "Men, I would like to present my wife, Katherine," he announced with a twinkling eye. "Katherine, may I present Taegan and Turquine, most recently of Dristan's guard and—"

"It did not take you long, did—" Taegan began, only to find his brothers fist in his belly.

"Really?" Katherine said, sending him a scathing look that her mother would have been proud of. "Can't you see me standing right here in front of you?"

Fletcher laughed. "Now you have done it. Riorden's lady will not let you get away with talk like that men, at least not when she is within hearing distance."

Turquine slapped his brother up the side of the head, for good measure. "Do not insult the lady! 'Tis his wife you fool, not some girl for wenching with!" he huffed.

"My apologies, my lady," Taegan muttered.

Riorden raised her hand, placing a kiss on its back. "As you can see, those two are a handful. This is Thomas, most recently of Amiria's guard," he continued. "And last, but not least, this is Ian of...where do you call home these days, Ian?"

"Wherever I can find a place to lay my head," he jested with a hearty laugh. "I thought I would head up to Edinburgh next to see what has become of the place since the last time I was there."

"Ian?" Katherine said softly and pulled on Riorden's sleeve until he leaned down so she could whisper in his ear. "Is this Lynet's, Ian?"

"Aye," he replied quietly. "As you can tell by his chin, he and I had speech together."

Ian rubbed his bruised face. "Speech?" he said aghast, "is that what you call it these days?"

"'Tis lucky you are not sporting a broken limb or two," Dristan said, butting into the conversation. "Riorden's gone soft since he left my hall, but I am sure he will be back up to my standards in no time."

Katherine smothered her laughter and once more looked at Ian to assess the man before her. She could see why Lynet was fascinated with him. She tilted her head, trying her best to determine what color she should call his hair. Red, definitely, but intermingled with brown and golden highlights. Eyes...well, his eyes were an incredible shade of hazel that she was sure had many a lady swooning just to have him look upon her. He appeared to be perhaps several years older than herself, which surprised her a little, thinking Lynet would be in love with someone closer to her own age. But he was as handsome as the rest of the men, towering over her own small height. She smiled as her eyes drifted to them all, who seemed to be amused at her staring so openly at their features. Yes, they were all cut from the same mold, the handsome rogues!

Katherine turned her attention back to the man who unknowingly held Lynet's heart. "Well, Sir Ian, I have heard much about you."

He looked startled, considering they had just met. "You have?"

"Yes...aye, I have," she stumbled, remembering she should beware of how she spoke to those who didn't know of her origin. "May we have a word, you and I?"

Riorden began to chuckle. "This should prove interesting," he mumbled.

"Shush, Riorden," Katherine said. "Gentlemen, if you would excuse us momentarily."

She bobbed a curtsey as they in turn gave a small bow. Disengaging her arm from Riorden's, she came up to Ian, raising

her eyes to his. "Shall we?" she asked, giving him no other opportunity than to offer his arm to her.

They didn't go far. The chamber was large, but it wasn't as
if it was crowded and they would have a difficult time locating
a place where they could have a private conversation. He led
her over to one of the walls where two comfortable looking
chairs were drawn up near a window. He helped her so she
could lower herself awkwardly into one of them, and she was
thankful for the opportunity, since standing for long periods of
time hurt her feet. She felt a twinge radiate across her belly and
tried to get comfortable. Ian stood there in indecision until she
motioned to the chair opposite her. "Please, don't feel the need
to stand, Sir Ian. Besides, I'll have a crook in my neck, trying
to talk to you if you don't take a chair."

"As you wish, my lady," was his reply as he sat. He was
clearly unsure where the conversation was going to lead him.

"So tell me, where do you come from besides being captain of
Amiria's guard?" she inquired. "I have already heard you spent
many years at Berwyck." Katherine folded her hands on the top
of her protruding stomach. Her action clearly made him uncomfortable, since his gaze immediately went to her belly. She supposed it was strange for him to see a woman so obviously
pregnant and not hidden away from prying eyes until she gave
birth. He cleared his throat and ran his hand through his hair.
Katherine tried not to grin.

"I grew up at Urquhart Castle in the Highlands of Scotland,
Lady Katherine, but have not been back for many a year," he
replied politely.

"And why is that? If I may ask such a personal question,"
she blurted out and then remembered herself. "Forgive me for
being so blunt, but I feel as if I know you already."

He shrugged. "Dristan mentioned you were...different," he began and then looked shocked that he may have offended her, "Not in a bad way, of course."

"Of course," she replied with a nod of her head for him to continue.

"My sire died several years ago. My older brother, naturally, inherited Urquhart and became head of the clan. Being a younger son, I could not bear to watch him squander what my sire had worked so hard to acquire over the years. I voiced my disapproval of his running the estate into the ground. For this, I was banished from my home, so I left without a backwards glance to make a better life for myself. I found myself at Berwyck, and the rest, I will assume, you may already know."

"I see. So you now find yourself wandering from place to place, earning coin at tourneys or hiring out your sword, I take it?" She watched him nod, but he didn't offer any further information. It was a tad annoying that she would need to be so abrupt. "May I be frank with you, Ian?"

He raised his brow at her for using his given name. "Do I have a choice?"

She gave a laugh. "Oh, we all make choices, Ian. The question is, when it comes down to decision making, what will be yours?"

"Since I do not know the question, how can I answer?" he said with puzzlement.

"Fair enough." Katherine paused to peruse the man before her. She could tell he was stubborn to a fault, just like someone else she knew. How much should she divulge? Perhaps not as much as she wanted to tell him. She suddenly had the feeling that Lynet would only want Ian to come for her because he wanted to, not because Katherine pushed him into it. It sounded too familiar.

Ian cleared his throat. "My lady?"

She shook her head and gave him a timid smile. "My apologies. Tell me, Ian, is there someone at Berwyck that still holds a special place in your heart?"

"So this is what has become the issue. Is Riorden asking you to find out if I am still in love with Amiria? If that is the case, you may inform him the answer is nay!" He folded his arms across his chest, obviously miffed she was treading on ground better left unturned.

"Actually, I wasn't thinking about Lady Amiria, but another." She continued to stare at him until it finally dawned on him who it was she was talking about.

"You mean...Lady Lynet?" He almost sounded more put out than when he mentioned Amiria's name.

"You do not care for the young lady?"

He stood and began pacing. "I told her not to wait for me," he muttered more to himself than for her ears. "I am much too old for the likes of her. She should be married by now with bairn's a plenty at her feet!"

"Well, she's not, if you would care to know, that is..." she left her words hanging in the air between them and wondered what he would make of them.

"She was but a young lassie of ten and four, the last I set eyes on her." He suddenly seemed lost in thought as past memories flashed inside his mind.

"And of marriageable age, although I must admit I think that is far too young to be married. A girl is little more than a child at that age. Surely you must realize Lynet is almost twenty...umm...a score of years now," Katherine said.

He stopped his pacing and returned to his chair. He opened his mouth several times until he let out a heavy sigh. "She must needs marry, but 'twill not be to me. I have no plans to settle down with a wife, as I have nothing to offer her, or any other bonny lass. She deserves more than I can give her."

Katherine had held such hopes that Ian held some form of affection for Lynet, and she felt sorry for the young girl whose heart would be completely broken. "I see." Katherine rose from her seat with Ian's assistance, and they began crossing the floor toward the others. "May I ask a favor of you, Ian?"

"Aye, Lady Katherine."

She halted her steps and turned to face him. "Please, send a missive to Lynet and at least let her know you have no plans to return for her. I should not admit this, but she has been waiting for word from you with the hopes that you might come to care for her. If this is not the case, then please tell the lady that you won't be returning to Berwyck."

"I do not wish to hurt her feelings, my lady."

Katherine looked sadly at the man before her. What a pity he couldn't see the gem that awaited him at Berwyck if he would only allow love back into his heart. "Better to hurt her feelings now, than for her to waste any more years yearning for something that will never be."

"I did ask her not to wait for me, Lady Katherine," Ian protested.

"That may be true, but again, it's all about choices. She made hers, just as you have made yours," Katherine replied forlornly. "It was good to finally meet you, Ian. I wish you all the best that life has to offer."

She patted his arm and returned to Riorden's side. She could feel Ian's gaze fall to her several times while the men conversed, and she could only pray that perhaps Ian might change his mind. Miracles could happen after all, and only time would tell if Lynet and Ian would find a way into each other's arms.

THIRTY-SIX

RIORDEN ADJUSTED THE BLANKET he had thrown across his wife's lap, even as he felt her shiver in his arms. They had been riding all day, and between the snow and the wind their progress was slow. He wished to go faster but was afraid of hurting the babe. It had been a hard day's ride, but soon he would at last set eyes on home, that is if he could keep the snow from clouding his vision to see where he was going.

Their company had parted ways at Bamburgh with Dristan and Fletcher providing escort, since Riorden had traveled alone. He had been given a sound thrashing from Dristan on the perils of traveling without a guard. Personally, Riorden had not given it a second thought when he had saddled Beast with all due haste. He had been on a mission of grave importance and currently she was snuggled within his arms. He was most thankful that he had gotten to Bamburgh in time.

Conversations had ceased hours ago when the weather had worsened. The only thing any of them could think of now, besides the cold penetrating down to their bones, was a blazing fire and thawing out in his hall with something hot to warm their innards. He was not prepared for the sudden gasp that came from his wife as she clutched her stomach.

"Riorden," she managed to grind out between her clenched teeth. Since she had her eyes squinted closed, 'twas apparent his lady was not well.

"What is it, Katherine?" Afore she could even utter another sound, he knew for a certainty what she was about to tell him. It scared the hell out of him as his eyes quickly tried to scan their whereabouts so he could judge the distance to Warkworth.

"I hate to be the bearer of bad tidings, but I'm in labor, and the contractions are starting to come closer together. I know you've been trying to be careful, getting us safely home, but unless you want your son born out here in the snow, you had best whip Beast into a frenzied gallop," she answered.

He quickly assessed her features and saw they were strained. "Just how long has this been going on?"

She looked at him wearily. "Awhile now, I'm afraid."

"And you did not think it of import to tell me?" he groaned helplessly.

"You can harp on me all you want later about my lack of judgment, but for heaven's sake, let's just get moving, and please hurry already!"

He would normally have given a retort to her comment, but felt that for now 'twas best not to rile his wife any further than she already was, given the circumstances. Dristan and Fletcher broke through the trees as they returned from scouting the area ahead. They took one look at the two of them and quickly reined their mounts back in the direction they had come.

"Aye, 'tis her time," Riorden answered their unspoken question.

"Then we must away and quickly," Fletcher uttered in concern for Katherine's welfare. "The way is clear. No one in their right mind would be out traveling in weather such as this."

'Twas all the words Riorden needed to hear, and he quickly flicked the reins, causing Beast to bolt forwards. He felt Katherine's arm grip about his waist to tighten her hold, although he would in no way allow her to fall from the saddle. From the looks on her features, she was far too worried about her labor than the normal dizzying heights that usually terrified her.

The countryside flew by in a white blur, whether from the speed in which they traveled, or the snow that continued to blanket the frozen ground. It seemed as if a lifetime had passed afore Riorden beheld, in the distance, the welcoming torches lit at Warkworth. The heavy, muffled sound of their mounts' thundering hooves marked their quick passage across the snow-filled fields. Once they reached the village, they were forced to slow their speed, and the sound changed eerily. 'Twas as if their horses' hooves were now being sucked down into the muddy muck below them. The normally solid dirt road had changed dramatically, with the passage of winter, into a mire of mud. But Riorden had a more pressing concern than how to improve the path through the village. Katherine's moans were a clear indication there was no longer any time to waste.

Dristan and Fletcher rode on ahead so by the time Riorden made it to the front gate, the drawbridge had been lowered, and an eager lad was near at hand to take Beast to the stable. Quickly dismounting, he reached out his hands, and Katherine eagerly placed her own palms on his shoulders. With no time to waste, he made his way steadily into the keep with his precious burden held close in his arms.

"Juliana," he bellowed, causing a frantic pause of alarm from the woman who was already in the process of bellowing orders to his staff to ensure the readiness of their lord's bedchamber for the birth of his child. Dristan and Fletcher were just now taking a seat near the hearth to warm themselves. He gave them no further heed, as all his attention was diverted to Katherine and the babe. "'Tis my lady's time," he called out for any who would hear his words and continued heading for their chamber.

Juliana continued shouting her orders as she followed quickly up the stairs. "Mabel, bring boiling water to your lord's chamber. Mary, please be a dear and bring me as many towels...um drying cloths as you can carry, or even clean bedding. Emily, I need your help, for I don't think Brie will be of much use if she ends up passing out in a dead faint!"

"Hey, I wanna help," Brianna shouted with hands on hips.

Juliana halted momentarily on the stairs and wagged her finger at the younger girl. "You faint or throw up and you go back to the hall, do you understand me?"

Riorden continued up the stairwell and had almost reached his chamber when a screech, like none he had ever heard afore, echoed through the passageway. Marguerite stood near her own chamber door with her hand clenched to her chest. The other rested near her temple and was shaking uncontrollably.

"She was supposed to be dead!" she mumbled, turning her head as if talking to another. "Do not tell me again how I am doomed. I paid good monies to ensure she would never again grace these halls. Why is she here, and not drowned at the bottom of the river? Stop harping at me and laughing in my head! If I could not have the man I truly loved, the very least you could have done, Everard, is left a clue as to where your coins were hid so I could leave this place a rich widow, you old goat. What should I do? Perchance, he will need a drink. That should do the trick so he will be mine yet again. Nay, do not tell me what to do," she began to cackle as she continued to have her seemingly one-sided conversation 'til she retreated into her chamber, slamming the door.

Riorden and Katherine could only stare at the closed door. "How long has she been doing that?" Riorden asked as Brianna opened the door to his chamber.

"Since you left," Juliana replied as she swept into the chamber. She began pulling down the coverlets on the bed afore heading towards the hearth to lay down straw upon the floor.

"She gives me the creeps," Emily said and gave her head a shake.

Riorden at last set Katherine upon her feet, and her friends promptly gathered around them.

"I hardly think we need to be worrying about the likes of her right now. We need to get Katie comfortable," Brianna interjected as she wrapped her arms around Katherine's neck with a sob. "You gave me such a scare that we had lost you. Don't ever do that to me again, or I swear I'll clobber you!"

Katherine let a snort escape her. "I won't. I promise."

Brianna looked her up and down afore a big smile lit her face as she returned to her old self. "Hi, sissy! How ya feeling?" she asked, as if she hadn't been ranting at her friend but moments afore.

Katherine gave a muffled laugh. "I've been better, but I must admit, I'm so glad to see everyone. I have missed you all more than any of you could even begin to imagine.

Riorden watched the four women envelope themselves into a sisterly embrace as they all began to talk at once. He hated to interrupt them, but he wished to take his leave and let the women attend his wife. "If you will excuse me ladies, I shall take care of the nasty business with Marguerite and then will await word from you down in the hall." He began to make a hasty exit when his wife shouted out his name, stopping him in his tracks. He turned back to her in alarm.

"No way are you getting out of here that easily, buster," she ordered, moving faster to his side than he thought possible. He tried not to laugh, thinking that she appeared much like a waddling mother duck, chasing after her chicks.

Riorden looked at her in confusion. "I only mean to be down in the hall with the men, as is proper during this time."

"Sorry...not happening. Your place is in here with me."

"But, Katherine—" he began in alarm 'til she grabbed a hold of his tunic.

"Remember, I'm a modern woman with modern ideas, dear. You were there during the conception, and so you'll be here during the birth," she demanded with clenched teeth as another contraction consumed her.

He looked on his tiny wife in alarm and then looked askance to her friends, who only nodded in agreement. "Is this the way of things in your world?" he wondered.

"'Fraid so," Emily replied with a smile.

"'Tis much to take in, and unheard of in this time, but, I will concede to my lady's wishes. Let us get her into the bed," he suggested.

"Sorry, Lord Riorden," Juliana answered, taking Katie's arm. She began walking by her side. "But that's the worst thing to prolong the delivery process. She needs to walk as long as she can."

"But she is about to have our child and must needs lay down," he protested in worry with the thought of his child being dropped on his head whilst being born.

Emily came over to him and gave him a reassuring pat on his arm, as if this simple act would calm his nerves. "She'll be in labor for a long while still, Riorden, Trust us when we tell you this is the best thing for Katie right now."

He shook his head in wonder. "I cannot believe the things you are telling me, but who am I to argue with four future women and their knowledge. If I could leave to attend to a matter or two, I will return momentarily, if that meets with your approval, Katherine?" he asked with a grin. She threw him a look, and he watched as she shuffled back to his side again.

"I love you, Riorden," she whispered and pulled his head down for a kiss. "Please just remember that, if I get grumpy in a while, okay?"

"I will remember," Riorden replied and kissed her lips once more, "and I love you, as well, *ma chere.* I will not be long."

"I'll hold you to your word," Katherine answered and went back to her pacing of the room.

Riorden left her in the care of her friends, knowing she was in good hands 'til his return. He was not looking forward to what he must do next, but whether she was sane or no, Marguerite would be on her way come the morn. At least, at her dower house, she could no longer cause any problems here at Warkworth. He stepped into the passageway and made his way to her chamber. 'Twas long past time to put his household in order.

THIRTY-SEVEN

Riorden opened Marguerite's chamber door, and a cold blast of air assaulted his senses. He gazed around with the distinct feeling the sensation had nothing to do with the temperature of the room. A fire burned brightly in the hearth, and the shutter was firmly in place at her window.

His eyes traveled to the woman who had meant all to him at one time in his life but no longer held any of his affections. His only feelings towards her were of anger and contempt. She had poisoned him into the stupor that had become his life of late. She had been the cause of Katherine's flight and near death in the icy river. And, if what he had learned recently were true, then she had even gone so far as to kill his sire. It could have so easily been him, as well.

He watched her for several minutes, unsure how to proceed with their discussion and whether 'twould send her over the edge of whatever sanity she still held onto. Such stability could not be abundant as she did not so much as even acknowledge he had entered the room. Her lips were silently moving as she sat at the edge of her bed, rocking to and fro whilst her hands shook, tugging at her hair. She was pulling at it so hard, he was surprised she was not yanking the long dark strands right out of her head by the handful. He pulled up a stool next to her side and sat.

"Marguerite." Riorden spoke her name softly so as not to startle her. It did not matter, for she continued to stare straight ahead with vacant, expressionless eyes.

"He never lets me rest," she whispered with a flash of anger and finally turned her attention to him, "and you are lost to me, yet again."

He was about to rant at her about how she made her choice years ago, but, for some reason, all the anger he had been holding onto no longer seemed to matter. What good could come of dragging their past through the mud, yet again? Their relationship was in the past. Let it remain there, and good riddance.

"I will provide an escort to take you to your dower house come the morn and also have someone come up to pack your belongings," he told her calmly.

"You will not take me there yourself?"

"Nay. You have done enough damage with your lies and deceit. It almost cost the life of my wife and unborn child. You are no longer welcome at Warkworth." He stood, not really seeing the need to have further speech with the woman who had almost cost him everything, including his future children.

He had just opened the door with his hand on the latch when she called out his name and he turned to gaze at her one last time.

"She will never make you happy, Riorden," Marguerite said whilst she raised her tormented eyes to him.

He pushed the door open wider afore answering her with a smile on his face. "You are wrong, as always, Marguerite. Katherine already does make me completely happy and will continue to do so for the rest of my days. No thanks to you, we have many years ahead of us to look forward to. Be prepared to leave come sun up and do not ever grace Warkworth again."

He began to walk through the portal to leave, but not afore he heard her final words. "Mayhap, I will at least find some peace away from this place."

Riorden shut the door and released the deep breath he felt he had been holding in for months. Peacefulness settled around his heart, even as he again felt a draft sweep through his body. He focused his vision down the passageway as a wisp of smoke began to take shape. He supposed he should not be too surprised that it took the form of his father.

"Well done, my son," Everard said with a proud look in his eyes. Riorden could only stand there speechless as he heard his sire's voice for the first time in years.

"Father," Riorden managed to at last gasp.

"We have much to discuss, once you have seen to your wife."

"Aye, but can I ask one question that has haunted me for years afore I go to Katherine?"

"You wish to know why I married Marguerite," Everard stated as a matter of fact, "putting a rift between us that I did not have the chance to mend whilst I yet lived."

"How did you know?"

Everard gave a short snort then recovered himself. "'Tis what I myself would want to ask. I would expect the same of my son," he murmured.

They walked side by side down the dimly lit passageway 'til they halted at Riorden's chamber door. He gazed down at his scuffed boots and hid a smile. Perchance, walking is not exactly what his sire was doing, as he all but hovered off the ground several inches. He at last raised his eyes to his father's and, for the briefest of seconds, saw all the agony the man had been feeling for many a year. 'Twas a mirror of his own feelings for the loss of a man he had looked up to and wished to become.

"I must humbly beg your pardon, Riorden, and ask your forgiveness for what I put you through all these years," Everard began. "'Twas not my intent to deliberately harm you, but I could see no other way to prevent you from making a terrible mistake by marrying Marguerite. I saw her for what she was, and yet, I knew you only observed what she showed you. I could tell you believed the best in her when nothing was further from the truth."

"I was even blinded to her true character when my own wife warned me to beware of the wench. I thought no harm would befall me," Riorden confessed.

"'Tis the conceit of men such as we, who think we are infallible and nothing in this world could be our downfall. Imagine my surprise to find myself done in by my own wife and doomed forever to roam my hall in such an existence," Everard replied and looked Riorden up and down. "But, if I could spare you the agony I now am in, then 'twas worth it. I would do anything for my sons, although you did not know it at the time."

"I have missed your council over the years," Riorden professed, "among other things. I suppose you will leave us, since this is perchance your unfinished business, and your soul can now rest in peace."

Everard gave a hearty laugh. "We shall see. I think I may stick around to see how my grandchildren turn out and see how you deal with the issues of being a father."

Aghast, Riorden barely could speak, especially when he heard Katherine on the other side of the door. "*Merde*, what do you know?"

His father's laugher rumbled deep inside his soul. "I think, I shall keep such information to myself, but you will certainly have your hands full, my boy! Now, go. Your wife needs you, and we will have plenty of time to have speech together later."

The door to his chamber magically opened without any assistance from Riorden. He looked back to reply to his father only to find him gone, and yet, he could still feel his presence. 'Twas a good sign that they would mend what had been broken between them. With a welcoming smile to his wife, he entered the chamber, wondering what these future ladies had in store for him. He had a feeling it had something to do with Karma. He could almost already feel the bite of its sting.

Thirty-Eight

G OOD LORD, I WANT AN EPIDURAL!"
"Sorry Katie, but you know that's not happening, even if I did have the ability to give you one," Juliana replied as she busily went about the chamber preparing for the birth.

"I swear this child is going to come out weighing at least twenty pounds."

Emily gave a laugh. "That's hardly likely, Katie. Just breathe during the contractions."

"This is entirely your fault," Katherine muttered, glaring at Riorden while he wiped at her brow.

"Kat, you are being unreasonable. Surely, you played your part in your predicament, as well," he answered. "Come, my love, let us take another turn around the chamber. It may ease your suffering."

"You have no idea of the suffering I'm in, and just so we understand each other, I'm never going through this again!"

"Yes, you will!" came the response in unison from the occupants of the room. They all laughed, including Riorden, who shrugged his shoulders when she glared at him. When she looked at her sisters of her heart, they quickly cast their eyes downward but kept the same shit-eating grins plastered annoyingly on their pretty little faces.

"Perhaps when I'm done having my child, the four of you will kindly fill me in on the private joke you all seem to be sharing at my expense!" Katherine huffed and clutched at her belly as another wave of contractions overtook her. After what seemed like an eternity, it finally subsided, and Katherine felt as though she could breathe again.

Juliana stood up from bending over the bed. "I think it's time we get her over near the hearth."

Riorden looked around the room in confusion. "But, where is the birthing chair?" he said quietly.

"Completely impersonal, although they were on track about the whole sitting up thing," Emily responded. "You know...it's all about gravity."

"Why would you have a woman lie down on her back the whole time, anyway? It certainly doesn't make any sense, does it?" Brianna added.

Julianna moved a blanket over several layers of straw near the hearth. A chair had been turned with pillows up against its back. "We've had to take into account how to go about having a medieval birth. Normally, in our time, Katie would be in a bed that would break down for easy access for the whole birthing process, but that's not possible here. We've made a few adjustments to the whole scenario, since your bed would be ruined afterwards."

"I will not fathom to even attempt to guess what you future women are chatting about," Riorden exclaimed as Katherine and her friends burst into fits of laughter...again.

Emily shrugged. "Childbirth is messy, my lord. There's no getting around it, I'm afraid."

Riorden paled.

"You're not going to faint on me now, are you? Don't you dare," Katherine warned as Riorden stood, shaking his head at the whole conversation. She squeezed his hand and gasped when her stomach tightened again. Everyone seemed to stop their conversations, waiting for her. "That was a strong one."

"My lord, if you will sit here against these pillows, then Katie can come rest against your chest," Juliana said, pointing to the floor.

"I do not know what you are having me do, and I would happily comply with your wishes if 'twill help Kat. I do, however, have need of my sword arm." He grimaced. "Unless you can persuade my lady to release my hand, she is going to break all my bones, and I will be of no use to her, or anyone else, in the future."

Katherine was almost embarrassed, since she hadn't realized she had been holding on to his limb with such a death grip. "Sorry," she mumbled and let go of the lifeline that had been of such help to her. It was so reassuring, knowing Riorden was being such a dear and staying by her side the whole time when, clearly, he would have preferred to be downstairs with the men.

"'Tis fine, Katherine. I but jested with you," he said as he pulled her against his chest and wrapped his arms around her and their child. He squeezed his hand into a fist a couple of times in front of her. "See, 'tis good as new."

She rested her head for a moment back against his shoulder. "Talk to me," she whispered softly.

"What would you like me to talk about?" he asked just as quietly, almost as if it were only the two of them in the room.

"Anything, just do it in French," she answered.

Katherine had no idea how long they sat there. It could have been minutes. It could have been hours. She only knew she was surrounded by the people who meant the most to her in this world. The contractions came and went until the urge to push overcame her. Again, time meant nothing to her. She had completely lost control as her body naturally took over to force out the child from her womb.

She was right in the middle of pushing when a commotion occurred outside their chamber. But she couldn't care less who it was, as her eyes were squeezed tightly shut while she was writhing in pain.

"Is this her bedroom?" a woman's voice was heard saying. "Oh, never mind." She apparently must have brushed past whoever had been barring her way as she pushed the door open wide. Considering the view, it was most embarrassing. "I see I'm just in time!"

Katherine's eyes flew open in surprise. "MOM?"

Her mother shut the door and threw her coat onto a nearby chair as she quickly made her way to Katherine's side. "Hello, baby girl. What are you doing on the floor?"

"MOM?" Katherine repeated herself.

The woman before her only leaned over to give her daughter a peck on her forehead with lips that were cold from the storm outside. She began to shake the snow from her hair. "What? Have you forgotten me, already, or is it a bad time for a visit?"

"What the hell are you doing here?" Katherine screeched as she blew out a gust of air, knowing another contraction was building up in her belly.

"I would think that's obvious. I'm here to see the birth of my grandson."

"You realize this is still like rustic camping here, don't you?" Katherine gasped until any further choice at conversation was taken from her. She began to push yet again while conversations continued all around her.

Emily gave a laugh as she answered Riorden's unasked question. "Mom's idea of camping is pretty much like my own. We prefer a nice hotel with a hot shower, don't we?"

Katherine's mother only stood there with a welcoming smile. "It's good to see you two ladies made it here. You gave us all quite the scare."

"How did you find them?" Brianna asked.

"I had some help from two very irate husbands who are downstairs waiting, rather impatiently, for their wives. You must be Riorden," she continued. "I've heard a lot about you."

"Madam," he murmured, nodding his head in greeting, as his hands were quite full.

"My, oh my, you really are just flat out gorgeous, aren't you? I know I had the video you and Katie made on her phone, but it's another thing entirely to see you in person. Juliana and Emily sure didn't lie when they described you. I can certainly see why Katherine crossed time for you," she said, taking a seat out of the way. "I just might have done the same, even if I would have to give up the luxury of indoor plumbing."

"Mom, stop! You'll embarrass him," Katherine said, between clenched teeth.

"Embarrass him? I doubt it, dear. Just look at him. He appears to have all the confidence in the world, but let's see how he holds up after he's holding his newborn son, shall we?"

Katherine may have groaned out a reply, or not. She only knew that Juliana called for her to push while she felt Riorden place a gentle kiss on the side of her temple. Juliana continued to give words of encouragement as her family stood to watch the miracle of birth. Katherine lost track of time until she let out a scream as she felt the baby expelled from her body. She sagged against her husband, much like a rag doll.

Katherine heard the baby's soft cry after being ripped from the warm, comforting surroundings he had known for nine months. She could hardly contain her joy as Juliana placed the babe on her stomach. The four weeping women crowded around the couple, and Juliana finished with quiet words to Brianna.

"She didn't tear, so that's good, but, if this happens the next time, you may have to put in a couple of stitches, here and here," Juliana pointed out. "I know you can do this, Brie, so just take special care to ensure everything is clean and sterilized, okay?"

"I can do it," Brianna said confidently as she was handed the tiny baby so they could clean him up.

Katherine lay there exhausted. She tried to form some kind of a response, but words escaped her. Everyone around her seemed to be in a haze as she drifted on a cloud, she was so tired. Riorden carefully lifted her, and a clean gown was draped over her shoulders while Juliana finished cleaning up the afterbirth. Placed onto the bed with warm blankets on top of her, she was handed her son, who she quickly put to her breast. She was startled at the feeling of the tiny baby when he began to nurse, and her eyes filled with unshed tears.

The chamber quietly emptied, leaving the three of them the privacy they stood in need of. Riorden came and lounged next to her in the bed, marveling at the tiny miracle they had created. He leaned over and tenderly kissed her lips.

"My thanks, my dearest love, for our son," he whispered, holding his finger out to the baby and watching the tiny little fingers grasp his father.

"Thanks for staying with me," she whispered.

"Ah, Kat, you have made me a most humble man this day."

Their eyes met, and she gave him a smile, while a tear of happiness slipped down his cheek. She brushed it away and turned back to their child. Held securely in Riorden's arms, she began to sing a lullaby until the baby fell asleep. At that moment, Katherine knew she had made the right decision to stay here, in the past. This day was a new beginning for them all. And this remarkable experience would be a memory she would hold dear in her heart for all of her days, one she would never forget.

THIRTY-NINE

MARGUERITE STORMED PAST TIMMONS as the door to the manor shut harshly behind her. Throwing her snow covered cape at a maid, she called for wine and moved into the small receiving room. The fire burned brightly and began to take the chill from her cold, weary bones.

It seemed the more miles she put between herself and Warkworth, the more her sanity returned to her. 'Twas a small price to pay, she supposed, but at what cost? She was still relatively young but without a husband. She did not relish the thought of petitioning the king to find someone to keep her in the manner she had become accustomed.

She saw Sir Nathaniel and Sir Ulrick enter the manor. They spoke to Timmons, and several servants began bringing in her luggage. Her gaze raked their bodies and she wondered how each might perform as a lover. They were both very handsome, and she would have attempted to catch their eye, except the looks they gave her told her she would be wasting her time. 'Twas clear they knew all too well her part in her late husband's demise, and her drugging of Riorden. She gave a heavy sign. It could have been worse, for Riorden could have had her imprisoned, and she could be wasting away in some dungeon.

Sir Nathaniel came to stand afore her, but she was unsure of what he wanted. Their trip to Dunhaven had been silent. After several miles of attempting to strike up a conversation with her escorts, Marguerite had finally given up. She basically felt as if she were being exiled, and her anger was ready to boil over at the smallest provocation.

"Well? What do you want?" she hissed. "Is it not enough that I have been sent from my home?"

"We shall leave come the morn, my lady," Nathaniel informed her. "I believe all is ready here at the manor, as instructed by Lord Riorden."

"As if he truly cared what happens to me," she murmured. "Be gone, and leave me in peace. I have no further need of you." He barely gave her a nod as he left her, sputtering about the manners of pigheaded men.

Sitting at the hearth, she began contemplating her next steps to ensure her future was secure. She hardly acknowledged the maid as she returned with a bottle of wine that she poured into a silver chalice. Taking the cup without a word of thanks, she tasted the heady wine as it slid down her throat. She sighed in bliss, thinking of all the ways she could win Riorden back, come the morrow.

Another maid came back, bringing with her a tray of tiny cakes for her to eat. Marguerite only stared at them with no appetite. Still the servant waited there for some kind of a response from her. "Can I not have a moment's rest in this godforsaken house? Leave me, and shut the door behind you. I do not wish to be disturbed by you or anyone else for the rest of the eve," Marguerite bellowed.

Looking down at the tray, she picked it up and hurled it against the wall, whilst the maid made a hasty retreat from the room. The door shut, and finally, Marguerite could relax to begin planning her next steps of her life. She took another sip of wine and ran her tongue across her lips to attempt to moisten them.

Staring into the flames, she blinked her eyes as her vision blurred. Her tongue became thick, her mouth dry. Wondering what was wrong with her, she began to cough and gasp for air. She reached for the chalice to bring it to her lips to quench her parched throat only to gaze at the goblet in shock. *Nay, it could not be!*

Marguerite let out a muffled scream as recognition of the cup registered in her foggy mind. She stumbled to the table that held the bottle of wine and peered at it, trying to bring it into focus. As much as Marguerite wanted to deny what she held, she could not, for 'twas the very same bottle that she had put the potion in several months ago. 'Twas meant for Riorden, and she had feared she had put too much into the bottle, as she had done with the wine she had given Everard.

Her breathing became rapid. She tried to call for help, but none answered her cry with the door closed and her voice nothing more than a whisper. She lost her balance, and stumbling, she fell to the floor. Clawing at her neck, she tried to catch her breath. But she could not breathe, and she swore she saw the shadow of death coming to claim her. As her body became motionless on the rug, Marguerite's last conscious thought was how Everard's laughter echoed in her head. Even at death's door, she realized she would never be free of him.

FORTY

KATHERINE GAVE HER HEAD A SHAKE, feeling the length of her wavy tresses swish back and forth down her back. Her hair was finally manageable after Mabel had assisted with its washing. She had been sitting before the fire, waiting for it to dry. While she had sat there, feeling toasty warm, she had begun wishing, for the first time in a long while, for the convenience of an appliance. It seemed as though it had taken hours for the water to work its way from her waist length hair, whereas five minutes with a hair dryer, and she would have been done.

With a shrug of her shoulders, she put the finishing touch to her attire in place by putting a ribbon in her hair while gazing down at the gown she had put on. It was a beautiful creation of heavy, white cotton with silken embroidery running the length of the skirt. A rose colored sash matched what she had just put in her hair and was located beneath her breasts. The long flowing dress was high-waisted, giving her the appearance that she hadn't gained all that much weight.

In reality, she was trying her best to hide, even from Riorden, how many pounds she actually had put on during her pregnancy. He had already made mention it hadn't mattered to him in the least, bless his heart, but Katherine knew she'd be working hard to get back into shape, just as soon as she could.

If she had a full length mirror to look into, she might be pleased with the picture she presented. Since that wasn't an option, she'd have to assume she looked as well as could be expected. Crossing the room, she reached for a small container of her favorite scent of Japanese cherry blossom. Riorden had been a dear when he found a bottle from this century that could hold the fragrance her mother had brought for her. He had taken the original plastic bottle and burned it so none could come upon something from the modern world.

Lifting the stopper, she inhaled and sighed in pleasure as the fragrant aroma of sweet flowers engulfed her senses. She only dabbed a tiny amount at her wrists and behind her ears, knowing this small luxury from the future would have to last her for perhaps months to come. She had decided to use it only on special occasions, although her mother proclaimed that every day was special, and she should use it to her hearts content.

She wiggled her warm feet poking out from beneath the hem, and looked around for her shoes. Espying them near the bed, she placed the soft soled slippers on her feet and, for the second time, wished for a mirror. The shoes were so feminine with the laced floral bow that she squealed in delight to be wearing something so dainty and pretty. Clothing in the future wasn't what it used to be, and she felt as though she were playing in some re-enactment guild with people who only got to dress like this on the weekends.

She twirled around the room with a small laugh. She wanted to look her best today, for she felt as though she was being released from a cage. Riorden had kept her bedridden for over a week to ensure she regained her strength after the birth of their son. Today was the first day he would allow her to be up and out of her bed to join in the company of the other men, who gathered regularly in his solar.

She had tried, without any success, to make her argument that times were different where she came from. He just as firmly told her that it wasn't her he was worried about, so much as the twelfth century men, who were still getting used to the idea of time travel and her being a woman from the future with different ideals.

She supposed she couldn't argue with him, especially when he put it so nicely. Though she understood his point, she was tired of being confined in her room like a disobedient child. As she stifled a yawn, she could almost see Riorden giving her an I-told-you-it-was-too-soon-to-be-out-of-bed look. She went to sit down for a moment and espied the manila envelope lying on Riorden's desk. Surely, it wouldn't hurt to have one more look at it before she must return it to her friends.

She didn't expect her hands to quiver as she flipped open the metal clasps to take out the contents. Peeling back the sheer film of protective paper, she slowly gazed at her future for the second time as she gently skimmed the surface with her fingertips. Chills raced down her arms as she stared into her own eyes, along with her children's, including the two who had yet to be born. It certainly wasn't every day that an opportunity such as this came to a person, and Katherine was unsure how to react as she witnessed what was in store for her in the years to come.

We all look so happy, even if we are much older, and why shouldn't we? She and Brianna had found their happily-ever-after with their knights, who took their breath away every moment they were together. Katherine still couldn't believe she wouldn't wake up soon to find it had all been a dream. She gazed down into the eyes of her husband in the portrait and a smile escaped her lips. They were just as blue and vivid, and she was content, knowing they had a lifetime to spend together.

A small rap at the door jerked Katherine out of her musings, and she quickly put the picture and envelope away. She didn't want to tempt fate any more than she had already done recently. A picture of this nature would be hard to explain, and no one would ever consider their story to be fact. It was just too unbelievable for most to wrap their thoughts around.

With her secret safe underneath the covers of the bed, she gave the call to enter and watched her mother slip into the room. Her mom was the last person she had ever expected to come traipsing through her door in the twelfth century, but she was glad for it. She hated the thought of her wondering for the rest of her life what had become of her daughter, or that she would turn out to be just another face on an episode of unsolved mysteries of missing people.

Her mom made a circular motion with her finger, and, with a girlish giggle, Katherine stood and twirled around so she could be inspected from head to toe. She watched the joy reach her mom's face as she clapped her hands together in approval.

"You look lovely, Katie. I've never seen you so radiant."

Katherine could feel the blush creeping up her cheeks from the compliment. "Thanks mommy."

"It looks like you got your wish after all, didn't you, baby girl?" she inquired.

Katherine couldn't figure out what she was talking about. "Did I wish for something?"

Her mother laughed. "You've been wishing on a star since you were a little toddler, wanting to play the damsel in distress with anyone that crossed your path. How many instances at bedtime did I have to pull you from the window sill while you talked to the Man in the Moon, asking him to let you live in another era?"

"You remember that?"

"How could I forget? I suppose I'll lay the blame at my own feet, having allowed you to watch all those Errol Flynn movies with me."

"Even you have to admit he was a pretty handsome Robin Hood, mom."

"At least you didn't run away with a pirate."

A snort escaped Katherine with her unexpected laughter. "I probably would've gotten sea sick and never survived."

They were silent for a few minutes as they were each lost in their own thoughts. She had been so blessed to have a mother who was also her best friend that thoughts of never seeing her again were almost Katherine's undoing. How would she go without talking to her every day? Mom must have felt the same emotions, since she reached over and gave Katherine's hand a gentle squeeze three times. It was their secret way to say I love you since she was a child. She returned the gesture as tears ran down both their faces.

"Be happy, Katie," Mom whispered honestly. "That's all I've ever wanted for you, and it's plain to see you and Riorden are madly in love."

"I will," Katherine said, feeling her emotions beginning to choke up inside her.

"I'm sure he's more than worth the sacrifice of the modern world." Mother and daughter embraced, perhaps for the last time. "I can tell he's a good man."

"He is, mom," Katherine declared brightly.

"Then everything is right in the world and meant to be."

Opening the chamber door, Katherine pondered her mother's words as they made their way down the passageway. Everything was so right in her world, knowing she was exactly where she was supposed to be. Smiling, Katherine knew her life with Riorden was indeed going to be the grandest adventure she could ever have wished for. She would be forever thankful she was still here, in the past with him, to enjoy the journey.

FORTY-ONE

RIORDEN SAT QUIETLY IN HIS SOLAR, holding his tiny son. He was so overcome with emotions, knowing this innocent babe was completely dependent on him, for 'twas only by a miracle from God that he had not lost them both. Oddly enough, he was calm with the thought of being a father. He must do something right in the years to come, for he was already aware that he would sire two more girls. Heaven help him when they came of marriageable age. No man would ever be good enough to wed with a daughter of his and would need to prove himself in the lists. He would ensure his sword was always sharpened in the years to come.

His solar door opened, and in walked Katherine and her mother, holding hands as they shared a laugh together. Looking at the two of them, you would never know they were mother and daughter, since they were as different as the sun was to the moon. His gaze leisurely slid down the length of Katherine's body. He swore she was even more beautiful in his eyes than she was afore she had gifted him with his son.

Their eyes met, and a slight smile lit her lovely face, as if she read his thoughts. Her mother went to sit with the others gathered here. But Katherine sauntered over to him as if they were alone in the chamber.

"Hello, my dearest love," she whispered softly in his ear. "I've missed you."

Not caring that others watched their display of affection, her mouth landed on his in a searing kiss afore he knew what she was about. The babe stirred and broke their concentration, afore Katherine gave the child a gentle caress and took a seat next to her dame.

He pondered the group of people who lounged here in his solar. 'Twas a peaceful setting and one he had longed for in the deepest recesses of his heart. 'Twas good to have Warkworth feel like home, again. Thanks to his wife, she had made it so, along with his sire, who hovered near at hand.

He watched as there was a silent exchange between his wife and Fletcher. Katherine had told him all of how his friend had been a support to her in the months since her disappearance. 'Twas clear that Fletcher had feelings for his wife, not that he could blame the man. She had assured him nothing had happened between the two of them, but that had not stopped Riorden from having a private word with Fletcher. At least, they understood one another, and they would be able to remain on good terms and continue to be friends.

No trace could be found of the scoundrels who had attempted to abduct his wife, leading to her jump into the river. Since it had been months since her supposed demise, there was nothing that could lead him to capturing the men. Riorden assumed they thought their job was a success with his wife's presumed demise. But he would remain diligent with his guards to keep a constant lookout for anything that appeared suspicious.

In the days that followed Riorden's son's birth, Nathaniel and Ulrick had returned from Dunhaven with the grave news that Marguerite was dead by her own hand. They had given coin over to ensure she had a proper burial and had returned, seeing no reason to stay. But even her death could not dampen the good cheer that had settled on Warkworth and its people.

Perchance, everything was not as cheery as he would like. Katherine had been extremely emotional after their child was born, but, mayhap, that was understandable. After all, 'twas not every day that her mother crossed time to see her, and it may be the last time they would be together. Riorden could tell mother and daughter were very close, and tears threatened to spill continually from both women whenever they were together.

Danior and Juliana, along with Tiernan and Emily, were bound to return back from whence they came as soon as they could travel safely to Bamburgh, after the storm's passing, or so was the plan. Katherine's mother would go back, as well. She had spoken only once about the nastiness of the garderobe and apparently this was reason alone for her to return to her own time, no matter how much she loved her daughter.

"Nay! You will not follow them," Fletcher firmly declared, breaking into Riorden's musings. "You have just had a child. Merciful heavens, how does Riorden deal with such stubbornness?"

"It's because he loves me so, isn't that right Riorden?" she asked brightly, batting her eye lashes at him and flashing a beautiful smile in his direction.

"Of course, I love you, but do not think you shall get your way with that pretty little look you are giving me," he replied with a roguish grin of his own. "You will not go traipsing about the countryside in the snow. You must needs say your farewells here."

"But, Riorden—" she pouted, sticking out her lower lip.

"Nay. My mind is made up. Besides, your son and I need you," he said meaningfully.

Silence descended on the room, as everyone seemed lost in their own thoughts until Katherine at last spoke up. He watched her carefully whilst she gazed at the women who meant the most to her with fresh tears freely flowing down her cheeks. "You won't be back..."

Her mother began to speak then closed her lips, obviously not knowing what she could say that would give her daughter any form of comfort. .Juliana, Emily, and Brianna reached out to her, and they all clasped hands with their sister of their heart.

"Jewels and I will take care of each other, won't we Jewels?" Emily said with a catch in her voice.

"And Brie lives not far from you, so you have each other," Juliana replied as her own emotions threatened to spill over.

Dristan took a sip of his wine. "Mayhap, your men there will do a better job of ensuring your safety so as you do not cross time and end up where you do not wish to be."

"They had better do a damn good job of it," Aiden replied as he flipped a dirk expertly in his hands and glared meaningfully at Tiernan.

The men chuckled at what they felt was amusement, although Riorden could not find the jest of the situation. He noticed Katherine beginning to already tire from the exertion of being out of bed, and he rose from his chair. "Katherine needs her rest, if you will excuse us."

Juliana opened her arms for the child, "We'll watch over the baby and will bring him to you when he wakes up for his feeding."

Riorden handed the infant over to the waiting arms of his godmother. Juliana held the babe most tenderly, placing a kiss on his forehead. "Hello James," she whispered and watched in delight as the child opened his eyes at her voice, yawned, and promptly went back to sleep.

Holding out his hand to his wife, he helped her rise from her chair, even as she gave a fond smile to those who had gathered together to celebrate the birth of his son and heir. They were almost to the door when her mother called out his name. She rose quickly to stand afore them and unexpectedly reached up to cup his cheek.

"I'm glad she found you, Riorden, even if it means I never see her again. She always wanted a knight in shining armor and told me she was born in the wrong century. I think perhaps she was right," she whispered, giving her daughter a kiss on her cheek. "You will take good care of her for me, won't you?"

He gave her a formal bow. "'Tis my greatest pleasure to see to her welfare for always, madam. I am happy my lady wife was able to see you again, if only for one last time."

Katherine wrapped her arms around her mother and whispered a hasty I love you. They made their way to their chamber, and Riorden saw his wife settled comfortably in their bed. Stripping his clothes from his body, he lay down next to her and felt a shock consume his body as she all but wrapped herself around him, now that their son was no longer between them. She must have felt it, too, given her words to him.

"I hope that never goes away."

"Aye, 'tis a way that Time reminds us that we were meant to be together."

"Even the little things in life can bring a small amount of happiness to your soul, and, sometimes, that is what matters the most." She spoke softly with a yawn, almost as if she were half between sleep and wakefulness.

"'Tis no small thing that has brought you into my life, Katherine," he said, kissing the top of her head. "Now, go to sleep and get your rest."

"But, I'll miss you if I go to sleep," her words were slow and lazy as she began to drift off into the netherworld.

"Nay, Katherine, you will not miss me, for we shall dream together, you and I, for even when we sleep, we are destined to be together, for always."

She snuggled deeper into his chest and grabbed at a length of his hair, twirling it between her fingers. "Yes, for always, Riorden," she murmured. "I'll see you then, in our dreams, my love."

Riorden gave a silent prayer of thanks to God above for giving him this woman in his arms to love. As he felt the last stages of consciousness settle around his soul afore sleep overtook him, he heard the softest of whispers coming from the angels in heaven as they answered his heartfelt words of praise. They were only three little words, but they were enough.

"You are welcome..."

EPILOGUE

Warkworth Castle
Summer

KATHERINE FELT THE WARMTH of the sun as it kissed her skin in a golden glow while she reclined in comfort on a blanket. Leaning on one elbow, her hand supported her head, while the other was busy twirling a blade of grass between her delicate fingers as she pondered life's mysteries. She sighed in pleasure at the view before her eyes, one she was very pleased to be witnessing.

It wasn't hard for her heart to beat madly in her chest, nor for it to feel as if it was flipping end over end in excitement. She was actually having a difficult time, trying to find her breath, and all because of what her eyes lovingly beheld. Her gaze swept the man before her as she all but stripped him of his clothing until their eyes locked knowingly. That same unexplainable feeling they had shared from the very beginning quickly passed between them, electrifying the very space separating them. She gulped in the air that finally managed to find its way into her lungs as a sudden rush of heated desire swept over her.

She gave him a seductive smile. His response was a slow, ever so slight, lazy grin. His intense expression spoke silently to her, as if he were reading her very thoughts. In that one instant, he gave her the resolution her heart had sought since she first looked upon his portrait in the future, the answer to what had haunted her at that time. How many times had she asked herself the same unnerving question and was unable to find any form of a solution that seemed logical? What had he been staring at? What had captured his attention so, causing his brilliant blue eyes to smolder across time as if he were beaconing for her to come join him? Until this very moment, she had been unsure of the response, but, now, she knew the undeniable truth. He had been looking...at her.

"There, *Monsieur!*" She exclaimed in delight, sitting straight upright and pointing to her husband. "Can you capture his expression just now?"

"*Mais bien sur que oui, Madame,*" the painter replied as his brush quickly flowed across the canvas to obey her request.

With a small glance at the portrait and knowing the artist's answer, *but of course, yes...*would satisfy her, she settled back down to continue to peruse the view at her leisure.

Once again, the future and the present fused. In the blink of an eye, a gilded frame surrounded Riorden's body until, magically, she found herself back in the future. She shouldn't have been surprised she found herself back in the room at Bamburgh where she had first learned Riorden's name. She saw herself reaching out to the exact same portrait of the very man who now stood impatiently before her. She could actually feel the cold stones beneath her as she had knelt on the castle's floor when her knees buckled by what was before her very eyes.

She could only marvel at what she saw. Here was the man who had filled her dreams her entire life, standing with Warkworth castle in the backdrop. Tears ran unhindered down her cheeks in remembrance of how the artist had captured him to perfection, especially the magnificence of his eyes. He was dressed as he had always been in her dreams with the lion head of his crest embroidered on his tabard. A dark blue cape enhanced his shoulders and fell to the earth beneath his feet. He held a sword in front of him, its tip gracing the earth. His hands rested one on top of the other on the golden hilt, adorned with a large sapphire blue stone of some worth. His hair blew gently in the breeze, and one could just tell by looking at the man that he had been none too pleased to have had to stand still for its painting.

"Katherine?"

Her eyes blinked yet again, and she watched in fascination when the walls of the castle disappeared from her vision to be replaced with the bluest of skies with white fluffy clouds above her head. Her mind registered Riorden had been saying her name, trying to gain her attention. He gave a flick of his wrist, dismissing the painter who quickly gathered his things and left. It broke the spell surrounding him as the portrait that was for one second before her vanished completely to be replaced with the living specimen of all knightly virtues she could ever wish to call her own.

He came to her with a slow and steady gait, portraying enough pure, raw energy to knock her off her feet, as he always seemed to do. At least she didn't have to worry about falling down, since she was already reclining as if she had been waiting for him. *Perhaps that was just it,* she mused. In some strange unclear way, Riorden had always been a part of her. Whether it was the past, present, or future, maybe everything was just somehow connected in the greater scheme of things, and how Time itself is perceived. She only knew for certain that she had been waiting for Riorden all of her life, and at last he was hers, and hers alone.

"Kat?" he said, gaining her full attention as he whipped off his cape, unbelted his sword, allowing it to fall to the ground, and settled down next to her.

"Hi," she whispered, reaching out to cup his face and marveling that he was in truth real.

"Hello," he murmured in a husky whisper. He reached out and tucked a lock of her hair behind her ear. She shivered in anticipation from his touch. "You were very far away, my love."

"Yes, I was just remembering the past and thinking how lucky I am to have you in my life."

"The past?" he asked with a raised brow.

Katherine gave a merry laugh. "Or maybe it was really the future. It's hard to tell sometimes, considering what we have between us."

"I pray they were good memories, then."

She gazed up lovingly into his eyes and was lost yet again. "Only the best," she replied, ever so softly.

Riorden leaned down and pressed his lips against her own in a sensual kiss meant to spark and ignite the fire within them. It worked, for Katherine felt as if there was a raging blaze ready to be released if he but gave the smallest crook of his finger. She sat up, and with a happy, cheerful laugh, began running through the field, thinking he shouldn't be so confident that she could be so easy to entice.

"Catch me if you can, Riorden!" She called out but shrieked playfully when he quickly made up the distance between them and caught her about the waist. He held her high above his shoulders and twirled her around and around.

"You are such a saucy little minx," he said, letting her slide slowly down the length of his body. It had the desired effect, and she wrapped her arms around his neck.

"Yes, but you love me," she said, skimming her hands up and down his chest.

"Aye, Kat. I do love you," he replied, staring into her eyes, "especially when you hear my heart sing."

She couldn't resist the smile that crossed her features at his words. "And can I listen to its song for all of ever, my dearest husband?"

The look he gave her spoke a thousand words. "Aye, my beautiful Katherine, for all of ever will my heart sing only for you."

Katherine gave a blissful sigh as they lowered themselves down onto the ground. She had found her chivalrous knight, and they had a lifetime of happiness to look forward to. Only God above knew for sure what He had in store for them in this strange and wonderful future of theirs. Yet Katherine understood the one most important fact where Riorden and their love was concerned. She knew without any doubt, if they had to search all of eternity, their souls would never rest until they found one another again, and, perhaps *that* was the best memory to look forward to of them all...

Author's Notes

I hope you've enjoyed the continuing saga of Katherine and Riorden on their journey to find love in ONLY FOR YOU. I must admit, these two characters are especially dear to my heart. So much so, that it was hard for me to say goodbye at the conclusion of this story. But never fear, dear reader, as with all my stories I've written thus far, you'll see glimpses of them popping in and out of my other novels from time to time. And just think of the stories I will weave about their children once they are grown...

I would like to clarify, from a historical perspective, some information about Warkworth Castle and its Hermitage that are both still standing today, as I mentioned in my previous notes in FOR ALL OF EVER.

I found this interesting information regarding the origins of Warkworth castle at http://www.english-heritage.org.uk/ which states: "Henry, son of David I, King of Scotland, has conventionally been credited with raising the motte and bailey (an artificial mound surrounded by a fortified enclosure) and the first stone buildings at Warkworth, after he became Earl of Northumberland in 1139. The first written record of Warkworth Castle, however, occurs in a charter of between 1157 and 1164, in which Henry II granted the castle and manor of Warkworth to Roger fitz Eustace."

Ask me why I originally chose Warkworth Castle as the place where my hero, Riorden de Deveraux, would claim his birthright, I couldn't say, except that I felt drawn to the place. It certainly wasn't because it's an easy word to pronounce when I have to pitch my novels. However, during my research into the castle and surrounding area, I was pleasantly surprised to learn about Warkworth's Hermitage that is located approximately one half mile away from the castle.

Accessible only by boat, the Hermitage was built as a chantry chapel around 1332/49 by Henry Percy II, son of the first Percy, Lord Alnwick, although parts of it were built at a later date. My research also found a story of love and sadness regarding the chapel, though many of the true facts remain unknown. It is believed by some that the chapel was created by Bertram of Bothal as a penance for having killed both his brother and his beloved Isobella of Widdrington during a rescue against Scottish kidnappers. This is when all the pieces fell into place with my own storyline, when I first had Katherine dreaming she was inside the Hermitage and Time returned her to the twenty-first century. Any details of a woman mourning her lost love throughout time is fictional on my part as the author of ONLY FOR YOU.

There are many websites dedicated to Warkworth Castle, the Hermitage, and the history during this incredible time period in England. You can also visit Warkworth and Bamburgh Castles, and I hope that one day I'll be able to check them both off my bucket list. In the age of technology in which we live, I continue to marvel at the amount of research that is available to the modern day writer with just a click of a mouse and the internet.

I hope you find these little tidbits of historical information interesting as I share some of my research about the areas in which I write and have my characters live.

ACKNOWLEDGEMENT

I continue to be humbly grateful to the multiple people in my life who have supported me during the writing of this novel and my path to becoming a self-published author.

To my family and friends, who continue to be my sounding board when I need them the most, I thank you from the bottom of my heart. Maybe one day I'll come out of my writing cave and be able to have sparkling conversations again. This is what happens when you wait a lifetime to begin a writing career. So much writing to do...so little time.

To my good friend and critique partner, Tricia Linden, who has become a true sister of my heart. You fixed this story big time with a major plot/character error that I didn't even see during its initial creation. Thank you for helping me keep this all together with your enthusiasm for my writing. I'm so glad we found each other!

For my amazing editor, Barbara Millman Cole, who takes my manuscripts and breathes that extra bit of life into my work in order to help me give my readers a quality product for them to enjoy. Thank you!

Thank you to my fellow authors at the San Francisco Area of Romance Writers of America who continue to share their knowledge with me and help me stay motivated to keep on writing. I am thankful, once more, to be associated with such a wonderful group of talented people.

I would also like to thank my readers who have purchased a copy of my work, especially those who have taken the time to write such wonderful reviews for IF MY HEART COULD SEE YOU and FOR ALL OF EVER. You are the people who are helping me find new readers who will enjoy my writing as much as you have, and you are also the reason that both stories became Amazon eBook bestsellers. Thank you all so very much!

You may be wondering what I have up next for you in 2015. I have a lot going on and plenty in store for you with both my medieval and time travel novels. I'm also working with a wonderful group of ladies who write in the Regency era. We call ourselves The Bluestocking Belles or Belles in Blue. In the coming year, I'll move history forward from the time period I've previously written in while I contribute to this amazing group with a novella in a boxset, due out in time for the holidays; support the Malala Fund, which is our mutual charity; and work on publishing ONE MOMENT IN TIME in early 2016. If you'd like to learn more about us as a group, you can find us at www.bluestockingbelles.com.

You also might be asking yourself where is Lynet of clan MacLaren's story from IF MY HEART COULD SEE YOU? Not wanting to disappoint my beloved readers, you'll only have to wait until this summer for A KNIGHT TO CALL MY OWN to be published. After that, I think I'll keep you guessing which of the knights from Berwyck will be featured in my next time travel. I just know you'll love both stories!

Thank you again for purchasing ONLY FOR YOU. If you enjoyed reading my novel, I would appreciate an honest review at whichever retailer you purchased it from. It's the best way you can support me as an Indie author so other readers can find my work. If you haven't stopped by my website, please do. You can sign up for my newsletter and/or my member's area to start a discussion on the forum page. In the meantime, I look forward to reading your reviews (yes...I read them all) along with your posts on our mutual social media platforms.

With Warm Regards,
Sherry Ewing

COMING SOON

A KNIGHT
TO CALL MY OWN

WHEN YOUR HEART IS BROKEN,
IS LOVE STILL WORTH THE RISK?

SUMMER 2015

OTHER BOOKS BY
SHERRY EWING

AVAILABLE IN PAPERBACK AND EBOOK
AT ONLINE RETAILERS

ABOUT THE AUTHOR

Sherry Ewing is a self-published author who writes historical and time travel romances to awaken the soul one heart at a time. Her debut historical romance, *IF MY HEART COULD SEE YOU*, hit Amazon's top ten bestseller list for the eBook only two days after the paperback release. Always wanting to write a novel but busy raising her children, she finally took the plunge in 2008 and wrote her first Regency. She is a national and local member of Romance Writers of America since 2012 and is currently working on her next novel. When Sherry is not busy writing, she can be found in the San Francisco area at her day job as an Information Technology Specialist. You can find out more about Sherry at her website at www.sherryewing.com.